I0618889

BEAT

A Novel

By

Alexandra Y. Caluen

BEAT

Copyright 2013, 2023 by Alexandra Y. Caluen

Cover design by RK Young

Cover photo by Damon Zaicmus
@touchdamonlight *unsplash.com*

This is a work of fiction. Characters, main events, and many of the named businesses, including the Underground Cabaret and its productions, are the product of the author's imagination. Any resemblance to real persons, events, or businesses is entirely coincidental.

BEAT

Just Dance – Lady Gaga

Waiting - Madonna

Owner of a Lonely Heart - Yes

Higher Ground – Red Hot Chili Peppers

Night and Day – U2

I'm a Believer – Smash Mouth

Make Me Feel – Janelle Monae

It is You (I Have Loved) – Dana Glover

Save the Last Dance – Michael Bublé

BEAT
Contents

Chapter 1

September 2011

It was a hot night in West Hollywood and the club was jam-packed, hot men spilling out onto the sidewalk. Mateo got carded at the door, as usual. Paid the cover charge and made his way through the crowd to the bar, where the bartender gave him a dubious look. "Your ID?"

Every goddamned time. "Just a second." Mateo unbuttoned the chest pocket of his tight, semi-transparent, short-sleeved shirt and pulled out his driver's license again. Made sure to flex a little, too.

The bartender eyed Mateo's biceps, then studied the ID. "This for real?"

"Dude. I swear."

"You look about fifteen."

"That's why I gotta hang out in bars, so I start looking my age." The bartender laughed as he handed back the ID. Mateo carefully buttoned it up again. "What's your name?"

"Jules."

"Hey Jules, nice to meet you. Strawberry daiquiri?" When his drink was delivered, Mateo pushed the change back across the bar with a smile, then turned around to survey the crowd. He let the heavy beat of the house music flow through his body, aware that people were looking at him. Exactly what he was here for, on his birthday, alone. He'd been mostly alone since he moved to Los Angeles, and he was tired of it. Officially. Tired Of It. He was officially here to get laid, even if the noise level, and the carnivorous quality of the crowd, were tripping him out a little.

As he reached the bottom of the drink, a good-looking blond guy caught his eye across the dance floor. Mateo took a deep breath, set down his glass, and made his way over. The blond guy looked him over approvingly. "Hey. You wanna dance?"

"Sure." Had to shout to hear each other, but this wasn't about conversation. They squeezed onto the dance floor. As he got into it, Mateo forgot his nerves. Dancing always did that for him.

"You've got some moves!" shouted the blond guy. "What do you call that?"

"Cha-cha." Mateo grinned, throwing in a couple of spins.

The blond guy caught him. Didn't have to shout with his mouth right against Mateo's neck. "Never seen you here before." He changed the cha-cha chassé to a grind, hand sliding under the shirt.

Music plus touch plus daiquiri meant Mateo was totally fine with that. "It's my birthday."

"No shit?" The blond guy turned to a jock grooving by himself nearby. "Birthday boy here!"

"Shots!!" yelled the jock, hustling off the dance floor to the DJ stand and then to the bar. In a second the music changed to the Beatles: 'You Say It's Your Birthday.' A space cleared on the dance floor around Mateo and the blond guy. The jock brought over three shots. They clinked glasses and drank.

Mateo sputtered. "Shit! What *was* that?"

"Jäger! Happy birthday!" The jock grabbed him by the ass and pulled him in for a kiss, then left the floor.

Mateo laughed at the blond guy. "He's crazy! That shit was heinous!"

The blond guy laughed back at him. "Dance it up, honey!"

Mateo rocked out to the Beatles, Lady Gaga, Katy Perry. Danced with one man after another, many of whom brought him shots, fortunately mostly not Jägermeister. Between the drinks, the dances, the gropes, and the kisses, he was having a blast. It felt like everybody in the whole place wanted him, and he was Here For It. Across the floor, a tall dark-skinned man watched with a smile. Mateo lifted his chin, lips parting to suck in some air, and the tall guy came out to the floor.

"Whoa, here comes Sam!" said the blond guy. Mateo had a moment clearheaded enough to wonder why that was worth saying. As if people should always notice this tall guy, Sam, when he danced.

The space around Mateo got wider and the DJ flipped over to a salsa track. Sam closed in, offering a hand. Mateo took it with the smile he couldn't help knowing was a killer. Sam gave him a spin and they started to salsa. By the time they were one minute in, nobody else was dancing. Sam had some serious skills. No wonder the blond guy got all excited. Mateo was excited too. This was the dance he'd hoped for every time he'd ever been in a club, fast and flirty and not nearly long enough. The other men clapped and grooved on the border of the dance floor till the music merged into another house track.

Mateo stayed next to Sam as the floor filled up again, pretending it was the crowd keeping them close. "Holy shit, you can dance!"

"You're pretty good yourself."

"Do I get a birthday kiss?" Mateo said recklessly.

"Okay." Sam leaned in and kissed his cheek.

It wasn't enough. "You've gotta be kidding me." Mateo put his hand on the guy's shoulder, stretching up for a proper kiss. A kiss that felt like the dance: heated, rhythmic, intentional. When he stood back he felt a little dizzy. Was he really that drunk, or did something else just happen? Sam was so still, so watchful, Mateo thought maybe he was really that drunk. "Uh, thanks. I think I need some water."

***

Sam watched as the birthday boy started toward the bar, weaving a little. Then he followed, a few steps behind, though he wouldn't have been able to explain why. Aside from the fact that he'd just had one of the best dances of his life with that pretty twink. Jules handed over a glass of water before the kid even asked.

"Thanks." Mateo glugged the water down, then noticed Sam, standing beside him again. Out of the swirling light show over the dance floor, he realized the taller man was a good bit older. His face was scarred and his nose had been broken. Aside from that, he was gorgeous; but Mateo had had too many drinks and his filter was off. "Whoa, what happened to you?"

Sam flinched. "Couple of fights."

"Sam here was an MMA fighter," said Jules.

"Shit, sorry." Mateo put his hand on Sam's arm. "I'm a little drunk."

That was so obviously true that Sam couldn't take offense. Plus the kid was touching him, which might not mean much under the circumstances, but at least he wasn't still under the lights grinding on one of those horndogs. He was here staring up at Sam, who had an apology to answer. "It's okay. I get that a lot."

8

"You're a fucking great dancer." Still touching Sam.

"Thanks. You too."

"Ugh. I gotta go." Mateo's hand slid off Sam as he turned around in an unsteady circle, looking for something.

"That way." Jules pointed to the bathroom. Mateo wobbled away. "He's pretty fucked up."

Sam glanced over. "He'll be okay."

"Maybe you should keep an eye on him."

"Why me?"

"Because you like him." Sam shook his head, smiling. Jules said, "He's probably a nice kid when he's not totally shitfaced." Sam laughed for real. "You should get him out of here."

It was a bad idea, and Sam knew it. That kid was out of Sam's league. He'd never seen anybody quite so...perfect. On the other hand, if Sam didn't take him home, somebody else surely would. Not all of them would take care of him. Pump and dump wasn't what the kid deserved on his birthday. Probably not what he wanted, either. "Yeah, okay."

Sam walked over to the bathroom and went inside. The twink had managed to do whatever he needed to do, but now he was leaning over the sink, both hands flat on the wet surface. Sam diagnosed an imminent blackout. "Why'd you want to go and do something this dumb?" he said softly. "Don't you know what can happen to a pretty boy like you?" He arranged arms around waists and started walking the kid out. Catching Jules' inquiring expression as they headed for the back door, Sam mouthed "So fucked up." Jules shook his head and turned back to his customers.

Less than twenty minutes later Sam stared down at the passed-out stranger on his bed and sighed. He'd picked someone up the last time he went to the club too, but at least that guy was conscious. "Don't sit on his face, Pachuco," he told his cat. "He wouldn't even feel it and you'd smother him for sure."

***

The next morning, Mateo woke up, fully clothed except for shoes, with a pounding headache, a hollow gut, and the taste of road-killed skunk in his mouth.

"Fuuuuuuuck." He thought he'd opened his eyes, but he couldn't see anything. "What the." Brushed a hand over his face and suddenly could see. There was a fluffy tail in his hand. He opened his fingers and turned his head in the direction of the tail. A large, long-haired, somewhat Siamese-looking cat lounged on the pillow beside his head, looking at him over its shoulder with disapproval. "Who are you?"

"That's Pachuco," said a low, quiet voice. "Hope you aren't allergic to cats."

Mateo turned his head the other way and saw Sam, sitting in a task chair at a compact desk, a few feet away from the bed. "I remember you. You're the salsa guy."

"You feeling okay?"

"I feel like ten flavors of shit," he admitted.

"Bathroom's over there." Sam watched as Mateo rolled onto his side and carefully sat up. The cat brushed by his arm and jumped off the bed; its slight impact nearly toppled him. "Want me to give you a hand?"

"Do you mind?"

"I've been there." Sam came over to help Mateo to his feet, across the room, and into the bathroom.

"Think I've got it from here. Thanks."

"No problem."

Mateo closed the door behind him and looked at himself in the mirror. He had a terminal case of bedhead, bloodshot eyes, and that skunk thing. After a long and heavenly piss, he splashed water on his face, ran his whole head under the faucet, and scrubbed his teeth with his finger. Then he dried off with a towel and went out. Sam was back in the task chair, apparently relaxed. Mateo didn't quite buy it. He leaned against a convenient wall. "I don't remember much about last night. After getting some water at the bar."

"You might have passed out a little."

"Did I do anything awful?"

"No. I just brought you home so you wouldn't get in trouble."

"Thanks. I appreciate it." He regarded Sam for a moment. The other man had an elegant stillness, and wary eyes. "I have a feeling I said something rude to you. If I did, I'm sorry."

"It's okay."

Mateo came closer. He lifted a hand and touched Sam's face, tracing the scar that ran from the outside corner of his eye across his cheek, nearly to the corner of his mouth. It was one of several marks on his mahogany skin. "How did this happen?"

No one had ever asked in quite that way, as if they were looking at a fine painting slashed by a box cutter, as if they were grieved by it. "MMA fight. Guy's hand whipped past and he had this sharp fingernail on his little finger. Cut me open."

"Mother*fucker*."

"Said it was an accident. Ref cut his fingernails, *all* of them, before the next round. And then I gave him the beat down." He couldn't help smiling.

Mateo laughed, then clutched his head. "Oh, shit, that hurts."

"You want something to eat?"

"I don't know." The thought was not immediately appealing. Why had he taken all those shots? What the fuck was he thinking? "I've never been that wasted before."

"You'll feel better if you eat a little something."

"If you say so. Guess it couldn't really be worse."

They went to the kitchen. Mateo hung back while Sam fixed a piece of toast with peanut butter. He gave Mateo a glass of orange juice mixed with Gatorade. "This'll taste horrible, but drink it." Sam started some coffee and had a piece of toast himself.

Mateo cautiously (and slowly) ate the toast and drank the juice, which did indeed taste horrible. "Do people do this shit more than once? Because *fuck*."

Sam turned his head away, hiding a laugh. "Some people do it every night."

"God," Mateo said, with feeling. "No. Never again. What time is it?"

Sam glanced at the clock on the microwave. "About eleven."

"Do you need me to get out of here?" Mateo was hoping not, because he didn't feel like he could face daylight. But the other man surely had better things to do than babysit an idiot.

"I'm off work today."

"Me too. Thought I was giving myself a birthday present, you know, a day off. Guess I was just being smart."

Sam smiled a little. "You'd never been in there before, had you?"

"They barely let me in *last* night!"

"Baby face."

"Yeah, whatever." Mateo would usually have done some kind of diva thing here, but he couldn't summon the will.

"What are you, Filipino?"

"Yeah. You?"

"Black and Chinese on one side, Mexican on the other."

"It looks good on you."

Sam wasn't used to being complimented. He knew people liked to dance with him, and his body got plenty of attention, but it had been a long time since he'd noticed someone looking at his face with appreciation in the light of day. "Maybe before my face got beat up."

"I love your hair." Sam ducked his head, fiddling with the end of his long black braid. "You don't get many compliments, do you?" Mateo said softly, wondering why not. He couldn't be the only one who thought this guy was gorgeous.

"I'm in the business of giving compliments, not getting them."

Mateo backed off a little. He asked where Sam worked, and found out he managed a tux shop in West L.A. That led into an easy conversation that lasted through another piece of toast and a cup of coffee for him, and a full breakfast for Sam. It wasn't until Sam was rinsing his plate that Mateo volunteered, "I work at a design-build firm in Santa Monica. Draftsman."

"I figured you weren't from this neighborhood."

"How's that?"

"You know, people are out and about a lot around here. I would have noticed you before." Sam poured them both some more coffee. "Feeling a little better?"

"Lots. Thanks." He smiled at Sam and after a moment, Sam smiled back. It took a solid effort not to sigh, swooning into his arms like a princess. "You probably have shit you need to do today." Not quite a question.

"Not really."

"Would you mind if I, you know, just hang out for a while?"

Sam took a second to respond. "Sure. I mean no, I don't mind."

"Maybe I could buy you dinner later. To thank you."

"You don't need to co that." Sam was more confused by the minute. Nothing about this morning was going the way he'd expected. He'd expected the twink to crawl out of bed, arrange transport, and disappear with a handshake, at most.

"I'd like to. I mean, if you don't mind being seen with someone who looks like he passed out in a bar last night."

Sam gave in, because he didn't mind being seen with this particular someone who'd passed out in a bar. Plus, he had to be honest. This particular someone was even cuter in daylight, which wasn't often the case. Why not give himself a few more hours to enjoy the sight. "Yeah, okay."

For some reason, Mateo felt like this was a major victory. "Did I ever introduce myself?"

Sam realized that he had no idea what the kid's name was. "No. I'm Sam Lee."

"Mateo de la Cruz. Nice to meet you." Mateo offered a hand. Sam took it as if it might be concealing explosives, lightly shook it, then let go. So cautious, Mateo thought, suddenly remembering the tactless question he'd asked the night before, but now it had nothing to do with the scar or the broken nose. What happened to this guy? What turned an MMA fighter into a great salsa dancer who was kind enough to take a drunk stranger home and not even mess with him? And why was he acting as if nobody ever stayed in this nice apartment? As if he'd thought Mateo would make tracks the second he was upright?

Sam Lee was the least obvious guy Mateo had met since moving to Los Angeles. Of all the guys who could've taken him home, it was the guy who—after that scorching salsa and dizzying kiss—left him completely alone. Barely even touched him. Mateo might've been annoyed about it if he weren't so damn curious.

Chapter 2

It was a strangely comfortable day. They didn't talk much. Sam put on a movie, and Mateo sort of watched it while Sam stretched. Minded his own business, pretending not to notice how flexible the other guy was. After the movie, and after another piece of toast, he took a nap. When he woke up again, Pachuco was stretched out along his side and Sam was doing on the computer.

"Damn, cat, you're hot." He petted the cat, who rolled over, purring, and gently bit his hand. Mateo laughed softly. "Shit, look at those fangs! Furry little badass." He looked over at Sam. "Whatcha doing?"

"Just monkeying around."

"With what? Or, you know, it's none of my business, just tell me to fuck off."

Sam smiled. "It's not top secret or anything. A friend of mine is in a cabaret troupe and she asked me to help spread the word about a show they're doing for Halloween."

"I miss dancing," Mateo said without meaning to.

"Yeah?"

He sat up a little. "Maybe that's why I got so crazy last night, it was so great to be dancing. I was on the ballroom team at Cal Poly Pomona. Used to dance six days a week. That salsa with you last night was the best dance I've had since I graduated."

Sam let that pass. "Your family out there?"

"Yeah. Had to move after graduation, though. I didn't come out till senior year. My pop was a little freaked. I needed to give him some space."

"That does happen."

"Luckily I have an older brother who's doing the right thing, you know, got married and already has a kid." The temptation to keep talking was strong, but he wasn't going to learn anything that way. Mateo petted the cat, waiting.

After a quiet minute Sam said, "I got into dancing some after retiring from the fights."

"Any ballroom?" Mateo couldn't help asking.

"Just salsa."

"I'll bet you'd be great at ballroom. Maybe I could show you a few things sometime." He couldn't help making that suggestion, either, though he instantly regretted it. For whatever reason, being flirty freaked this guy out.

Sure enough, Sam demurred. "I don't know."

Mateo changed the subject. "Aren't you awful young to be retired?"

"I'm thirty. Was on the circuit for five years. Didn't want to go into coaching."

"So now you're a fashion guru."

Sam laughed. "That's a good way to put it. Sounds a lot hipper than just, manager of a tux shop."

"Whatever works."

"I ought to introduce you to this guy I used to work with. He's a salsa dancer."

"You're not listening to me. I want to dance with *you* some more." Exasperated this time, not flirty.

Apparently that worked; Sam laughed again. "One of my straight friends. I saw him not too long ago and he told me about a dance studio here in WeHo somewhere that's gay-friendly."

Mateo perked up. "That would be cool. As long as you come with me." Sam didn't answer and Mateo didn't press it. He petted the cat some more. "Hey, you getting hungry?"

Sam wasn't sure what was happening, but he wasn't ready to see the last of this kid. "I could eat."

"What's good around here?"

"You like Italian?"

"Love it. Gimme that pasta. But no wine tonight, please!"

Sam said, "Yeah, I'll bet." They got themselves together. For Mateo that amounted to finger-combing his hair, feeling grateful his facial hair was practically nonexistent, and deeply appreciating his fancy and functional deodorant. For Sam it meant a quick shower and shave, then changing into oatmeal-colored jeans and a long-sleeved knit pullover that just about killed Mateo because its open stitches let him see the skin underneath. He wondered if Sam realized how sexy it was.

When Sam chose that top he was mostly thinking it was warm outside now, but would be cooler when he was walking home. The knit was the perfect weight for this kind of weather, and he liked the ocean-blue color. But he couldn't help noticing the way Mateo noticed it, which had nothing to do with practicality. They went out, walking along the boulevard. Mateo asked Sam about the neighborhood. Kept him talking all the way. Sam didn't even think about how nice it was to have a conversation like this; he was too preoccupied by how nice it was to be walking with someone who looked like this. Every time some other guy's head turned Sam thought, yeah, he's with me. Of course, every time that happened he also thought, it's only dinner.

***

14

The evening out was, again, strangely comfortable. The restaurant was full of all kinds of couples and families. Mateo felt at home, in a way he didn't in his own neighborhood. Even in yesterday's clothes and not exactly at his best. They talked easily about nonsense like movies and music. Mateo played it safe with fettucine Alfredo; Sam had vegetable lasagna. Was he vegetarian? No, just liked it better than the version with meat. One of the many pieces of trivia Mateo collected, confirming that he liked a lot of things about this guy. If this had been a real date, he'd've been thrilled.

After dinner, they walked back up the boulevard. Sam was thinking the kid would probably go now. "Where did you leave your car?" He hadn't even thought about it till that moment, across the street from his building.

"I didn't drive here last night. Took a taxi."

"Were you figuring on getting shitfaced? 'Cause, you know, good job."

Mateo laughed, incautiously. It didn't make his head fall off this time. "It was a possibility. And to be honest, I thought I might get picked up."

Sam wished he hadn't been honest. It was annoying to think the only reason the kid was here right now was overdrinking. He might've chosen to go home with somebody else, if he'd been capable of making a choice. "I'll bet that happens a lot."

"Not as much as you'd think. I don't really go out much. And never like last night. I'm kind of embarrassed. Actually I'm *really* embarrassed. That was not a good scene. Thanks a lot for, you know."

"You're a nice kid. I didn't want anything bad happening to you." Both those things were true. "I don't get a chance to help someone stay out of trouble very often." Also true.

"I appreciate it." They'd reached Sam's place. Mateo stopped a few feet back from the door. "So, should I get out of here now? Or...can I come in for a while?" Sam stopped too, surprised. Mateo stepped closer and put a hand on Sam's chest. Pressing a little with his thumb, so his skin met Sam's through the open knit. "What do you think?" he said softly.

"You already said thank you."

"Fuck that. I want to put my hands on you." He fit action to words, sliding both hands around Sam's back and pressing his own body close. He didn't know where this was coming from, maybe just the whole quiet day of feeling the other man's vibe and watching him move. Plus, wasn't getting laid the whole reason he went out last night? And didn't it suddenly seem very necessary? He couldn't stand the thought of leaving without at least saying, "I want to put my *mouth* on you."

Sam's head went back and he sucked in a deep breath. Then he looked down at Mateo's face. This was surely not a man who'd ask twice. He wouldn't have to. How was Sam supposed to say No to that? And why the hell should he? Lifting one hand to Mateo's smooth neck, Sam shoved his fingers up into that rumpled black hair, bent his head and went for it.

Mateo opened his mouth immediately, relieved and thrilled and excited. Tasting garlic and red wine on Sam's tongue, feeling hard muscle beneath that sexy knit thing. He never could remember, later, exactly how they got inside. The next thing he knew he was flat on his back on the couch. Sam was pressing him down, kissing him, propped on one elbow, unbuttoning Mateo's shirt with the other hand.

16

Then that hand was skimming over his skin. Sam made a low sound. He moved away; Mateo made a sound of protest, then squeaked because Sam's mouth was on his chest and he'd never felt anything like it. But he was starting to freak out a little, because he was suddenly very aware of how powerful Sam was.

Mateo was not a featherweight and he thought he could get out of this if he wanted to, but it would take the kind of force that was basically violence. Now that Sam wasn't kissing him he was able to think. Nothing Sam was doing was unpleasant. Quite the opposite. It was only that Mateo didn't really have a lot of experience, and he couldn't help wondering if Sam might want things from him that he wasn't prepared for. He'd thought he was prepared for anything.

Sam interrupted his racing thoughts. "What's the matter," he said softly. He'd shifted to one side, no longer covering Mateo's body. His hand was still on Mateo, lightly on his ribs, thumb caressing as if unconsciously. "Are you okay?"

Mateo swallowed. He could feel Sam's erection against his leg and was embarrassed to realize he'd lost his own. Wasn't breathing right. Tried to steady that. "I want you," he said. "I do. I'm just, I haven't done a lot of this. It's been a while and I'm not sure what you want and could we talk?"

"Of course." Sam didn't move for a second. He was remembering a moment very much like this, about six years ago. Then he shifted a little more, stretched out beside Mateo, leaving his arm draped over. Their faces were close together. "Did someone hurt you?" He said it softly.

"Not intentionally." Mateo believed that. "He didn't know what a beginner I was."

"What do *you* like?"

17

Mateo had to think about it. "I like kissing." He turned his face toward Sam, who picked up the cue and kissed him again. "I especially like kissing you." Sam smiled against his mouth. Mateo kept his eyes closed. "I like giving head. I like getting it. I like a hand. Your hands are so smooth."

"I have to handle fabrics all the time. Have to help people dress. Can't be all rough, so I go to a nail salon. How about rimming?"

Mateo barely knew what that was. "I don't know. I don't think anyone's ever done it."

Sam stifled a laugh. "Nobody ever ate your cute little ass?" The stifled, slightly-hysterical giggle from Mateo told him the answer. He indulged in a minute or two of petting that cute ass, stroking the firm curves of it, dipping his fingers under Mateo's waistband to brush across the very top of his cleft. The resulting low yummy sound told him it wasn't something this guy was turned off by. And Jesus, he hadn't been this turned on for ages. He resolved the current kiss when he realized his big hand was pulling Mateo's hips tight against his own, to no protest whatsoever. "Maybe we could try it, see if you like it. You don't like being pinned down." That wasn't a question.

"I never thought about it before. It's always been, you know, one up one down, or face to the wall, or hands and knees."

"No one ever looked you in the face? What a waste." And what a thrill. Here in WeHo, Sam was rarely the more experienced partner. This might be his chance to do exactly and only what he liked best. So long as Mateo liked it too. And there was something else he needed to say. "I go to the clinic every six months and get tested. It's safe for you to be with me.

18

I have condoms. But if you're nervous, if you only want to use hands, or if you only want to kiss, that's okay."

"Oh Jesus." Mateo hadn't even thought of asking. He wondered if he would have been assertive enough before anything serious happened. He had been before, but then he wasn't with somebody like this. He didn't know if there even *was* somebody like this, except Sam. "I get tested too. Should've said. No issues here. I feel like such an idiot." Sam kissed him again. "I'm sorry, did I kill the vibe? I did, didn't I."

"No you didn't. I'm glad you said something."

Mateo hadn't, actually. Sam had listened to his body. He wasn't the least bit scared now. "Could you touch me some more? Would you?"

Sam sat up, and for a second Mateo thought it was all over. Then he was being pulled to his feet and walked through to the bedroom. "This will be more comfortable," Sam said. "Hey Pachuco. Watch yourself." Mateo snickered at the cat's offended expression. Stripped off his shirt and threw it somewhere, took off his shoes, shucked off his jeans as Sam watched. When he hooked his thumbs in the waistband of his briefs and started to push them down, Sam took over. He knelt on the floor at Mateo's feet, ran his hands down and then up his bare legs. All over him, touching everything he could reach, everything except what Mateo expected him to touch. What he increasingly wanted him to touch. "Sit yourself down." As if in a dream, Mateo did. He watched Sam strip, which, Holy Mother of God. His erection was like the rest of him, long and solid, standing tall with tidily-trimmed black hair at its root. Mateo wanted it in his mouth, but Sam went to the nightstand and took something out of the drawer. "Scoot up a little, baby."

Mateo did, getting all the way on the bed. Sam knelt beside him and leaned in for another kiss, one hand on his face. Then still kissing, stroking down his neck and chest, putting a little pressure on his shoulder. Mateo lay back. Sam had both hands on him now, but not pinning him. Petting him. There was no other word for it. Hands everywhere, and then his mouth everywhere. A hand behind a knee to bend it, opening it away from Mateo's body Mouth on the inside of the thigh, and a sound that said Sam didn't at all mind the musky state of things down there.

Mateo was lightheaded with arousal. The mouth and the hands at his groin, on his balls, on his cock. "Holy *fuck*." A muffled laugh. Then fingers caressing lower, a little lube. Not penetrating, only stroking. Teasing. It felt incredible. Mateo opened the other leg to give Sam more room to work, heard an approving sound, didn't know what to do with his hands. He settled for grabbing the pillows and pulling them under his head so he could see what was going on down there. He felt like he was being worshiped. He felt like he should be taking notes. "Oh God. I want you in me."

***

Sam wanted that too, but first he wanted to make this beautiful man come. He wanted to hear it and taste it. All that sensitive golden skin, all for him. He heard Mateo whimper and knew he really did want it. A little more lube, and the slow introduction of a finger. A gasp, a twitch, and the knees open wide. Mateo curled his back a little, asking for more. Sam gave it to him. He still had that perfect cock in his mouth, one hand around the base with his thumb below Mateo's balls. The whole package was so gorgeous he could have spent an hour on this, but it

20

wouldn't be long now. One foot was in the air, then on Sam's shoulder. Another finger went in and Mateo moaned. Sam went for the magic spot, tasting how close Mateo was, feeling his body jerk, listening to the vocal breaths as he peaked. Then there was the spasm and the cry and Sam nearly came himself as he swallowed. He withdrew those fingers once the climax was over. Mateo breathed, "Oh my Jesus. Please. Please kiss me."

Sam let go so he could say, "If I kiss you, I'll be in you."

"Please. Kneel up a minute so I can see you."

"Watch it happen, baby. And if you don't like it, say so. I'll stop." It might kill him, but he would stop. He made eye contact, waited for Mateo's nod. His eyes were sleepy, bottom lip red as if he'd bitten it.

Sam rolled on a condom and slicked himself up, aware of Mateo's gaze. Then another caress with the lube, and this beauty let Sam do it, the most intimate thing Sam could imagine. Fucking him face to face. He pulled the pillows out from under his head and went flat, wrapping his hands around Sam's arms, holding on for dear life.

He went slow, as slow as he could, letting the heat and the pressure do half the work. Then Mateo's hips moving with him, and a sound that clearly meant *More*. His legs were crossed over Sam's back. One arm wrapped around Sam's head, and the other flung out, hand gripping the blanket, his head pressed back. Sam had his mouth on Mateo's throat when he came. The sound he made wasn't even close to a word.

They rested for a few minutes after Sam disengaged. He lay in Mateo's arms, feeling the younger man stroking his hair, knowing he should get them into the shower. Almost afraid to break the spell.

"We'd better clean up," Mateo said drowsily. "I'm going to be asleep in five seconds and I want to suck your cock when I wake up." Sam started laughing, rolled off the bed, helped Mateo up. They staggered to the bathroom.

Chapter 3

Two Sundays later, confused and upset, Mateo was on the phone with his sister Kristine. Sitting on the balcony of his small apartment, letting the ocean breeze wash past him into the un-air-conditioned living space, talking about what happened on his birthday. "So what do you think?"

"He's never even picked up?" Kristine couldn't believe anyone would not call her brother back. She would have been inclined to call the guy names if Mateo hadn't sounded so down.

"I guess I should stop calling. I just really liked him. I kind of fell in love with him a little." Only to Kris would he have admitted this.

"Well, he rescued you, kind of."

"Maybe that's it. My princess fantasy." Had he managed to make this sound like a joke?

Kristine played along, laughing, then suggested, "You could go by his store sometime."

"I don't want to *stalk* the guy. Maybe he didn't really like me." The thought hurt, and it didn't fit with the way Mateo had felt. Or the way Sam had acted. But what did he know about how thirty-year-old guys conducted one-night stands, after all. That was his first time with someone older than twenty-five.

"Everybody likes you!" Kristine said loyally. "You said he's older, right?"

"Seven years."

"Maybe he thinks he's too old for you."

"Or I'm too young for him." Mateo suspected there was a difference. Had he ever mentioned his age? For all he knew, Sam thought he was only twenty-one. Maybe when Mateo said he moved after graduation, Sam thought he meant this year. Oh, God, and then Mateo went and freaked out.

Kris interrupted the doom spiral. "It may not even be about you. Maybe he's actually in a relationship and you just, like, tempted him. With your cute self."

Mateo made a *pfft* noise. "It's not necessarily a blessing, this face. Well, *you* know, you've got the same one."

"You know good and damn well it's not as special on a girl," she said dryly. Kristine had been called beautiful plenty of times, usually by someone who wanted something. When people said it about Mateo, it was always with disbelief.

"Yeah, whatever. He said I probably get picked up a lot. I didn't tell him I hadn't gone out like that in a year." Because the big city was scarier than he'd thought, and he was here all alone, and he didn't belong at home but he didn't belong here yet either. And he didn't know where to start, especially since the one person he'd really clicked with apparently didn't want to talk to him again. He honestly didn't know why. The next morning, Sam waited with him for the taxi and kissed him goodbye as if seeing each other again was a foregone conclusion. And then nothing. As if seeing each other again was never on the table.

Once again, Kris broke into the doom spiral. "But he was nice to you, right?"

"He called me beautiful." He knew he sounded wistful.

That struck at Kristine's heart. She suddenly wondered if anyone had ever said that *to* her brother before. "Oh, Mateo."

Once he got off the phone, Mateo went for a run. On the way back from the beach, sweaty and gross as he was, he stepped into the nearest grocery store and filled a handbasket with healthy food. Noticed the cashier eyeing him, smiled back, and thought about asking when his shift ended.

Maybe in a few days, when he'd need to stock up again. He'd make a point of not being sweaty and gross. Because life went the fuck on, didn't it. So what the hell. "This your usual shift?"

The cashier pushed Mateo's loaded bag over to him, holding on till Mateo reached for the bag, fingers brushing his. Smiling coyly. "I'm on Sundays through Thursdays. Got class Monday and Wednesday nights at SMC." Cleverly filling in an essential piece of information: old enough.

"I'll remember that." Another smile, letting his gaze drop to the college boy's mouth. Mateo wasn't looking for true love, not while his own heart felt bruised, but this one as good as said he'd be free on Tuesday or Thursday night. And didn't they say the best way to get over someone was to get under someone else?

It was summer, dammit. He was single, dammit. He could chalk the whole Sam thing up to experience, which he needed, and try to learn from it. Make the most of being single during summer in the big city. It was perfectly reasonable for a twenty-three-year-old gay man to have meaningless hookups.

The problem was, he never quite got used to it. Didn't quite have a handle on what he wanted. He'd been taught the straight way of doing things: go on dates, get approved by the other person's parents, get more serious, get engaged, get married, have some kids. None of which he wanted, not then. As a horny, lonely, closeted teenager, all he really wanted was someone to get off with. In college, out to his classmates, he found those people. Some of them were friends, too, and their joint activities would've been called dates if they were straight. But most of the straight kids were looking for Mx. Right. Mateo and his queer friends were locking for Mx. Right Now. Not one of them planned to stay in Pomona. They scattered after graduation. Mateo wasn't even in touch with any of those people.

So he needed new people. Obviously. And it was perfectly reasonable to try them out the way everyone expected from a young single gay man. Even if he'd begun to think he might want more, or should expect more, or maybe deserved more.

***

Three weeks after his night with Mateo, Sam was out at brunch with his friend Rory and her girlfriend Dana. They were giving him shit about once again having no date. "Jesus, Sam," said Rory. "With your body you ought to be in pornos, and every time I see you you've got another lock on your chastity belt."

"It's not all about sex," he said prissily.

Dana shook her head. "Yes, it is."

Rory grinned smugly. "Didn't you say you'd met someone a few weeks ago?"

Sam didn't want to answer that. "You know just because I don't bring a date wherever, that doesn't mean I'm not fucking anybody."

"I stand corrected." Rory raised her coffee cup in a salute.

Nevertheless, Dana persisted. "No, but seriously. What happened with that guy? Did you call him?"

"He called me a few times." She made an encouraging gesture. Sam looked away, then down. "I didn't pick up."

Both women said, "*What*?!" in such outraged tones that half the other customers looked over.

"Are you insane?" Rory demanded. "You, the bulletproof monk, like someone enough to take him home from a club, and he calls you, and you don't answer the frickin' phone?"

"He's just a kid. And he's gorgeous. He's probably got a different guy every night." He knew that wasn't true. Even if it *was* true, it wasn't fair. Not with as much fucking as Sam did, starting the minute he thought he could get away with it.

Dana was not having it. "He called *you*, you idiot!"

Rory was also not having it. She and Dana had been trying to get Sam into a good relationship almost since they'd met him. "Okay. I'm trying not to smack you right now. Tell us everything."

Sam sighed. "It was his birthday. Some guys got the shots thing going at this club. You know the one. He got pretty wasted. I took him home so none of *them* would. We spent the next day together. He took me out to dinner. And then, well."

Dana nudged him under the table. "All of it."

"Jesus! Okay, so he asked if he could come in, and we kissed, and we went to bed, and it was *heaven*, all right, and he left about five in the morning because he had to get home and get ready for work, and he called and I didn't pick up because, goddammit, I am too old for him and my face is fucked up and every time we walked down the street people would be looking at me and thinking, why is that beautiful boy with *that* mess?"

He stopped and looked away. There were tears in his eyes. The women said nothing for a minute. Then Dana reached over and took his hand. He wiped his eyes with the other.

Rory sighed, half guilty and half exasperated. "Sam. Thirty is not old, you asshole. In case you've forgotten, I'm thirty-four. And one of these days you're going to have to realize that a few scars do not make you ugly. If I were straight, I would do you in a hot minute." She paused to consider this. "Okay, we'd both have to be straight." He laughed a little.

"She's right, you know," said Dana.

"Do you think I don't have that shit, too? Here's Dana, with that body, and that face, she's like the Hollywood lipstick lesbian and she's with *me*, for fuck's sake. I'm short, I'm chunky, I shave my head, I've got ink all over me."

"You're not chunky, you're *curvy*."

"Thanks, sweetie. But you know what I mean." Rory turned back to Sam. "I'm, like, the Obvious Dyke. She could be on a sitcom. In fact, she *was* on a sitcom. And the point I am trying to make is that who we fall in love with doesn't necessarily track with how we look."

"And this guy liked you enough to stay with you all day, and take you out to dinner, and go to bed with you *sober*," Dana pointed out. "It's not like he humped you while he was drunk and then made a getaway as fast as he could"

Sam almost laughed again at that, but he shook his head. "I don't know."

Rory smacked him on the shoulder. "If he calls again, you'd better pick up."

"And if you *don't* pick up you'd better never admit that he called you."

"Or we will kick your frickin' ass," Rory promised.

"He liked Pachuco," Sam said softly.

Dana sighed. "Oh, Sam."

Chapter 4

November 2011

Sam was never a talkative or effusive man. His co-workers at the tux shop didn't seem to notice that he was even more quiet than usual in the weeks following That Night. Their customers were nearly always first-time, one-time people, so none of them noticed either. Dana and Rory did, of course; they kept trying to cheer him up. His friend Vince also asked him what had happened.

"What do you mean?" Sam was stalling. They'd met up at the Italian restaurant, in walking distance from both their apartments, as they did every two or three weeks on average. It had been a bit longer than that this time. Vince was deep in love, and up to Halloween had been deep in preparation for a performance with the Underground Cabaret. He was giving Sam a sardonic No Bullshit Please look. Sam sighed. "I met someone this summer."

Vince gave that a few seconds. When no more was forthcoming, he said, "And? Did he turn out to be an asshole?"

"No. Nothing like that."

Another pause. "Should I be concerned?"

"He was perfect. Young, fun, smart. Beautiful. We met at that club I told you about. It was his birthday." Now that he was talking, he couldn't seem to stop. "Guys were buying him shots. He got really fucked up, and I took him home so he'd be safe." Vince's face betrayed surprise. Sam shrugged, a little embarrassed. He knew most people didn't understand how hard it was for him to truly connect. They only knew that he didn't. "When he woke up, we talked. We both had the day off. We just hung out. He took me out to dinner. We ate here." He looked around as if to verify it was the same place. "And then he, he asked if he could come back home with me."

"Uh-huh." Another long pause as Vince deduced what happened next. "And he was perfect?" Sam nodded. Vince was trying to figure this out. He'd found his perfect partner only months ago and hadn't stopped talking to her since. But clearly Sam was not talking to this guy. "Did he not take your calls or something?" That would make him an asshole, and Sam said he wasn't, but otherwise Vince didn't know what the hell could have happened.

Sam was staring across the room. "I didn't take his calls."

"What the fuck, Sam." Vince couldn't figure this out at all. Sam was obviously miserable, maybe heartbroken, but it sounded as though he'd done it to himself. "I'm assuming you had some reason. Did you catch him kicking your cat?" Again, asshole, but Vince was trying to elicit some response.

Sam was gazing at him now. "I'm too old for him. I have a lot of baggage. I'm kind of a mess."

"Sam, for fuck's sake." Vince had heard from his new love Kelli on the subject of Sam. Old and mess were not included in the description. Not to mention Sam was actually younger than Vince. He frowned a little. The mystery guy had to be at least twenty-one. "How old is he?"

"Twenty-three." Which didn't sound that young, except when you compared it to thirty.

"Sam! For fuck's sake!" That almost got a laugh. Vince was exasperated. "Tell me you're having second

31

thoughts."

"Second, third, twentieth."

"Do you still have his number?"

"No." Sam planted his elbows on the table and dropped his head into his hands.

"God damn it." Sam nodded. Vince thought for a second. "You know his name, though." No sound, no movement. "He lives in L A." Silence again implied assent. "Are you going to try to find him? It couldn't be that hard." The number would be on his call records, even it if wasn't in his phone anymore. This guy was really conflicted. Vince didn't understand it.

Sam took a deep breath, let it out slowly, and raised his head. "By now he's probably decided it's not worth the trouble. I wouldn't blame him. He knows where I work." That escaped him. Mateo knew where he lived, too. Sam acknowledged, to himself, that by not answering the phone he'd put the younger man in an impossible position. "I should have talked to him."

"Yeah, you should. Well." Vince drank the rest of his wine. "He knows where to find you. Maybe he'll try again once he's over being mad." Vince would have been more hurt than mad, if Kelli hadn't taken his call. And they hadn't even been to bed on their first date. "I'd like to know why you'd blow something up like that. I mean on one level it's none of my business, but you're my friend and I'm not understanding you right now."

"I don't understand myself sometimes." Sam drank the rest of his wine. As if that were a signal, the server came over to see if they wanted anything else. Neither of them did. They fake-argued over the bill before agreeing to split it, as usual.

Ordinarily that would have meant the end of the evening, but Vince wanted to get to the bottom of this while he had the chance. Kelli had just moved in and his place was still a chaos zone. "Can we talk some more? I could walk back with you. A little extra exercise won't kill me."

Sam knew what Vince was trying to do, and he appreciated it. He didn't want to go into his history any more than he ever had, but something had to give. Maybe Mateo would never come back, even if Sam dug through his mobile bill to find the number, stopped being such a passive-aggressive coward, and called. And he might truly be too old and messed up for Mateo, but surely he wasn't too old, or too messed up, for everybody. "Yeah, okay. Let's walk."

They headed out, moving down the street at a good pace, but unhurried. Sam knew he needed to speak first. "I have some history," he said before they'd gone so far that it was awkward to say anything at all. "Everybody does, but I really suck at talking about mine. I grew up in foster care. Never really had someone I trusted to talk to, so I never learned how." Vince didn't say anything. Sam glanced over; as if he could feel the look, Vince made eye contact. Everything about him said to keep going, so Sam did. "I told you about doing MMA. That was when I had my first real relationship. And I say real but I have no idea if that's even what it was. I know he didn't love me. I think I wanted someone to belong to. It was sex, occasionally falling asleep together, and not much more. We were both still in the fights and nobody was out." Another shared glance. "After I quit the fights and moved here, I met some people. I was out, obviously, because that's easy here. Hooked up whenever I wanted. Had kind of a boyfriend for a

33

while. But I still wanted to belong to someone and that still wasn't happening." Words were pouring out now. "It's like, plenty of people want to fuck me but nobody wants to stick. That's been my whole life, except a few years up in Berkeley, the last family I lived with. So I don't know how to do it. I don't know how to belong. And that guy, it was so easy and cool and sweet with him, I'd give anything to belong to someone like him, but we're so different. And I got scared." He finally stopped talking. Swallowed hard, realizing how much he'd confessed.

That was a lot. Vince thought about it for a minute. They were almost to Sam's place. "What made you take him home?"

"Jules. The bartender. He gave me a guilt trip."

"Okay, but what made you care if he was safe?"

"The way we danced."

Oh. Now it made sense. Vince and Kelli had basically fallen in love dancing, so he knew all about that. "A good dance. A good day. A good dinner, and a good night. Did you think it was too good to be true?"

"I think I must have."

"But he called you."

"A few times. I'm such an asshole." Vince choked back a laugh. Sam didn't blame him. "That's what Rory said."

"It might be a little harsh. Sam, look. I think you should find his number and call him. But if you really think it couldn't work out, for whatever reason, maybe just start thinking about who you want to belong to. Where you might find that person. But you've got to be open-minded. I sure as shit didn't expect to find mine in the bar at Monsoon."

They'd arrived at Sam's apartment. He stopped at the door, knowing Vince would want to turn around now and go home to Kelli. "Thanks for this. I know you're right. I'll be thinking."

"Give me a call next week, let me know where you're at. Maybe you could come over and we'll play you the video from the show."

"Yeah, okay." Sam never went to the Cabaret. Rory and Dana never stopped giving him shit about it.

"Take it easy." They shook hands.

"You too." Sam watched Vince walk away, then opened his door and went in. "Hey Pachuco." The big cat was on the coffee table. He jumped down and went to Sam, making a face that said You Are Late. Sam laughed softly and picked him up. "I know I'm late." He put his face in the cat's fur. An hour later, he was forgiven. Why couldn't humans be as easy as cats?

***

April 2012

Mateo resolved not to let his disappointment about Sam ruin his life. It surely wasn't possible that the best night of his life had already come and gone. There had to be more out there. More great dancing, more great sex, more sense of belonging.

He tried, he really did. There were quite a few dates, most of which didn't go beyond a hand job and a "See ya." He couldn't help comparing the guys to Sam, and none of them came close to measuring up. There was one guy who had some of the same qualities, and Mateo gave that a good solid effort. They had enough dates to meet a few of each other's friends and refer to each other as boyfriends. First date: hand jobs. Second date, exchanging a little more

35

information: blow jobs. Third date: all the way, and it wasn't horrible. Objectively fine. If there hadn't been Sam, Mateo wouldn't have known anything was missing. At least the guy took it well when Mateo made a few suggestions for how this particular bottom might get off. But after a few more dates, when the guy pressed for a commitment, wanting to move in together, Mateo said no, and the guy said they were done. After the fact, Mateo wondered why. They hadn't even known each other for six months. The invitation had felt really premature, and frankly unwelcome. Then he realized that if it had been Sam he would have said yes—even after only that single, thirty-six-hour encounter—and he knew he was in trouble.

That was when he decided to look elsewhere for a while. He remembered what Sam said about that dance studio in WeHo. Obviously he wouldn't find Sam there. He was determined not to go looking for him. But he might at least enjoy some dancing again. He'd always felt like he belonged on the dance floor.

It wasn't at all convenient. He lived and worked in Santa Monica, forty minutes from West Hollywood. An experiment with a closer studio didn't work. He wasn't made to feel unwelcome, exactly, but nobody seemed thrilled to meet him. Mateo needed that. He missed his family (especially his baby sister), he didn't know what he'd done wrong with Sam, and he needed someone to smile when he came in.

****

There were four group classes to choose from at Shall We Dance. Mateo knew from experience that there was nothing like a group class for getting acquainted fast. On the night he dropped by the studio, the class was billed as Intermediate Ballroom,

36

which could have meant a lot of things. He was greeted by a good-looking woman who said, "Hi, I'm Julia," and asked about his background. When she heard he'd been on the Cal Poly team she told him to join the current class. "You won't have any trouble catching up," she said, and he didn't. He had a blast. Everyone there was nice. The women were happy to dance with someone who had some experience. So were the men who danced the follower part, even though a couple of them were taller than Mateo.

There was a shuffle midway through, when some students switched roles; that was even more of a kick. Mateo hadn't danced follower since college, except that one dance with Sam. "My God this is fun," he said out loud, about ten minutes before the end of the class.

The guy he was dancing with, a straight guy who looked to be around forty years old, smiled and said, "I'm glad you're enjoying it. You're Mateo, right?"

"Right. You're, give me a second. Aaron?" Mateo wasn't quite sure. He'd heard an awful lot of names.

"Very good. You'll be a real asset if you decide to come back."

"Oh, honey, you couldn't keep me away." He made sure to commit himself before he left, paying for the last two classes in the series and for the next six weeks.

Julia caught up to him after he changed his shoes. "You got the schedule, right? We'd love to see you at the social this weekend."

"Yeah?" She looked as though she sincerely wanted him there. Mateo would have cancelled a date to be at that Saturday social dance. "Then I'll be here." She gave him a hug and told him to drive carefully. He went home feeling more like himself than he had since moving to L.A. And feeling like himself finally felt okay.

***

The next Saturday night, Mateo had barely changed his shoes before an older man asked him to dance. "Good evening," he said. "I am Dmitri Vasko. Julia tells me you join the Intermediate class this week."

"Oh, you're the boss! Everybody's like, Dmitri said this. Dmitri does it this way. We all want to dance like Dmitri." The studio head looked amused. He took Mateo out on the floor for a rumba, and they didn't say anything else for a while. Mateo was paying attention to the lead. This didn't feel like a test, exactly, but he knew there was a lot they could tell each other this way. Dmitri's hold and his lead were both definite and light. Intentional and inviting. He was probably thirty years older than Mateo, as old as his father, but he moved like a much younger man. Only a couple inches taller than Mateo's five foot eight; their faces were close; he could very easily have put on the vibe. Mateo would have been disappointed if he had. This way he could absorb what was happening and think about it later. It had been a long time since he danced with someone so much better than he was. "God, you're good," he said, almost without meaning to. There was something very close to a smile from the boss. "I heard about this place from a guy who lives in the neighborhood. He has a friend who trains here. He didn't tell me the guy's name, though."

"You will meet everyone in time," Dmitri said. "If you like it here."

38

"I love it here. I saw on the calendar that you're doing Rising Star Smooth." He didn't ask why someone Dmitri's age was doing Rising Star.

Dmitri heard the question anyway. "My partner, she is new to ballroom. She is excellent."

Mateo heard: we won't be in Rising Star for long. "I kind of miss competition. But I need to get back in the groove. It's been a couple of years."

"Will be on calendar, when Michelle and I have an event. Or when others from the studio compete." The implication was that Mateo was welcome to go and observe, possibly to cheer the studio's dancers on. The rumba was over. Dmitri glanced around. "Come and meet my students Vince and Kelli. They compete at the L.A. Salsa Challenge soon. They danced at the House of Blues." There was a clear note of pride.

"No way!" Mateo followed along. Dmitri took him to a great-looking couple, both smiling as if they couldn't think of anything they'd like better than to meet some random newcomer. After a minimal introduction, Dmitri left them, placing his hand on Mateo's back for a second in a way that said he was one of them now, before he walked away. "Who even *is* that guy?" Mateo said, watching the boss, trying to disguise the emotion that touch elicited, then offered his hand. "Mateo de la Cruz. Nice to meet you."

"Likewise. Vince Conner, and this is my fiancée Kelli Lopez. Dmitri is a special person. I hear you were referred by a friend?"

"Kind of a friend. Guy I met last summer at a club in the neighborhood. I was hoping we would be friends." Mateo prayed he didn't look as desolate as he felt. He'd managed to almost forget how this all started. "How'd you find it?"

"I've lived down the street for years but managed to miss it until some friends of mine started taking lessons. Those two." Vince pointed at two women dancing together. "Vicky's the Glamazon and Sharon is the blonde."

"Then when *we* needed lessons, obviously we were going to take them here," Kelli said. "Vince and I put together a thing for the Underground Cabaret last Halloween. Have you been to any of those shows?"

"Never have."

"Oh honey, you *have* to. They're *insane*. The club where they perform, it's about to get completely renovated and expanded, it's the coolest thing ever. The next one's in June. You have to go." Kelli held onto both of Mateo's hands as though the world would end if he didn't see that show.

Mateo couldn't help smiling, couldn't help laughing. She was so pretty, and probably ten years older than he was, and she was acting like he belonged right here. "Will you be dancing then?"

"No, we did the one that just closed. Dammit! You should have seen us! We were so cute!" They both snickered while Vince produced a fake-embarrassed eyeroll.

"Dmitri said you were competing at the L.A. Salsa Challenge. When is that?"

"Next month. We're doing this chanson mambo, I dig it the most, and I have the best dress in the history of dresses. You should come see us! Vince, honey, why don't you go dance with somebody while I give Mateo the four-one-one " He leaned in and kissed her cheek, patted Mateo's back, and wandered off. "God I love that man."

Mateo laughed again. "So tell me all about the

Cabaret." He led Kelli over to a couple of vacant chairs and they settled in.

When he got home that night he looked through his closet, thinking he needed some better clothes. He was going to start hanging out with grown-ups, people who lived grown-up lives and worked for what they wanted. He'd send a text to Kristine and get her advice. She was the fashion expert in the family.

Kris very kindly didn't suggest tracking down the guy from last fall who worked in a tux shop. Instead she asked, "What were other people wearing at the social dance?"

"All kinds of stuff, but reasonably covered up. Not like at the gay clubs."

"Oh, so your fishnet crop tops won't cut it."

"Obviously, or I wouldn't have called you," Mateo said, rolling his eyes so hard she probably heard them rattle. "Look, you already sorted me out for work clothes, and dancewear is easy. I can literally go to a dancewear shop and get clothes to go dancing in. What I'm after is clothes for an adult social life. Going out to dinner at a decent restaurant with people older than me, versus going to pick up burgers and eat in someone's backyard."

"What people older than you?"

"Well, there's this guy, he's half Mexican and his fiancée is Nuyorican and they're about ten years older than me, but they're super nice, and it seems like they're at the dance studio a lot. I mean," he faltered, "maybe they were just being nice? But she sort of invited me to come and see them compete. And the studio owner kind of said that too."

"And you're trying to build a community for yourself," Kris said, catching on, "so you don't want to roll up at their competition in icky gym clothes or boring work clothes or slutty club clothes."

"Exactly," he said, too relieved to even object to the last item. Because truth, his club clothes were slutty.

"You want them to see you as an interesting adult."

"Exactly!"

"Which is what you are. Let me pull together a vision board for you, and then I want to hear all about your shopping trip."

"I wish you could come over here and shop with me." He meant it, too. "Someday? It's not *that* horrible a drive."

"It isn't," Kris said, "it's just my horrible schedule. Someday. And hey. I'm really glad you're meeting some nice people."

"Me too. It's about time, right?" Mateo changed the subject then, encouraging Kristine to bitch about her horrible schedule and gossip about their older siblings. Just like being at home.

Chapter 5

Sam came very close to calling Mateo. More than once, he looked at his phone records, wrote the number on a sticky note, put it on his desk and almost called. But he didn't know what to say, what he *could* say, and ultimately he chickened out. He was mad at himself about it. Felt like his inability to do this was some kind of character defect, even though his logical side argued that no one ever taught him how. Logically, this idea that relating to other humans should be natural and easy was very flawed. All you had to do was look around to see how many people failed at it, many of them in much worse ways than Sam failed. The logic didn't make the failure any easier to bear.

In years past, he'd have covered up the failure with a series of meaningless hookups. Now he thought that was another failure, a way to avoid taking chances. Deliberately avoiding situations where you might learn how to handle another person's heart pretty much guaranteed you never would. The silent argument he'd always made to himself was: at least I won't get hurt. But he did, because he didn't get what he wanted, and he ended up feeling used even when he was using someone else. No more.

He'd always worked out his feelings at the gym. It was the easiest, most obvious way, one that had served Sam well for over twenty years. Even there he was reminded. It wasn't that anyone at the gym was like Mateo. It was that almost every time he was there, some guy tried to pick him up. It didn't make him feel good. He'd never had more than a five-minute conversation with anyone there. Nobody approached saying, hey, I'd like to get to know you, how about dinner sometime. It was always hey, you're hot. Want to break the rules in the steam room. Want to shower with me.

And even that, Sam felt, was somehow his fault. Because he was so uncomfortable with small talk. He didn't know how to do it, and he could see how impatient other men were with him when he tried. He couldn't help thinking of that almost-painless day with Mateo, and the genuinely easy conversation over dinner. That couldn't possibly have been the best day of his life. He was too young for everything to go downhill from here.

That fearful thought made him even less receptive, bringing his temper closer to the surface. He never lost control of it, but when the guy who never racked his weights wouldn't leave him alone in the shower room Sam finally reacted. He stepped close, very much not in a way that said, sure, let's get it on right here. It was menacing, and after a second the guy realized it. He took a step back, smile fading. "Hey," he said. "I just want to get to know you."

"That's not what you said." Sam's voice was low, soft, and cold.

The guy looked like he was remembering and regretting exactly what he'd said. He stuck out a hand awkwardly, as if to shake. "Cory Perez."

Sam didn't take his hand. "Sam Lee. UFC, two thousand three to two thousand eight. Don't."

The guy swallowed, letting his hand fall. "Sure. Sorry." Sam didn't say anything else, only took a couple of steps back before turning away. The word got around fast. No one approached him anymore. He did his workouts in peace, hating himself all the more because now nobody even smiled at him.

44

He had to do better. Didn't want to go back to Vince and ask for lessons in being human. Sam should be able to get this by himself. He wasn't stupid. He wasn't incapable of reading social cues. He only needed to stop being afraid of doing something wrong. If he couldn't stop being afraid, he could at least stop letting that shut him down.

Sam thought about what Vince had said: who do you want to belong to. Where might you find that person. It should be someone physical, someone who would understand actions as well as words. But someone whose physicality wasn't bound to aggression or violence. Sam didn't want a combative person, or someone who used action *instead* of words. He wanted both. Where could he learn to talk to people who were physical? It was a real question. Not at the dojo, where no one but the sensei really talked. Not at the gym, at least not until he figured out how to make his own approaches, in a way that would signal friendliness. A way that would make amends for brushing Cory off harder than he'd needed to. A way to show all the others that they didn't need to be afraid of him.

The answer came like a revelation: try dancing. It worked with Mateo, so maybe it would work again. He felt like going out; it had been a long time, and he was so tired of himself. Even Pachuco was starting to look at him sideways. He didn't want to go to that same club, because it really was a place to pick someone up. It was loud and unsubtle; you couldn't talk even if you wanted to. But there were other places to dance.

He tried a few bars and restaurants that played salsa music and had dance floors. After several weeks he was in a groove. Dancing made him feel good. He was dancing almost entirely with women, and whether they could tell he was gay or not they all seemed to know he wasn't there for anything more than dancing. They talked to him. He got better at it, figuring out how to ask the right kind of questions, telling himself that talking to men didn't need to be any harder than this.

It was painful, sometimes feeling like he was literally breaking through a glass wall, but he practiced. Struck up conversations at the grocery store, or at BevMo or Petco or wherever else he went. And he learned. One of the things he learned: almost nobody objected to a conversation, even with a tall dark-skinned man with scars, when it began with a smile.

By April he thought he was ready to start a more difficult conversation. By then he'd been in the fortress of solitude at the gym for so long it was almost as though nobody even saw him. Sam told himself the worst that could happen was nothing changed. He was in the weight room at the same time as Cory, by design. When he got done with his reps he racked his weights, wiped his bench, and sat down on the floor by the wall. He didn't obviously watch, simply waited until the guy finished, noting that Cory now racked his weights too. Maybe somebody else said something. He gave Sam an uneasy sideways glance as he wiped his bench.

Sam said, "I owe you an apology." Cory looked totally surprised. Sam didn't wait for him to say anything. He went straight to the toughest thing he had to say, the thing most likely to end in some kind of insult. And he went there with at least a ghost of a smile. "I want to be in love. There was someone last year and I fucked it up, and for months after that I fucked everything up. I don't want to do hookups anymore. But I'm sorry I came at you like that. Could I buy you a coffee sometime?"

Cory was clearly thrown, but he didn't seem offended. After a moment he said, "Thanks for that. Nobody I talk to knows what your deal is. Are you even gay?"

Sam smiled for real. "Yeah."

"I thought so! I just, Jesus. When you did that I thought oh shit, I got this all wrong, he's going to kill me."

"I'm really sorry. I'm just barely housebroken." Cory laughed. Sam was relieved. "I'm done here today, and I've got some time. If today isn't good, some other time. Or if you don't want to, no worries."

"Today's good." Cory draped his towel around his neck. "I'm not going to the office today."

"What kind of work do you do?" Sam asked the question as he stood up, and the conversation lasted for two hours. When he thought about it later, he realized it was almost as easy as his dinner with Mateo. He went to work that afternoon feeling like he'd done something right. Maybe even something good.

Barely a week later, Cory asked if Sam would be interested in helping a friend tear down part of a garage. "Do what now?"

Cory grinned at him over the barbell. "This dude I picked up once offered to help a friend turn his garage into a casita kind of deal, and he mentioned it to me when he was in the other day, so I'm going over there Saturday. Are you working?" Sam shook his head. "Ever done demolition?"

"Sort of," Sam said. "One of the foster homes I was in, the guy volunteered with Habitat for Humanity. I wouldn't say I could build anything, but I can handle tools alright."

"Then you'll be fine with a sledgehammer. Know anybody else who could join? It sounds like the guy has a tight timeline."

"Why's he doing it now?"

"Long story. Short version is a homeless vet needs a safe place to stay for a little while."

Sam blinked, surprised. Remodeling a garage was not the easiest way to house someone, so it must be the way this particular vet could accept. "Okay, I'm in. Hang on." He went to get his phone, sending a quick text to Vince, who (Sam happened to be aware) also knew his way around a hammer and who (it turned out) was at loose ends on Saturday.

They rolled in together in the morning, surprising the homeowner and pleasing his friend. At the end of a long day of hard work, Sam felt true satisfaction. Not only had they done something good, he'd cemented another adult friendship.

And over the next two months, things kept getting better.

***

Sam had an invitation from Rory and Dana for the fourth of July. When he asked what he could contribute, Dana said they were going with a Polynesian barbecue theme, so he brought a fresh pineapple and some pork tenderloins. Rory did a soy-ginger glaze for the pig and pineapple both, serving them up with shrimp skewers, veggie kabobs, and coconut-guava rum punch. "Damn, girl," Sam said after a glass of that. "It's a good thing I walked here."

"That is UFC-level punch, isn't it," Dana said. "You look great. What's new?"

He knew they were both hoping to hear he was seeing somebody. But they seemed happy enough to hear that he'd made some friends at the gym, out dancing, and even at the dojo. "I'm learning how to human," he said.

Dana gave him a thumbs-up. "It's amazing how hard that is. When I was chasing Rory, I had to get a friend to help me." She told the story of her then-roommate, who'd acted as the go-between for a crucial information exchange. Then she said, "What's next?"

"I don't know. Kind of in a wait and see mode. I wouldn't say I'm all that good at talking yet, but at least I'm talking." He told them about Cory, and what a relief it was to fix that.

"But he's not for you, huh." Rory slurped some of her punch. "Wow, I really did make this strong. Or is he?"

"No, I don't think so. I told him I want to be in love, not hook up. He was all, okay, I respect that but I don't want that, nothing personal." Sam smiled at his friends. "And for once it didn't feel personal. So we can actually be friends, and I can give him shit about it when he makes some lame-ass pass."

***

Mateo was in Pomona for the Fourth. It was just as well his parents didn't ask him if he was seeing anybody, because he would have had to say No. They didn't ask him much of anything, actually, which let him know he wasn't quite forgiven, which was equal parts upsetting and infuriating. It was still good being with his family. He hadn't been out there since

Christmas; the whole place felt different. The house was redecorated. They had a new dog. Otherwise, the backyard cookout was very much as in years past. It was completely normal for Mateo to end up in a corner of the yard, trying to stay cool, talking to Kristine. "I can't believe you're still single," she said. "It can't be because nobody's chasing you."

"Eh. I'm kind of staying away from the places where people would chase me. Spending most of my free time at the dance studio. Getting back in the ballroom groove."

Kristine was glad to hear it. "I was going to ask! Are you planning to compete again?"

"I don't know yet. The boss guy is amazing. There's an older lady who does Latin with some of the guy students. I'm sort of sniffing around what other people do. Back in May two of Dmitri's students won a thing at the L.A. Salsa Challenge. I went to see that, and they were *so* good." He'd been too shy to join the group from the studio, which was stupid. Next time, maybe. "And a bunch of people there work with this semi-pro company called the Underground Cabaret. Their show last month was *amazing*."

Kristine wanted to hear all about that, especially because talking about it seemed to make Mateo happy, which he had kind of obviously not been up to now. Since he hadn't busted out a dating story of any kind, and had so promptly steered away from the subject, she started to wonder if he even *was* dating. Her adorable brother couldn't possibly stay single for long. Though it was none of her business, and she had her own problems. Kristine was heading into her senior year at Cal Poly and everyone was letting her know they expected her to get married right after graduation. In order to stop thinking about that, she changed the subject to his apartment in Santa Monica. "Is it totally awesome being so close to the ocean?" she asked wistfully.

"It's *cold*," he said. "Compared to out here. Had to buy a quilt! And I toast marshmallows on the cooktop."

"You do not," she said, laughing.

"I totally do. I make my little adobo burrito for dinner and then I make a cup of decaf, dump some cocoa mix in it, and toast a marshmallow." He didn't add that it was as close as he got to a hug most of the winter, because while that was true, he got a lot of hugs now at the studio. Didn't want to sound pathetic, or like he was regretting moving to Los Angeles. Things were definitely better than they had been before Shall We Dance. Still a long damn way from perfect.

He wasn't ready to admit how close he was to giving in and going after Sam again. If that was even the right way to think of it: Giving In. Maybe what he did before was Give Up. He knew where to find the guy, after all.

On the other hand, the last six months had kind of helped him find himself. He knew what he *didn't* want now. Not a bad place to be, considering he'd had exactly no one to help him figure all this shit out. His job was copacetic, there were suddenly a lot of people he could call friends, and pretty soon he'd be ready to think about trying again.

Chapter 6

September 2012

Mateo was tired, hot, and hungry, but he was focused. He was at the studio, practicing a paso doble routine with another of the regular students. Dmitri was coaching them, having encouraged the pairing. He'd implied that the other students would benefit from seeing a same-sex routine. As they finished this run-through, he said, "Once more. I video for you. Mateo, keep your head up. Richard, stronger center. Places, please." When they finished this time, the other students in the room applauded. Dmitri nodded and switched off the camera. "I send you the file tonight."

"Thanks, boss," Mateo said after catching his breath. "We were thinking we could submit it to Underground Cabaret for their Halloween show." It was almost a question.

Dmitri looked pleased. "Yes, of course."

Mateo looked at Richard. "Want to get some dinner?"

"Not tonight, thanks. I've got a date."

"You've always got a date!"

Richard smiled. "What can I say, I'm in demand."

They gathered up their gear and headed out to their separate cars. Mateo got into his with a wave that he knew said Won't Ask Again. It wasn't the first time he'd suggested doing something social with Richard, but it would definitely be the last. He couldn't tell if the other guy was genuinely not interested, was playing hard to get, or was playing it off because they were both so active at the studio. It could get messy if they got involved and something went sideways.

Which it probably would. Mateo had given up on hookups after one too many nights thinking Why Did I Bother. He'd given up on dating because he couldn't stop thinking about Sam.

He ordered some takeout at a Mexican joint and drove back to Santa Monica with the sun in his eyes all the way, feeling lonely and frustrated. When he got home, he called his sister. "Hey Kris. I just wanted to warn you I'm about to go stalker."

"*What?*"

"Remember last year when I had that one-night stand?"

"Ooh, yeah. You never heard back from him, huh?"

"No. And I can't get him out of my head. I went back to that club last week and didn't see him. I don't want to hang out there hoping he'll show up, and I don't want to call him in case he doesn't pick up again. So I've just about decided to go by the place he used to work and see if he's still there."

"Go for it," she said instantly.

"You don't think I'm being obsessive and weird?"

A dismissive huff. "No. I think you're in love."

Mateo wriggled, uncomfortable, even though he suspected she was right. "You don't think one day and one night is kind of a short amount of time to fall in love?"

"No. You know that line from 'Silk Stockings,' it's a chemical reaction, that's all. Nothing you can do about it." Kristine sounded utterly convinced.

He loved her so much. "God, only you."

"Oh, like you haven't memorized that movie."

Mateo laughed. "Shut up."

"Let me ask you something."

"What."

"How many dates have you been on in the last year or so? I haven't heard of many."

"There were a few. Actually more than a few." All a complete waste of time.

"You even kind of had a boyfriend for a while there, right?"

"Kind of, yeah." Mateo still couldn't believe how clueless he'd been about that. The other guy had been falling in love while Mateo had been...not. Hadn't even noticed. He felt a little guilty about it.

"And you're still hung up on this guy." Mateo didn't precisely answer, but he made a sound that Kristine could interpret as assent. "So, if what you're waiting for is permission to go after what you want, you have it."

Thank God for that. "I may be calling you in a few days crying to bail me out."

Kristine made an exasperated sound. "I really don't think he'll call the cops on you."

"You'll be the first to know." With that, Mateo disconnected. Stared at the phone for a second, then opened a browser to look up the tux shop again. Told himself it made sense to double-check the hours.

***

Late the following Saturday afternoon, Mateo walked into the tux shop on Westwood. He was nervous, so he kept his sunglasses on. Looking around the store for a minute, seeing no one, he huffed out a breath. Then he heard a low voice, as of someone on the telephone in the office, and took up a position by a display case full of ties and cufflinks. After a minute,

54

Sam came out of the office, looking elegant in a suit and tie. He stopped short, staring at Mateo, who was glad he'd worn something other than a tee shirt with his jeans. The tailored silk and linen shirt from Tommy Bahama was clean and pressed. Mateo took off his sunglasses. "Hi, Sam."

Sam couldn't have been more astonished if Giorgio Armani himself had walked in. "Um. Hi, Mateo. Can I help you?"

"Yeah, actually." He walked straight up to Sam, grabbed him by the back of the neck, and kissed him. After a shocked second, Sam's arms went around him. They lost themselves for a long moment.

When Sam broke the kiss, he didn't let go. "What are you doing here?"

"I can't get you out of my head. I think I'm in love with you." Shit, didn't mean to say that. Mateo kept eye contact with a superhuman effort.

This was the very last thing Sam ever expected. He heard the words but could barely process them. Tried to come up with a sensible reply, but failed. "I don't know what to say."

"You could tell me why you never picked up when I called."

"Oh, shit. Because I'm an asshole. At least that's what my friend Rory says. And she's always right." He was still holding Mateo. Never wanted to let go.

Mateo laughed, lightheaded with relief because Sam was still holding him and he felt relaxed. He looked happy, which made Mateo extremely happy. "Did she ever tell you to call me?"

"No." Not in so many words.

"Then I've got a bone to pick with her. Sam, *why*? We had such a great day. And night." And oh God, shut up.

Sam gazed at him. "Are you busy tonight? Could we go somewhere and talk?"

"I'll stay right here until you're done."

"I won't disappear. I promise. We close at six." Sam reluctantly released Mateo. He wanted to kiss him again. His gaze dropped to Mateo's mouth. There was nobody else in the shop, so fuck it. He bent for another kiss, a light kiss, not starting anything. Only promising. Remembering. Getting reacquainted. Easing back wasn't at all easy.

The kiss didn't last long enough, but Mateo didn't let himself cling. "I know when you close." Mateo took a seat on a chair behind the display case as Sam turned away to do whatever he needed to do. Pulled out his phone and sent a text to his sister: **He didn't kick me out!**

Told ya. Dork.

OXO. He checked his messages, rolled his eyes over a last-minute request from his employer, checked his calendar, read a few news articles. He was about to mute the phone when an incoming text message beeped. He opened it up. "Hey! Cool." A quick call to Richard, who didn't pick up, so he left a message. "Richard, the Frankenstein routine passed the audition. Dress rehearsal is Saturday before show date. Eleven a.m. at the club. See you at Dmitri's next week." He disconnected.

"Who's Richard?"

Mateo looked over at Sam, who was locking up the front door and not looking at him. "I wish that were jealousy talking."

"It is."

Mateo smiled. "Richard's my dance partner. For now. For a show. I've started dancing again and I'm working with a girl, too, but there was this casting call and I'd met Richard at the studio and I really don't care about him. I want to talk about you. I want to talk about *us*."

"I do, too."

"Well, let's go." Mateo stood up and headed for the back.

"Should I follow you?"

"No way, you're coming in my car so I can keep an eye on you." Sam laughed, following him out the back door, locking it behind them.

Mateo's heart was pounding from nerves and excitement as he drove west. He couldn't believe that worked. Like, it Totally Worked. A glance over at Sam showed him an apparently calm face but tense hands. He wasn't looking at Mateo when he asked, "Where are we going?"

"Well, first we're going to my place so we can talk. And then we can talk about where else to go."

"Okay. You're a little bossy." Smiling now.

"I've been wigging out about you for a year, and now I've had my hands on you again, and I'm so horny I can hardly see the road." He was, too. He'd always liked a tall man. An athletic man. A long-legged man. And then there was that mouth. Jeez, he had to stop this or he'd crash for real.

Sam was baffled. He spread his fingers, made fists, relaxed. "I'm sorry I didn't pick up your calls."

"My sister said maybe you thought I was too young for you."

"Well, I thought I was too old for you.

57

And…you're beautiful, and I'm not."

"Bullshit!" Mateo glanced in the rear-view and side mirrors before making a dive for the curb lane. Sam looked startled and a car honked behind them. Mateo pulled over on a yellow curb and slammed the car into Park. He turned to face Sam, deadly serious. "Sam, I am twenty-four, not sixteen. And I'm just a regular guy, not a supermodel. That night with you was the best night of my life. I want you. *You.*"

"I never thought…"

"Honey, somewhere down the line, someone did a number on you. But it's going to be my mission to make you believe you are everything I want."

Sam reached over and touched Mateo's face. He ran his hand through Mateo's hair. Mateo turned his face into Sam's hand and kissed the palm. Sam leaned close and kissed him. Finally, he drew away. He glanced at the driver's side mirror and smiled. "You'd better peel out." A parking enforcement vehicle was in view, a few cars back.

"Yellow line is fine after six. That metermaid's out of luck." Mateo put the car in Drive, signaled, waited decorously for a gap in traffic, and pulled out. They didn't talk for the next few minutes, but they were both more relaxed now.

Mateo found a parking spot a block from his apartment, hung up his permit, and got out of the car. Sam followed slowly. "If you don't pick up some speed, I'm going to think you don't really want to come with me."

Sam shook his head. "I still can't believe this is happening."

"Believe it. And something else you can believe is, I've never done anything like this before. I had to ask my sister if I was turning into a stalker. Come on, big guy." He held out his hand to Sam, who took it. They walked up to the building, then up the stairs. Mateo unlocked the door and pulled Sam inside. "I'll give you the quick tour—"

Sam shut the door and leaned back against it, pulling Mateo into a bear hug. Then he dipped his head to kiss Mateo's neck. His hands wandered. "Fuck the tour. God, you feel good."

"This way," Mateo said, breathless. He backed away, holding Sam's hand, and started toward the bedroom.

Chapter 7

Sam had never come back to a lover after a lengthy separation, so he wasn't familiar with reunion sex as more than a concept. In the future, he would always think of haste. Frenzy. Kisses that bruised, clutching hands that left marks. Clothes dropped heedlessly to the floor, stumbling through a doorway, crashing onto a bed.

It was good that they were both in such a hurry to get off. This was no time to discuss what or who they'd done since their last time naked together. No time to fumble for lubes or condoms, no time for prep, no time for anything except bare skin and friction. By the time they achieved full body-to-body contact, they were both dripping with precome. That was all the lube Sam needed, or at least all he wanted to bother with. Enough to keep their two urgent erections from going up in actual flame as they ground against each other. Enough to let him focus on Mateo's mouth, the desperate sounds he made, the sweat that bloomed on his skin, the dizzying scent of desire.

From the moment they started moving through the apartment, they didn't exchange a single actual word. Not until they both lay still, gasping for breath, overheated and messy. Sam slowly catalogued his parts. Legs tangled with Mateo's. One arm wrapped tight around the other man, slick with sweat in the hollow of his back, that hand gripping the outside of a butt cheek. The other hand in Mateo's hair, holding his head against Sam's chest. Then, of all the words he might have found, the one he managed was, "Amazing."

***

Mateo peeled himself off Sam after a while, likewise amazed by that episode. They'd simply ripped their clothes off, fallen onto the bed, and pressed against each other, moving against each other, kissing. Mateo couldn't remember coming that fast since he was about twelve, and Sam had been only seconds behind. Mateo kept one hand on that hard, dark body as he settled to one side. Said the first thing that came to mind, as if they'd been in the middle of a conversation. "I've been thinking about it a lot. For the longest time I thought I must have done something wrong."

Sam stirred. "You didn't do anything wrong. You were perfect."

Mateo patted him. "After a while I thought, okay. He's older, he's got history, maybe it wasn't me. My sister thought maybe you were in a relationship."

"You told your sister about me?"

"I told her everything. I told bits and pieces to anybody else who would listen. The head guy at that studio, he's my father's age. His, I don't think she's his business partner, call her his associate. She's old enough to be my mother. I won't lie, I threw myself at them. I didn't even realize how much I missed my parents until I met those people. Anyway, Julia, she said what was his home like. And I realized you didn't have family stuff. No pictures. Almost nothing personal, and nothing that might have come with you from your parents' house."

Sam was astonished all over again, that Mateo had noticed and remembered. He didn't know what to say, as usual. Didn't want to go into his history right now, but was determined to say something. "I never really had a home till I moved to WeHo."

"I thought maybe that was it. And maybe you'll tell me about it sometime. But after I stopped trying to date I kept thinking about that."

"You weren't dating?"

"I was for a while. I was like, okay, that hurt but it didn't kill you, get back out there. I had sort of a boyfriend for a while, and then I stopped."

"What happened?" Sam's voice was soft. He wasn't sure he had the right to ask.

"He wanted me to move in with him. And I said no, it hasn't been long enough, I'm not ready for that. He pulled the plug, and I thought what the fuck. But then I realized, well, never mind." Mateo didn't want to go there yet. "Anyway I realized I needed to take some time off."

"I never have dated much, but I took time off too. I was so mad at myself for not having the guts to take your calls. I thought, I need to get better at this. He didn't deserve that, nobody does, I need to fix it." Sam turned his head. Mateo was watching him, listening. Sam smiled a little. "God, you're beautiful. Anyway I have a friend who would have walked me through it. The salsa guy. Vince."

"I know Vince! I met him at the studio."

"He's great, isn't he? Helped me a lot when we worked together before. Taught me how it works in a real job, how to conduct myself. I didn't want to lean on him this time. So I put myself through, like, social school. Went out dancing a lot. Talked to a lot of women, they were a big help. They're all like, ask me this. Tell me that. Why, where, who. You can't put anything over on a woman, not if you want her to dance with you." Mateo made a sound that was half amusement, half agreement. Sam ran a finger up his golden flank. "So I tried it on a guy at the gym, and we got friendly. Started talking to more of the guys there, and at my dojo. Talked to the ladies at the nail salon." He gazed at Mateo, lifted a hand and traced a knuckle down the side of that pretty face. "I thought I'd never see you again, but at least I wouldn't do that to anyone else."

"You really thought I'd give up?"

Everyone else did. Or maybe *he* did. "I almost called you so many times. But then so much time had passed that I thought it was too late. I thought it would be an insult to call you after all that time."

"Sam, for fuck's sake." Sam laughed. Mateo made a querying face, so Sam told him how Vince had said that. Mateo leaned in to kiss him again. "I told Vince some stuff. I wonder if he knew I was talking about you."

"He probably did."

They got up after a while. Mateo made them each a cup of tea, took a bowl of trail mix into the bedroom and lit some candles. They flickered in the slight breeze making its way to them from the living area's open windows. Mateo sat there with his half-empty mug, looking at Sam, gloriously naked beside him on the bed. "Your body is amazing. Tell me the secret, aside from being six foot one."

"Tai chi."

"Really? No, fuck that. You've got the dojo and the gym plus you're dancing." Mateo ticked them off on his fingers. "It's being six foot one. I'd be the Pillsbury doughboy if I didn't do every damn thing."

"You would not."

"Oh yes I would. Here." Mateo found his phone and pulled up a picture from his college graduation.

He handed it to Sam, who looked at the family lineup and said, "I see." Mateo snickered. His brother and his father were both shorter than he was, and distinctly rounder. "I'm guessing they don't work out that hard."

"Well, they're married. They say they don't have time."

Sam made a dismissive noise. If you wanted to stay fit, you found the time. "You're doing good. I lift weights. Do some yoga. Basically all I do aside from my job is work out." Sam wasn't as heavy as he'd been during his fighting years. Now he was slim and sleek. He liked his body, the way it worked, the way it looked both naked and clothed. He realized it was safe to say that to Mateo, so he did.

Mateo, glad he'd hung up Sam's suit before going to make the tea, confessed, "I don't even own a suit."

"I'll take you to Men's Wearhouse sometime and hook you up." Mateo laughed and nodded. Sam was smiling. "Be your fashion guru."

"Then I can go in and ask for a raise. This place I'm working, I think they got me for a little under market." Mateo shrugged. He was doing fine. His own apartment, a decent car, and no trouble paying his student loan. "So tell me about dancing?" He held out the bowl of trail mix.

Sam took a handful. "About once a week. I haven't been back to the club, though."

"I *know*. I went looking for you there. That surfer dude tried to pick me up again. You owe me a night at the Mayan, or Monsoon, at least."

Sam smiled. "Let's go next weekend."

"It's a date."

"How about you? You said you're dancing again too. You found the studio."

"Yeah, it's literally down the block from that Italian restaurant. Everyone there has been awesome. You used to work with Vince?"

"He worked at Men's Wearhouse part of the time I was there. But tell me about Frankenstein." Sam couldn't imagine what that was about.

Mateo waved a hand; it wasn't important. "So Vince and his hot girlfriend, actually she's his fiancée, did you know that? Oh, sure you did. They have an in with this group called Underground Cabaret and told me about an open audition for a Halloween show. I'd been working with Richard for a month or so, just goofing around, and asked if he wanted to put something together. So we took that song and we're doing a paso doble."

"That's the bullfighter one, right?"

"Yeah. Our coach emailed me a video for the audition, I can show it to you if you want."

"Definitely."

"The show is October 30 and 31. I'd love it if you could come. I'd like you to meet the girls who run the thing. Though I think you already know one."

"Yeah, I do. My friend Rory's their stripper, and her girlfriend Dana works the pole from time to time."

"Are they gonna be happy about this?" He was really asking if Sam had mentioned him before.

Sam knew it. "Yeah, they are. They couldn't believe I didn't answer your calls."

It seemed almost funny now. "I couldn't either! You have anything you need to do tomorrow?"

"Well, I'd better get back home sometime and check on Pachuco."

Mateo looked guilty. "Oops, yeah."

Sam laughed. "Don't worry, he'll be pissed but he's got one of those auto-feeders."

"So we could go out for brunch?"

"Sure."

"Then I've actually got some work, some dumbass thing that really could wait for Monday but nooooo, they want it sent by six tomorrow."

"But you don't have to work on it tonight?" Mateo made a face that said Hell No. Sam touched him again, because he could, poking a fingertip into that not-at-all-doughboy belly. "Do you want to go get some dinner?"

"Actually not feeling very hungry right now."

"All that gorp."

Mateo smiled wickedly. "No, that's not it." He set the empty bowl down on the nightstand and ran his hand up Sam's leg. Sam caught the hand and pulled him up to lie alongside him. Mateo threw a leg over Sam's and skimmed a hand down his body, loving the contrast of their skin colors. "I love the way you look. Believe it yet?"

"I'm getting there." He pulled Mateo up for a kiss, and then somehow flipped him over so they were back to front.

Mateo giggled. "Is that tai chi?" He wriggled his butt against Sam's dick.

"No, that's me getting a hold of this." Both hands on Mateo, stroking down his sides to his hips. One hand closing around his cock, which immediately reacted. Filling, lengthening, pushing insistently upward. He let it rise, stroking, thumbing the head.

"Oh…okay," said Mateo, his head falling back against Sam's shoulder. "I guess that's…holy *fuck*."

Sam laughed softly, his other hand skimming over Mateo's smooth chest, head turned to see Mateo's eyes close, his lips part, his throat work as his breath caught. Sam was fully aroused again too. "What do you want, baby?"

"You."

***

Pachuco had things to say about being left alone so long. Sam gave the cat his attention for quite a while, feeding and grooming while talking nonstop about Mateo. "You know what I realized?" He stretched out on the couch with the cat on his chest. "He's the first college guy I've been with. All those other guys were like me, made it through high school by the skin of their teeth or not at all. Everybody had a job, but none of us thought we were professionals. We all had this chip on our shoulder. But I'm the one wearing a suit." Pachuco was purring, enjoying Sam's hands and voice. "He's like, how'd you put that tie with that suit. I was cracking up." Sam petted the cat some more. "He makes more money than me now. Good thing I saved when I was doing the fights." He wasn't worried about it, though. He'd thought he might be, thought that not being a college man himself could be a disadvantage. But Mateo didn't care. Nothing they talked about was beyond Sam's grasp. School might not have done much for Sam, but it seemed all the reading he'd done since then accomplished something. There were things he could teach Mateo. He couldn't wait to begin.

***

Over in Santa Monica, Mateo was thinking too. Part of his brain was always free to think while he was producing a drawing, and what it chose to think about this time was the future. He was thinking that he and

67

Sam might actually *have* a future. He'd managed to not use the L-word more than the once, but he knew Sam heard it. Sooner or later they'd get to the bottom of the inferiority complex. Their nineteen-hour second date had gone a long way to convincing both of them that something was very right. Without actually interrogating each other, they'd arrived at an understanding that each man was solvent, each man had savings, each man had solid career prospects and health insurance and a retirement plan. Mateo couldn't even remember how the subject of money came up. Maybe when they were walking back to his place from breakfast. Sam had insisted on paying. He'd been funny about it: he was wearing a suit, after all. Mateo had made a joke about being his girlfriend. Sam put an arm around him and said, "You're my boyfriend. Aren't you?"

Mateo turned his head for a kiss and said, "Yes." Going from All Alone to Sam's Boyfriend in less than twenty-four hours felt like winning the biggest trophy in the history of trophies. "Oh fuck," he said out loud, looking at the graphic on his screen, making a correction. Better keep his mind on his business for a while.

He was getting ready to go for a run the next day when his phone buzzed. He wasn't expecting another text from Sam—they'd just finished organizing a salsa date for Wednesday night, as apparently next weekend was too far away—but he was perfectly willing to put off that run and flirt with Sam some more. The message wasn't from Sam, though; it was from Kristine: *So why haven't I heard from you??*

Oops well been kind of busy

Busy getting busy?

Mateo didn't bother texting back. He switched modes and called. His sister picked up immediately. "Tell me all," she demanded. "He didn't throw you out. Then what happened?"

"Then we talked, and I brought him back to my place, and we got busy, and then we talked again, and then we got busy again." Kristine was giggling. Mateo was grinning. "He stayed all night. Took me out for breakfast. Asked me if I was his boyfriend now, and I most definitely said yes. We're going out dancing later this week."

"That's all good. That's great! So why the hell did he not answer your calls?"

"He's got this inferiority complex. It's a long story. I don't know all of it yet, but I told you he was a fighter, right? MMA. He's got some scars and he's really self-conscious about them. Plus he thought he was too old for me. I was like, bitch, please." Kristine was cracking up. Mateo could have talked about Sam all night. "I'll send you a picture in a minute. I was about to go for a run and then I swear I was going to call you."

"If he was there all night Saturday, I'm surprised you're even walking today."

Mateo cackled. "How much detail do you want? 'Cause I will spill every last filthy bean."

"Not that much," Kristine decided. "Only you're happy, right?"

"Oh my God Kris. So happy." He debated for barely a second before saying, "I told him I thought I was in love with him."

"Oh my Jesus Mateo. What did he say?"

"Nothing. But I know he heard me. And he didn't run away. I mean, that was right when I got there. I

opened my mouth and that fell out. I almost died."
Kristine laughed again. They talked for a little while
longer. Mateo tried to get a hint of what was going on
in his sister's love life.

"Don't ask," she said. "If I start unloading you'll
never get your run in. Besides, it's not important.
There's nothing bad." Nothing really good either,
from the sound of it, but Mateo knew better than to
push. He promised to call every week, sent the
promised picture, got off the phone, and went for his
run on the beach.

***

Meanwhile in West L.A., Sam was at work,
having a typically quiet evening shift. He was
seriously tempted to text Mateo again, but there
wasn't really anything new to say. In order to pass the
time he sent a message to Vince instead: **Hey amigo
guess what. I'm getting a second chance**

The reply was fast. Predictably, Vince didn't need
more details: *Last summer's guy came back?*

**Yes he did. Showed up at the store on
Saturday**

Going to work it out this time?

**I think we already did. I spent the night at his
place. I'll bet you guessed it was Mateo**

*Sort of. Was hoping. He's a nice guy. Good
dancer too*

**We're going out Wednesday. Oops someone
just came in, ttyl**. Sam slid his phone into his pocket
and went to greet his customer. Throughout the
browsing and the conversation and the transaction, he
was low-key thinking about how maybe he and Mateo
could go out with Vince and Kelli someday. A double
date, like grown-ups.

Sam had never thought of himself as particularly domestic, but after seeing Mateo's place he looked at his own with fresh eyes. The only things the younger man had that said Home were a few framed snapshots of friends and family. Aside from those, his apartment could have been a hotel room, if the hotel had a really good computer and stereo. It wasn't all that different from the apartments of other men Sam had known. Now he realized how different his own was. He didn't have the family history things, but (in addition to having color on his walls) he had books, art, rugs and pillows. Plus, of course, there was the cat.

He mentioned it to Rory and Dana when he saw them on Tuesday. First they had to get the whole life update out of the way, which started with "So Mateo came by the store on Saturday." The resulting puzzled expressions led to, "The guy from last year," which led to a long-ass story with an embarrassing amount of detail followed by some hugs. Then he said, "He noticed that I don't have any family stuff. I'm going to ask the Lees to send me a good picture I can print up and get framed."

Dana smothered a surprised reaction. "That's great. I know they're important to you."

"They are, and I've got pictures in my phone, but I kind of wanted them to know I want to put one out where people can see it. Then I thought I could send them a picture of my place, and they can see where they are in it. Is that a good idea?" Sam knew his foster parents had at least one picture of him in their home.

"That's an awesome idea," Rory said, after a second to clear her throat. "Have they ever seen your place before?"

71

"No. I'm going to tell them I'm in love. Mrs. Lee, she asks once in a while, if I'm seeing somebody special." Neither of the women commented on the L word, though he could tell they were both dying to. "That's what he said. He said, I think I'm in love with you. And I think I must be too. Don't you?"

"Um, yeah." Rory gave him a fondly exasperated look. "I'm glad you're not scared to say so."

"Well, I was scared to say it to *him*." Both women laughed. Sam was smiling. "I'll get there. He's so, I don't know, easy. I mean I feel like I can say anything. I'm not used to it yet."

"It's only been five minutes," Dana pointed out. "Give yourself a break. You've come a long way since this time last year."

He really had. Some of the process had been uncomfortable, even painful, but every other thing he'd learned was that way. No surprise that this was the same. After he sent the email to Mrs. Lee, he decided to write to his first sensei, the man who began Sam's training as a martial artist. Walked down the street to the drugstore and picked up a Halloween greeting card, and then had no idea what to write inside. He finally settled for:

Hi Mr. Mendoza, Just felt like getting in touch. I'm doing well. Still doing tai chi and staying out of trouble. Hope you and Mrs. Mendoza are well. Would be great to hear from you sometime. Here's my new email address. Take care – Sam Lee

He sealed the envelope and put a stamp on it before he could talk himself out of it. The Mendozas didn't know he was gay, as far as he knew. He'd left their home before he was ready to talk about anything that sensitive. They exchanged Christmas cards, always civil, never very personal. This desire to tell people about Mateo might be the end of even that limited correspondence, because if things worked out there was no way Sam couldn't say something about it in the Christmas card. It was the biggest and best news he'd had since his promotion to manager. It was basically the best news of his life. Sam simply didn't know if the Mendozas would agree with that, but he wanted to tell them anyway. He wanted to tell the whole world.

Chapter 8

October 2012

A few weeks of being Mateo's boyfriend later, Sam had managed to introduce him to exactly none of his friends. When they got together they couldn't seem to keep their hands off each other, which was thrilling but also slightly embarrassing. Someday soon, he thought, they'd be able to conduct themselves decently, and then some kind of social life could begin. If Rory and Dana hadn't already figured out that Sam's Mateo and Shall We Dance Mateo were the same guy, they were bound to when Sam showed up to see the Underground Cabaret's Halloween production at Chrome.

After going inside, Sam stood on the catwalk for a minute, taking in what he could see of the club. Looked over the railing, down into the main floor. It was already filling up. He went downstairs, where he found an empty two-top near the bar and hitched himself onto a seat. A server arrived within seconds. "Hey there. First time?"

"Yeah."

"Are you expecting somebody else or can we seat someone with you?"

"No, that's fine. I mean yeah, you can seat someone else here."

"Great, we're gonna be packed. What can I get you?"

"Um, is there a special tonight?"

"Tequila Sunset, featuring jalapeño vodka, OJ, grenadine, and cheap-ass tequila."

Sam laughed. "I'll take one of those. And water."

"You got it." She zoomed away.

Sam looked around and saw Rory poke her head out from the wing curtain. She spotted him, grinned, and waved. He waved back and she disappeared. In a minute she came through the stage door and scurried through the crowd. She was wearing jeans and a Jack Skellington tee shirt, which meant Sam felt right at home in his Beetlejuice-inspired jacket. "To what do we owe the honor? You've never come to our show before! You didn't say you were coming!"

He'd meant to, but they got to talking about other stuff and it slipped his mind. "Mateo's dancing tonight. Paso doble? Frankenstein?"

"Mateo? Holy shit! Your Mateo is *our* Mateo?"

Sam smiled. "Yeah."

"Can't believe you didn't mention that interesting fact." Sam made an apologetic face. Rory rolled her eyes. "Like oh by the way the perfect kid is dancing in your thing. Does he know you're here?"

"Yeah."

"I have to reconfigure my whole worldview now. Gotta run. Don't take off after the show." She grabbed his braid to pull him down for a kiss, then hustled back to the stage door, where she checked in with Kim, that night's director. "Anything you need from me?"

"No, I'm good. Except who's that guy you just talked to?"

"Over by the bar? That's my friend Sam. He's got a thing with Mateo."

"Ooh, pretty Mateo." Kim peeked around the curtain and looked again; she'd mostly noticed the jacket and the hair. "Damn. Pretty Sam!"

"He doesn't think so. We're working on him."

Dana came up. "What are you talking about?" She peeked around the curtain too. "Oh! It's Sam!"

"He is fucking *fine*," Kim said. "Like Desmond Richardson, Keanu Reeves, and Danny Trejo all mixed up. I would sit on that face any day. Do not tell Hector I said that."

Rory snorted out a laugh. "Andy's going to be bitching at me for not introducing them earlier. I told Sam to stick around after the show. Dana, he's here for Mateo. I mean, he's *with* Mateo. Mateo's the guy."

Dana said, "The guy from last year? Mateo is *that* Mateo?!" and did a happy dance.

***

Back on the club floor, the waitress had returned with Sam's drink and with someone to share the table. Sam nodded a greeting and turned away, taking what turned out to be an incautiously large mouthful of his drink. "*Damn.*" He coughed a little.

The newcomer said, "What's that?"

"Tonight's special. They're calling it a Tequila Sunset. It's got jalapeño vodka in it, and they were not shy."

"Is it good?"

"It's kind of nasty, but I like it."

The guy laughed. Then the background music and the lighting changed to indicate that the show was about to start. The first half had everything from a stripper (not Rory) to a group doing 'Monster Mash.' At intermission, Sam looked over to find another Tequila Sunset on the table in front of the other guy. He pointed to the cocktail and said, "You weren't kidding. It's got a bite to it. Good show, huh? My name's Andy, by the way. I do their posters."

"I'm Sam. Nice to meet you. A couple of friends of mine are in it. I'm kind of kicking myself that I've never come to see them before."

"A friend of mine runs the video. You should check out some of the back issues. Which artist is your friend?"

"Rory Atwood, mainly, and Dana. We've known each other for a while. Tonight there's a guest act I'm here to see, too."

"Rory's the best. Her number in the 'Blue' show was fucking hilarious."

Mateo said the same. Sam really needed to catch up with this shit. The lights went down again. The act opened with a group using kung-fu movie-style flying rigs. Sam had just finished processing the martial-arts adaptation to the stage, surprised by how well it worked with music, when the 'Frankenstein' music started.

The lights came up on Mateo, doing a short solo before his partner joined him onstage. Both wore black pants and vests with full-sleeved white shirts that kind of said Pirate. They were the same height, but Mateo generated lifts and throws with apparent ease. Flung himself through the air with abandon during side-by-side work. Sam was seriously impressed. He applauded and whistled as the men closed the routine with a paired lunge, miming an exchange of death blows.

As the applause faded, Andy said, "I'm guessing one of those guys is your friend?"

"The leader. He's my lover." It was the first time Sam had said that out loud. And he'd meant to say boyfriend, but at the moment that didn't seem serious enough.

"He's a lucky guy."

Sam gave Andy a startled glance before turning back to the stage. The show ended with a group routine, and then there was a curtain call for all the performers. After the curtain closed, a lighting stencil displayed the Underground Cabaret logo. The house lights came up. Andy slid off his barstool with a smile and a wave, disappearing into the crowd.

Background music started pumping again. Sam stood by the table and started on his second drink, a much tamer screwdriver, waiting for Mateo. Dana found him first. "Good you're still here," she said as Rory joined them.

"Rory told me to wait. It was a great show," he told her.

"Glad you enjoyed it. How'd you like your boy?"

"He's really good, huh? I saw the audition video, but it's way different on stage."

"Which is why I always say you should come to our show," Rory said, nobly refraining from adding You Jerk. Sam heard it anyway.

"So tell us all, amigo." Dana helped herself to his screwdriver and gave him an expectant look. "Everything you left out."

"I didn't leave anything out," Sam protested, even though he knew she was only busting his chops.

"Except that little part about who the fuck he is," Rory. "But I guess we changed the subject."

Sam smiled. "I did. I went off on a tangent."

"You look really happy."

"He's pretty great." Mateo was sidling through the crowd toward them. When he finally got there, Sam bent to kiss him. Neither of them noticed Rory and Dana making *aww* faces at each other.

"Sorry it took so long, I had to shake Richard off," said Mateo. "He wanted to meet you, but no. What did you think?"

"It was fantastic."

"You know, with a few lessons, you could throw *me* around like that." Mateo batted his eyelashes.

Sam gave in, whether to the eyelashes or the hand on his ass he couldn't have said. "Okay, okay. Set it up."

Mateo pumped his fist. "Yes!" Rory and Dana were laughing when Andy came up to them.

"Hi ladies. I wanted to talk to your friend here about something," he said, indicating Sam.

"He is *not* single," Mateo said emphatically.

"Yeah, I get that, dammit, but here's my card." Andy handed one to Sam. "I'm a photographer. I've been looking for a specific type of male model and I'd really like to do a session with you."

"With *me*? Um. Okay."

"No cost to you, you get to choose which images I use, and a free set of head shots out of the deal."

Dana said, "That's worth some money."

"I'm not an actor." He didn't much like having his picture taken, either, but Mateo was making an encouraging face. That's the face Andy should be photographing. Though, come to think of it, Sam had some people who might like an up-to-date picture.

Andy shook his head. "Dude, this is L.A. You never know when you might need a head shot."

***

Over the next couple of weeks, Sam and Mateo had dinner with Vince and Kelli, hearing about two shows and a competition they were rehearsing for;

met up with Rory and Dana for brunch, swapping stories about jobs; bounced between their respective beds in Santa Monica and West Hollywood; and cemented their status as boyfriends. Sam interrogated himself about the distinction between Boyfriend and Lover. Mateo fretted and dithered about how (or whether) to invite Sam to Pomona for Thanksgiving.

He'd been trying to come up with a way to say This Is Serious. Or, at least, I Am Serious. A way to hint that an invitation to live together, or an equivalent statement of seriousness, would be welcome from Sam, as it hadn't been from that other guy, without actually saying that. Suggesting that they go to the California Star Ball, where a lot of the Shall We Dance people would be competing on Thanksgiving weekend, was his fallback position. The ballroom studio and its people were increasingly important to Mateo. If Sam was willing to spend a whole evening in that environment, it would mean something.

He knew Sam wasn't always great about hints, and that he also wasn't always great about verbalizing his feelings. If he disliked something he was apt to say nothing. But since he was habitually quiet, that was not always a reliable indicator. Mateo couldn't let it go any longer; he'd have to just be brave and ask. They were at Sam's place, they'd had dinner and a drink, they were on the couch with Pachuco sort-of-watching a movie, and the vibe was about as relaxed as it was ever going to be. Mateo put a hand on Sam's arm, stroking up and down. "I was wondering."

Sam was getting better with things like tone of voice. He looked over. "Wondering what, baby."

"If you had plans for Thanksgiving." Sam's expression was almost funny. It was like he'd never even considered having plans for Thanksgiving.

"Because if you don't, I'd love to take you out to Pomona with me. Kristine is dying to meet you." He couldn't say that about the rest of the family, because they didn't know about Sam. They didn't know Sam existed. But if Kristine knew Sam was coming, she would make sure everyone else was informed, and also that they would all be nice to him. Mateo had no clue what Sam was thinking. "Do you have to work the whole weekend? Or do you hate that idea?"

Sam answered immediately. "No, I love that idea. I do have to work, but we're closed Thanksgiving Day. Really?"

"Yeah, really." Mateo would happily go to the Star Ball by himself. Going to Pomona by himself would not have been happy. "You're my boyfriend. You're important. I want them to meet you." What he meant was I Love You, but he wasn't quite *that* brave.

Sam had a feeling there was some subtext there. He really sucked at subtext. He'd never even heard of it till a couple of years ago. But the words were plain enough. "I'll go anywhere you want me to go. Your sister will be there, right?"

"Oh yeah. Well, she might have to split the day because her boyfriend probably wants her at his parents' house." Mateo rolled his eyes. He wasn't all that thrilled about this boyfriend. "My other sister will be there with her husband, and my brother will be there with his wife and his kid. Not, like, the whole time. Everyone will be in and out. There might be a minute when we're all sitting at the table together, but it's usually this ridiculous noisy standing and eating and walking and eating and talking and eating thing. Seriously, it's a mess, maybe we should just go to Denny's." Sam laughed. Mateo was half-serious. "But I actually do want them all to meet you because you

81

are in my life and I hope you will be for a long time and—"

Sam interrupted that high-speed babble by kissing him. By the time they stopped kissing, Pachuco had exited the couch with a hateful mutter, and there was no question that they would both go to Pomona.

***

Vince heard about it the next day, when they ran into each other picking up take-out from the Italian restaurant. "Hey Sam, good to see you. I meant to ask, what did you think of the Cabaret?"

"Now that I've finally seen a show?" Sam was smiling. "You and Kelii were amazing. I'm feeling like an idiot for never going before. Can't even remember what my reasons were."

"Rory says they were all lame." Vince leaned on the wall, smiling back at his friend. "She says you only showed up because of Mateo. How's that going?"

"God, he's great. He asked me to come to his parents' house for Thanksgiving. I was so surprised."

"Why? He's crazy about you."

"I can't get used to it. I always want him around, and he never seems to get tired of me. When I'm at his place I don't want to go home. When he's at my place he doesn't want to go home."

Vince was familiar with that. "You should move in together."

"I would love that. If he moved in with me. I don't know how to ask. I'm so afraid he'd say no. He told me about this guy he was dating who asked, and Mateo said no." Having never lived with a roommate, much less a boyfriend, Sam was not at all confident about making the offer.

"Sam, for fuck's sake, all the guy talks about is you. He would not say no."

"But he works over in Santa Monica, and it's only been a few weeks." Sam really wanted to be convinced.

Vince was exasperated. "It's been more than a *year*. And you did all that work on yourself. You really leveled up." He tipped his head to one side, realizing this was a good time to ask the question. "Why'd you do that, anyway? I mean, it's good that you did. But if you thought he was never coming back."

Sam rolled his neck, wriggled his back, lifted into a better posture. He suddenly realized that he always did this, made himself taller, when he needed to say something serious. Vince was giving him a sardonic under-the-eyebrows look that said he understood the body language. And of course he did. "There's a huge horrible difference between never having something, and losing something." Instant comprehension on Vince's face. Sam added, "Even if he never came back, I didn't want that to ever happen again with someone because of something I did. I didn't want to cause that. It wasn't just me being unhappy because he wasn't there. It was me hurting him. I didn't want to, never wanted to. It was just pure clumsiness. Incompetence. So I had to fix it." He shrugged. "I don't suppose I'll ever get as good with words as you are, or as he is. But I told you about Cory. I was clumsy with him too. And it was so fucking annoying." Vince almost laughed. "Physically, it's so easy. When I'm moving, people understand me. I thought, if I can do that with my body it has to be in my brain somewhere, and if it's in my brain then I ought to be able to get it out my damn mouth." Vince

83

did laugh then. Sam shook his head, smiling. "Maybe I'll ask him after Thanksgiving. How did you ask Kelli?"

"I kind of didn't. We were mutually bitching about how we always had to decide where we were going, and it was just like okay, your place or mine." He was smiling all over again at the memory. "Then I made it official. And you know, that's when I told her I loved her. I said it and immediately thought, damn, why haven't I said this before. Have you guys said it yet?" Vince could tell from Sam's expression that they hadn't, or at least that Sam hadn't. "You do love him, right?"

"Of course." Sam had no doubt about that, even though he wasn't entirely sure what the word meant. If it meant caring more for someone than he ever thought was possible, then that was the right word. "Knowing Mateo, he'll say it first."

"Well, if he does, I recommend saying it back immediately."

Chapter 9

Kristine swore that everybody knew Mateo was bringing Sam, and she promised everyone would be on their best behavior. That didn't necessarily mean much. Best was a relative term. Sam laughed when Mateo said that, and he only then noticed the unintentional pun. "Well, you'll see," he said. "I've been home a few times since I moved to L.A., and it's always been weird. You know how people look at you and you can tell what they're thinking? I can tell my parents are always thinking, he has sex with men. They're going to see you and picture that."

Sam looked over from the driver's seat. They hadn't talked about this, or at least not in this explicit way. "You're sure you want to? Because we don't have to."

Mateo turned in the passenger seat. "Yes we do. Yes we fucking do. This is who I am. You are the person I, the person I'm with." He came so very close to saying The Person I Love. Still wasn't sure Sam was ready for that. "I know they'll do their best. If they weren't prepared to try I would have heard about it. Someone would have said something." He'd almost expected it. Kristine must have been busy. "Anyway yes. I want you there." He knew that was the real question.

"Okay, baby. But you say the word and we're out. They can't hurt me and I won't let them hurt you." That wasn't really something he could promise, and Mateo probably knew it. If the family was unwelcoming or mean, it would hurt both of them.

Fortunately, that didn't happen. Everyone was civil, and no one was mean. Some of them seemed uneasy, and it was very easy to imagine that they were doing exactly what Mateo said: picturing the two of them together. There was also some apparent surprise and discomfort over Sam's tall, dark physical presence. "I never even thought of that," Mateo said, about an hour after they arrived, when they'd gone out to the yard for a moment alone. "Nobody in the family has ever dated someone who wasn't Filipino."

"How'd your brother and sister meet theirs?"

"At church. Kind of the opposite to how I met you." They'd told that story. Mateo didn't mention exactly how drunk he was when Sam took him home. It was pretty clear this wasn't a family of party animals, so Sam didn't fill in the blanks. Mateo did say he went home with Sam, and his mother might have crossed herself, but nobody said anything. Nobody except Kristine, later in the day, when her boyfriend Justin brought her home.

"Thank God you're still here," she said, dragging them both out into the yard again. "Everybody being decent?"

"Everyone's been great," Sam said. "The food's good, too. I wasn't expecting a whole roasted pig."

"That's only for very special occasions. We'll be eating that for a week. Please take some home with you. God, is there anything to drink?"

"Always." Mateo studied his sister, then went to the cooler by the patio door and fished out a can of beer for her. "What's up?"

She drank half the beer, smothered a belch, and sighed. "Justin's parents spent two fucking hours discussing our wedding."

"What?! I don't see any goddamned ring!"

"Exactly, thank you, and all three of them are acting like it's a foregone conclusion. I swear if I hadn't been deflecting like a Jedi they would have chosen names for our first three kids." She drank the rest of the beer. Mateo and Sam exchanged a glance. "I love him. I do. But give me a minute, you know? I haven't even graduated yet. I don't have a job yet." She was working at In-N-Out Burger, which was not a bad college job but definitely not what she was going to college for.

Mateo heard the subtext: I haven't had a life yet. He patted her shoulder, unsure what (if anything) he could or should say. That was the second reason he'd fled Pomona himself: to get his life.

Sam came to the rescue. "How'd you get them to stop? I would've wanted to say, you're getting a little ahead of yourselves."

Kristine laughed. "I wanted to say exactly that, believe me. Told them I had to get home because Mateo brought his gorgeous boyfriend and I don't want to miss them." Sam smiled at the compliment. "You are gorgeous. He told me you were tall but none of the pictures he sent showed you standing side by side. You make us all look like midgets."

He snickered. "No. You're not that short."

"When she wears her trampy heels she's taller than me," Mateo said. "You can't marry Justin, Kris. You can't make another generation of short Filipinos." Justin was five foot six to Kristine's five foot five.

"I don't want to go through life never wearing heels again, that's for sure." She gave Mateo a dirty look. "And who are you calling trampy? Mr. Goes Home on the First Date."

"Your heels!" he protested. "I said your *heels* are trampy." Then he looked at Sam, who was trying not to laugh, and said, "I was totally trampy. And I'm not sorry."

"You should have been trampier," Kristine said. "Sam could have come out here *last* Thanksgiving."

"It was my fault, not his." Sam put his arm around Mateo. "I'm lucky he came back at all."

"He couldn't stay away." Kristine patted her brother. "He was toast. I'm so glad you guys found each other."

"Thanks Kris." Mateo didn't mention she was the only one here who'd said so, but he knew she heard it anyway. He and Sam didn't stay much longer. Getting back to Sam's place, where they could kiss and touch without feeling like people were judging them, was a relief.

***

Sam had to get to the tux shop early for their Black Friday sale; he left Mateo in bed, trying and failing to get back to sleep. Eventually he sighed and sat up, pulling his feet out from under the cat. Stared around Sam's room, wished he didn't have to leave, and thought about his weekend.

His office was closed, projects all delivered by end of business Wednesday. Three days on his own. There was always new work stuff, and if he got bored enough he could start on some of that. Wasn't in the mood to shop. Some new movies were out, but he wanted to go with Sam.

"That's the whole problem, Pachuco," he said out loud. "I want to do everything with Sam. I'm being that clingy bitch who won't let a man have his life." Time to get his ass moving. Get home, go for a run, get cleaned up. Find dates to propose for their first few lessons at Shall We Dance. Then go down to California Star Ball and watch all his new friends do their thing. He could sit there and think about what Sam might enjoy most.

By Saturday night, sitting with Aaron and watching the professional events, Mateo had a few ideas, mixed up with a few concerns. "He was a pro athlete. A fighter on the UFC circuit. So I know he's competitive, but we can't compete together." He gestured at the dance floor, crowded with boy-girl couples.

Aaron turned to make eye contact. "You could do pro-am at the same events. I mean, at least you'd be going to the same things at the same time and you could cheer each other on."

"Yeah, I guess."

"And there's queer Dance Sport too. A couple of Dmitri's students are training for the Gay Games."

Mateo blinked. "The huh? Wait, there's dancing in the Gay Games?"

"That's what I said!" They both snickered. Aaron added, "You still thinking about teaching someday?"

"Yeah, kind of. I mean, it seems like the obvious thing. My job is copacetic, not planning to quit that. I wouldn't want to dance and teach full-time, because fuck being self-employed."

"God, for real."

"But yeah, I really love it and if I were teaching I'd always be getting better, right?"

"Probably so. How does Sam fit into that?"

"That is the whole entire question." They were quiet for a few minutes as another event went forward in the loud, colorful, freezing-cold room. Mateo pulled his fleece jacket up over his shoulders again.

The impulse to take lessons with Sam was initially about dancing together. Socially. But also, maybe, he admitted in the privacy of his own head, to nudge him into some kind of performance.

Being a professional athlete was performance. Doing a routine together at the studio (or, in a shiny pink imaginary world, with the Underground Cabaret) might work for Sam on the same level as doing belt tests or exhibitions at the dojo. He'd probably always be good with going out dancing with friends at the local clubs, but if Mateo pitched it right, he might get interested in more.

"I should bring him to one of these," he said, half to himself.

Aaron heard him and nodded. "Totally. Let him see how tough it is. He sounds like a guy who enjoys a challenge. Julia had to talk me into it, but I love having this as my sport."

"Oh yeah." Mateo was getting excited now. He'd have to do some more research. Find out exactly where and how two men could compete together, as partners. The events probably wouldn't be as big as this, on a giant gleaming floor in a hotel ballroom, but if it were all men like them? What a trip!

* * *

Meanwhile, up in West L.A., Sam couldn't help wondering about the dance competition Mateo talked about. Saying he knew all these people who'd be there, and he wanted to see what they were doing. Cheer them on. Get inspired.

Sam's experience of dance contests was limited to the casual throwdowns that happened at the salsa clubs once in a while. He knew the big clubs hosted events with dozens (or hundreds) of competitors, but he'd never gone to one of those. Then there were the even bigger, fancier events like the Salsa Challenge Vince and Kelli did in May. They were doing another one this weekend, up in San Francisco. He'd been a little envious, he realized. Vince was out there competing for a trophy, if not for money. Sam hadn't done anything like that for a long time, despite his sensei's hints.

Now that he thought about it, he couldn't believe he'd never asked about Mateo's competition dancing in college. The man brought it up at the very beginning, after all. Made it clear dance meant something to him beyond a way to get close to someone in a club.

The next morning was a good time to start that conversation. Sam didn't have to be at the shop till eleven. Once they sat down with their breakfast, he said, "Tell me about this thing you went to last night. How was it different from what your team did in college?"

Mateo turned to look at him, surprised and delighted. "You really want to know?"

"Yeah, I do. Tell me everything."

A quick pounce of a kiss, then Mateo sat back, grinning, and started to talk.

Chapter 10

December 2012

The reaction when Sam took Mateo to his gym was kind of ridiculous. "I should have expected that," he told his lover when they finally got clear of the mob. "It's always busy this time of day, and these guys are always like this."

Mateo was halfway to cracking up, but he was glad to be there with Sam and not alone. "That was kind of intense. My gym is so, like, sedate."

"Your gym isn't the live version of Grindr." Sam's tone was dry. Mateo snorted out a laugh. Sam petted his hair for a second. "I guarantee you're going to get some kind of proposition before we leave."

"Jesus, really? When I'm here with you? All I want to do is lift some weights." Mateo wasn't averse to being admired, and he knew Sam liked it when he *was* admired, but still.

"Let's do that. Then we can go get something at Bossa Nova on the way home."

"Oh my God, Sam. Do *not* let me get the chocolate mousse." They went about their workouts to a soundtrack of minor catcalling and the occasional wolf whistle. As they headed for the shower Mateo said, "I have never felt so much like a girl. Jesus H. Christ. I'm gonna tell Kristine about this and she's gonna say, do you get it now, you clueless motherfucker."

Sam was laughing as he pushed open the door to the shower room. Then he said, "Oh lord, not you."

Cory was toweling off, naked and grinning. "You had to know I'd make a pass. Good God Almighty. Is this your guy? The one from last year?"

"Yes. Hands off unless he touches you first." Sam noticed Mateo's startled expression. "You don't actually belong to me, baby."

Mateo wanted to contradict that, loudly, but settled for glaring at the naked guy, who was not at all put off. Cory said, "The three of us could have a lot of fun."

"Sam, what the fuck." Mateo was appalled.

"If you want to." Sam shrugged. He didn't know what the rules were. Didn't know if Mateo wanted to look outside. They hadn't discussed fidelity, or exclusivity. Or much of anything, really.

"You are all the man I need." Mateo turned to Cory, who was at least holding the towel in front of his privates now. "Thanks but no thanks, no offense."

"Hey, nothing ventured." Cory obviously wasn't offended. In fact, he looked as though he might have won a bet. He turned away and headed for his locker, swaggering a little.

Mateo was a guy, so he low-key appreciated that bare ass, then transferred his glare to Sam, who made an apologetic face. "I don't want anyone else. And I don't want to share you." He didn't care if that other guy heard him.

"I don't want to share you either." Sam realized that Mateo was genuinely upset. "Come here, baby." He opened his arms. Mateo stepped into them. Sam spoke softly into his hair. "I'm sorry. I thought I should stand back. It's not for me to say who you could be with."

"I don't want to be with anyone else. I want to belong to you. I do." It was muffled against Sam's shoulder.

"Did you want me to punch him in the face?" Sam felt Mateo laugh. "Because I could do that."

93

Another laugh from Mateo, and a "Hey!" from Cory.

Sam said, "I want to belong to you too." Mateo looked up then. Sam couldn't think of a single reason not to kiss him. After a minute he said, "Fuck this place. Let's go shower at home. We can get Bossa Nova to deliver."

They were at Sam's place, clean, and fed before Mateo gave in to curiosity. He might not have if they hadn't been in bed and already warmed up. Lying on their sides facing each other, each with a hand wandering, sharing light and promising kisses. "Have you ever done that? A three-way?"

Sam moved back enough to make eye contact. He smiled. "I wondered if you would ask. Yeah, once."

"Did you like it?"

"I got off." That didn't quite answer the question. "I was in the middle." He could see Mateo thinking that through, or maybe picturing it. "Do you know what that means?"

"I think so? One in your mouth and one behind?"

Sam stifled a laugh. His lover could be a little prissy sometimes, which considering his supply of swear words was hilarious. "That's right."

He asked again, "Did you like it? Because I thought you didn't go for being the bottom." But he suddenly realized that was an assumption. They'd never discussed it. Mateo always behaved in a way that invited Sam to take charge, and Sam always did.

"Sometimes I've liked it. You remember what you told me." This wasn't easy for Sam to say. But he wanted, oh, everything. He wanted everything.

"Somebody hurt you. Intentionally?"

"No. I was a beginner, like you. And I weighed about fifty pounds more then. He assumed I would like it hard."

"Ew, damn." Mateo ducked his head to kiss Sam's chest. Smooth muscle under that mahogany skin. He'd seen pictures of Sam at his heaviest. Bulky, intimidating, with his hair shaved close: no one's idea of a guy who would take it. "Did he back off when he realized?"

"He never did. He was high."

Oh, goddamn. Mateo had never thought to ask. He'd smoked a little dope here and there, but never since he'd been in Los Angeles. Always felt like he needed to keep his wits about him. And he'd never caught a hint that Sam used any kind of drugs. "Were you?"

"Not then. When we did the three-way, yeah." Sam decided to turn it around, since they were talking. "Have you ever been the top?"

"No." Mateo stalled there. He wasn't sure if it was a good or a bad thing that he didn't have that experience. "I've only been with three other guys where it went past hands and mouths. All those guys were bigger than me, but they weren't super experienced either. And I look like a girl. I don't think it occurred to any of us that I would be the top."

"You do *not* look like a girl." Maybe he had when he was a kid. Not now, not with this body. The guys at the gym hadn't been drooling over Mateo's face. Sam shook that off. "Did you want to?"

Mateo had to think about that for a while. Had he wanted to penetrate those other men? No, not really. Had he *ever* wanted to penetrate another man? Not really. That wasn't what he pictured, or imagined, when he was attracted to someone. But now that they were talking about it, he couldn't deny he was curious. Sam's tone, and the way he brought it up, kind of implied he wasn't averse to the idea. Sam had taught Mateo a lot about ways to play. Maybe he'd been hoping all along that someday Mateo would do to him some of the things he did to Mateo. He finally said, "I didn't then." Then he panicked a little and derailed. "You don't use anything now. Dope, whatever."

"No. That was only when I was on the circuit. Everybody used something. Speed or weed or juice. Painkillers and alcohol. There was a lot I didn't want to see or feel sober."

"Oh honey." Mateo pressed close.

Sam held him tight. They were both pretty thoroughly turned on. "I want to feel everything with you." He hoped that was clear enough. Mateo didn't say anything—he was busy kissing Sam—but he reached down and caught Sam's leg, pulling his knee up over his own hip. Brushing his fingers over the curve of Sam's ass, the inside of his thigh, the crease of his groin.

"I've never even had a finger in you." Mateo was so hard it hurt. Their hips moved, a slow grind. Sam took his hand out of Mateo's hair and reached behind him to the nightstand. Held the lube while Mateo got some on his fingers. Made a muffled and unmistakably hungry sound when those fingers went to work.

Mateo realized he'd learned a few things, glad he'd been paying attention at least half the time. When he was only half out of his mind with arousal and wanting and Sam. Sam, who was panting into Mateo's hair, who definitely wanted this. Mateo wanted to try it the way they'd done it that first time, face to face.

He kept hold of Sam's thigh and exerted himself, pushing them over, settling between Sam's legs. "God, you're so gorgeous." Sam was still holding the lube, but his eyes were closed. Both knees up, lips parted: he looked close to climax already. "Do you want to come before?" A single shake of the head. Mateo thought of seeing Sam come while he was inside and nearly lost it right there. He bent close for a kiss, deep and hot, feeling their erections both throbbing between them. Wished for a moment they were the same height, but he'd make this work if it killed him. And maybe now that they'd said those things about belonging to each other, they could get tested again. See if they had the option of ditching the condoms. He grabbed one off the nightstand and rolled it on, then took the lube out of Sam's hand. Slicked himself, braced himself on one hand, and began. Sam's foot hooked over his back. Mateo hoped he was doing this right. The sounds Sam was making were not discouraging. "Oh God," he said as he pushed further in. He had to put his other hand down.

"Oh *Jesus*." Sam's other foot came up, locking his legs around Mateo. "Fucking *hell*." He kept talking as Mateo started to move, slow and shallow at first, then deeper, faster, harder. Sam was pulling him in with those strong legs, saying all the filthy things that Mateo would have said. Begging, gasping, and finally moaning, head pressed back, neck arched, body convulsing around Mateo's.

"Jesus fucking *Christ*." It was that convulsion, that vision, that sent Mateo over the edge. If this was what Sam felt, no wonder he liked topping. He thrust hard, let the climax take him, said something loud that probably wasn't a word. Collapsed onto Sam, face against his neck, boneless and exhausted. Needed to get out. How'd Sam do it? He reached for the memory, the understanding. Propped himself up a bit to disengage, stripped the condom off into a tissue, then collapsed in Sam's arms. "Wow, Sam."

A breath of a laugh. "Yeah." Sam turned his head to kiss the side of his lover's face. "You did good."

"Mm-hmm."

"I'm going to love thinking of that. When those meatheads at the gym look at you. I'll be like, you wish you knew what we do." Mateo giggled.

Chapter 11

A couple weeks later, with Christmas on the horizon and no particular plans for it, Mateo and Sam were lounging at Sam's place, reading the Sunday paper in bed. Pachuco lay across their legs. "That cannot be comfortable," said Mateo. "His spine is draped across four shinbones."

"I think cats can turn into Jello at will."

"Man, I guess. So let me run something by you."

"Whatcha got."

"I absolutely hate living so far away from you."

Sam looked up from the paper. He'd never had a live-in boyfriend before. His relationships had been so not-that-way, he'd never thought of asking before Mateo. He'd been thinking of very little else since talking to Vince, and now he knew a hint when he heard one. "Move in with me." He smiled.

So did Mateo. "Wow, that was easy." They both laughed. "I was thinking of trying a work-from-home deal with my job. What I do really doesn't have to be done on-site, and half the time I'm working at home anyway because of their fucked-up deadlines."

"Think they'll go for it?"

"Only one way to find out. If they don't, though, I might have to scramble for a minute." Mateo had landed the job on his first interview during senior year, but he knew it might not be so easy next time.

"I've been swinging this rent by myself for a long time. And you could probably find something else close by pretty easily. Aren't there a lot of architecture type firms down along San Vicente and Melrose?"

"Yeah. Would that be okay with you?"

"The company that owns the tux shop would cover you on my insurance." Sam suddenly realized what he'd just said, and what it meant: if they were registered domestic partners.

Mateo dropped his section of the paper and turned onto his side, dislodging the cat. Wrapping his arms around Sam, crumpling the rest of the paper between them. "I love you."

Thank the Lord. "I love you, too." Mateo's face was tucked into the curve of Sam's neck. Sam held him there, eyes closed, some deeply-held tension finally unraveling.

Before they had a chance to enjoy the moment, Pachuco grabbed Mateo's foot and bit it. "Ow! Little fucker!"

Sam laughed. "He wasn't ready to transform from Jello to cat."

"Watch it, bitch," Mateo said to the cat. "I'm gonna outrank you pretty soon." Pachuco was unimpressed. Mateo fished the newspaper out from between him and Sam and dumped it on the cat, who immediately started killing it. "Oops. Hope you were done with that."

"Close enough," Sam said, kissing him, bearing him down against the pillows, angling their bodies away from the cat tornado. Mateo was laughing right up until Sam sat up again, astride his hips, and wrapped a hand around both erections.

"Are you gonna jerk us, big guy?" Mateo propped himself on his elbows and watched, breathing hard, as Sam started to work them. "I'm going to go so fast," he warned.

"Good." Sam bent forward to kiss him. "Me too."

***

"Are you *sure* you don't want to meet up for some after-Christmas shopping? Because it'd be way more fun with you." Mateo, after Kristine's ten-minute tale of woe, thought she really seriously needed to get out of Pomona for a minute. Like, immediately.

Kris sighed, made a mournful sound as if about to bow out yet again, then suddenly said, "You know what? Fuck it. Fuck all of this. I do not need to go to Justin's parents' house *again*. I want to go shopping with you. Is Sam working?"

"Always. He's too easy on his assistant manager. Where do you want to go? The mall in Santa Monica, or the one in Century City, or how about the Beverly Center?"

"Is that the one from 'Clueless'?"

"No, the 'Clueless' one was out in the Valley, and fuck the Valley. Let's go to Century City. We can drink coffee, get a million samples at See's Candy, watch all the rich people, and criticize what they're wearing."

"Oh my God yes. What's better, Saturday or Sunday?"

Mateo countered with, "New Year's Eve? We don't have plans to go out, do you?"

"Justin's suggestion was church," Kris said, tone dry as Death Valley.

"Fuck him!"

"Did that, rethinking it."

He cackled. "Listen, we should do that. Go shopping, then you could come and crash with us instead of driving home on the drunkest night of the year."

"Uh, what? Did you say crash with *us*?"

"Oh." Mateo grinned to himself, then said, as if these five words didn't set off fireworks in his head, "I'm moving in with Sam."

***

After negotiating a new deal with his employers (reported with pride to his family, who had amazingly little to say about the reason he'd be working from home), Mateo gave notice on his apartment and packed up to go, happy to surrender his deposit in exchange for getting out fast. He dumped a carload of electronics and clothes in the living area at Sam's place two days before Christmas. "Let's deal with that later, I'm hungry."

Sam, who'd had a very busy day at the tux shop, blinked at the amazingly small stack of bags and boxes, thinking that later sounded good. "Want to go down to the Italian place for dinner?"

"Great idea. I'll learn to cook one of these days, but for now, pasta is where it's at."

They walked down to the restaurant, waited a short time for a table, and were seated. After ordering, Sam asked, "Anything else to bring over?"

"Nope, I've brought everything I need. Mostly clothes and music, and the computer stuff. I sold everything else or gave it away." Mateo shrugged. His furniture hadn't been worth the cost of hiring a truck, having already seen heavy use in both his older siblings' first apartments. What neighbors didn't want went out on the curb.

Sam was guiltily glad he wouldn't have to rearrange much. "I made some space for your work stuff." Their drink order arrived while they were discussing how best to deploy Mateo's computer equipment. Then Sam mentioned that Andy, the photographer they met at the Halloween show, had been in touch to set something up.

"Any idea what the project is?"

"Not really. You don't think it's porn, do you?"

"If only! We'd be moving to a penthouse!"

Sam laughed. "Shut up. You gonna finally tell me what you want for Christmas?"

Mateo swallowed some of his wine and sat back. "Yes I am. Now that we don't have to waste time driving back and forth, let's set up those lessons at Dmitri's place."

"Little pit bull." Sam had a drink, half-laughing again. This kid was unstoppable.

"I know you're just humoring me. But you'll start to like it. Bet you." Mateo smiled.

"I'm not taking that bet. You've been right about everything so far."

After a quick glance around to make sure he wouldn't whack a server, Mateo made a grand, televangelist gesture. "That's because I *believe*, loverboy." He put both hands on the table, leaning in a little. "I do believe. I believe in us."

"So do I, baby." Every week, every day, every minute together made Sam feel more confident. There were still moments of doubt, when he wondered if the ease of their time together owed something to suppression. Was Mateo not saying what he wanted, or doing what he wanted, because he wanted to please Sam. The question simply wouldn't stick. Sam knew what it felt like when someone was trying too hard, and this wasn't that. This felt like neither of them had to try at all. He took one of Mateo's hands and lifted it to his lips. "I love you." Every time he said it, it got easier.

"I love you too. What do *you* want for Christmas?"

Sam gazed at him. "Already got it. You in my bed every night."

"Ooh." Mateo wriggled, delighted. "Maybe some new sheets, then?"

***

The day after Christmas, Sam woke to the sensation of a kiss on his cheek. He smiled before he even opened his eyes. "Rise and shine," said Mateo. "I know you're opening today and it's gonna be a madhouse with your sale." He moved half on top of Sam. Both their bodies were very willing to make Sam late. Mateo kissed his mouth and then (regretfully) moved away again. "I'll get your breakfast while you're in the shower."

Sam sat up. Mateo was still close enough for another kiss. Sam cupped his face, stroking a thumb along his cheekbone. "I can't believe you're going to be here every morning."

"Believe it. When you don't have to leave early, I'll wake you up some other way." He stood up, tugged Sam to his feet, stood still for a hug and one more kiss. Sam patted his ass before heading to the bathroom. Mateo pulled on some sweatpants and a tee shirt and went to the kitchen, pleasantly aroused.

He loved knowing that they would really have a routine now, a domestic life together. Stability. Something close to what his parents had, always there for each other. Working from home was awesome, but doing it with Sam at the beginning and end of every day was going to be fantastic. He knew his lover usually stopped at a drive-through when he had an early start. They could do better. He'd planned ahead. Learning to cook was something he fully intended to do, and he'd begun practicing already. He had the fresh-made breakfast burrito packed in an insulated bag before the shower shut off. When Sam came out to the kitchen, dressed and ready, Mateo handed him the bag and a travel cup. "Your green tea."

"You don't have to do that, baby." Sam paid for both with a kiss.

"I want to. Get on out of here. Be thinking about how I'm going to love you up when you get home. Mmm. 'Everybody's crazy 'bout a sharp-dressed man.'" Sam was laughing as he went out. Mateo closed the door, turned around, and addressed Pachuco. "Just you and me, you furry bandito. Let's see how we get along now that this is *my* house."

Chapter 12

January 2013

Mateo had just returned from a run when he heard Sam pick up another call from Andy. Instead of diving straight into the shower, he sat down nearby to listen in. Sam made it easy and put the call on speaker. "So have you got a date for me?"

"Can you do next Saturday or Sunday?"

"I'm working Saturday, but Sunday's good." Mateo was imitating a begging puppy. Sam gave him a look. "Um, can Mateo come along?"

"Sure. Tell him no flirting, though."

"Yeah, that'll happen," Sam said dryly.

Andy laughed. "You've got the address, right?"

"Any trick to finding this place?"

"Don't map it on anything but Google. You can park along the main entrance road. It looks like shit, but it's safe."

"What should I wear?"

"This is for a series of figure studies."

"In other words, not much."

"Just be comfortable."

Sam sighed. "Right. See you next Sunday." He hung up and looked at Mateo. "Why do I get the feeling I'm gonna be naked?"

"If I bring along some tequila, will it seem more natural?" He put a hand on Sam's thigh. "You're okay with this, right?"

"Yeah, I'm okay with it. I wouldn't do it otherwise. It might be interesting."

"You always dodge pictures, though."

106

Sam gazed at him, thinking about his work, and his friends, and this beautiful young man who so very clearly couldn't get enough of him. "It's time I stopped doing that, isn't it?"

The following weekend, they drove out to the artists' colony in an old brewery complex north of Downtown. Found a parking space, located the building where Andy had his loft, then headed up three flights of stairs separated by weirdly sloping hallways covered with flyers and posters for various events in and out of the complex.

Mateo stopped to look at a poster for something called a Happening. "This place is a trip."

"It's a little chaotic. I don't think I could hack it."

They found the correct door, which was standing open. Andy was at a desk at the end of the room, but stood up as they came in. "Hey guys. Any trouble finding the place?"

Sam shook his head. "No problem."

"Come on in, I've got some coffee going. Help yourselves."

"Great, thanks," Mateo said, looking around. He didn't know what he'd been expecting, but somehow the space surprised him.

"Sam, I take it you're a martial artist?" Andy had closed the door and turned to join them. Sam was wearing his gi over a tank top and boxer briefs.

"Yeah, done a bit here and there."

"Let me tell you how I work." They all got their coffee and sat down on a couch under a huge whitewashed window, in front of a large open-front white box standing in the middle of the big room. "What I like to do is get my subject talking about himself, or herself. This particular series is called 'Cut

107

Open' and I'm hanging the show in March. I want you to be as relaxed and natural as possible. Move around however you want inside the space. I'll ask you questions. I'm going to be taking video at the same time, but that's only so I can review it later and capture anything I might miss while I'm looking through the DSLR. Also, so I can connect what you were talking about with the images. I won't keep the video once the project is finished; you can have it if you want it. Here's the image rights contract and waiver; you should read the whole thing. If it's cool, sign and date it." He handed over a closely printed sheet.

Sam took it but didn't read it right away. "Cut Open, huh."

"Yeah. Everybody I'm working with has taken some kind of visible damage. What I'm trying to do is find the images that express how people have coped with and overcome things."

"Any chance I could see some other things in the series?"

"Sure. Here's a dozen or so." Andy retrieved a folder from the desk and handed it to Sam.

Sam leafed through the 8x10 prints slowly. "These are really good."

Mateo leaned in. "Can I see?"

"Sure," said Andy.

Sam passed the folder to Mateo, then turned his attention to the contract. Andy didn't interrupt him. Eventually, he took the pen Andy offered, signed it, and handed it back. "Seems fair."

"I appreciate it. Okay. The bathroom's over there, I'm going to move the lights into position, and Mateo?"

"Yeah."

"You can sit anywhere behind the camera." Sam went into the bathroom. Andy looked at Mateo. "You may hear things you haven't heard before. Sometimes this is like a therapy session. If you could avoid reacting, it'll really help keep Sam in the moment."

Mateo nodded seriously. "I'll do my best." He made a dash for the bathroom himself when Sam emerged.

Andy said, "Sam, I've been friends with Rory for a long time. I asked her why she hadn't introduced us. She said you didn't like having your picture taken, and she knew I would want to, even before I had the idea for this show. So why did you agree?"

Sam took a moment. He wanted to answer, didn't want to take too long because Mateo would be returning to the main room, but wasn't sure quite how to say it. "It's hard to feel like you're not enough when someone like that wants you," he said at last. Andy's reaction puzzled him; it seemed those words were painful in some way. But he didn't say anything, only nodded.

When Mateo returned, Andy took a seat by the cameras. Sam went to stand in the middle of the white box, looking watchful. "Okay, Sam. Do whatever you want to do. I'd like to hear about where you grew up."

"Okay. Um. I was born in Oakland."

"Can you tell me about your parents?"

The bare facts were all he had. For a while, he'd felt guilty about them, as if he should've chosen better parents. "My mother was a crack addict and my father was her dealer. I went into the system pretty young."

"Foster care?"

109

"Yeah. My first family was all right." Sam began moving through a tai chi series. His speech was slow, his voice in its lowest register. "They had two of their own kids, and two foster kids. I lived there till I was eight. Then their older kid, a son, he started running with a bad crowd. He got picked up for vandalism and the system took us foster kids away." He continued moving slowly, breathing steadily. "The next place, the man of the house was a martial artist. He started training me. Boxing, kickboxing, tae kwon do, judo, karate. He was a hard man, but he was fair."

"Was there physical discipline?"

"Oh yeah. But, you know, it never came as a surprise." He smiled. Then he untied his belt and took off his jacket, moving into a new series. "I probably could have stayed there till I was eighteen, but the lady of the house got cancer. The system took me out because my sensei couldn't be home enough to suit them. So, the next place was fucking horrible. I was fourteen. These people ran kind of a farm. They had way too many foster kids, and it was all for the government payments. It wasn't abusive, exactly, but maybe like being a dairy cow."

"How long did that last?"

"Not long, less than a year. Two of the older kids got into *big* trouble, stole a car. Actually, carjacked this lady. Everyone got pulled out." He went down to the floor and into a deep forward bending stretch, exhaling. "But then I got a home. Two professors from Berkeley. Their youngest kid had just gone away to college and they actually wanted an older teenager. The guy, he'd been into martial arts before and somehow the system made the match. They were great, they did their best. But I wasn't much of a student and I didn't want to go to college. I graduated

110

high school, barely, then went to work at a dojo and eventually started competing."

Sam had begun a yoga vinyasa. Andy gave him a minute, then asked, "Are you still in touch with them?"

"Yeah. I took their name when I turned eighteen, that's where Lee comes from. We'll go there for Thanksgiving this year. Went to Mateo's family last year. That was nice. Haven't done a family Thanksgiving since I left Berkeley." He pushed up from the floor into a back bend.

"When did your nose get broken?"

"My motherfucking *first* professional MMA fight." Sam dropped to the floor, half-laughing, and lay still. Hands on his chest, head turned toward Andy. "All the other scars, the little ones, were from MMA fights too. The bad one's from the last fight."

"You won that?"

"I won them all."

***

Mateo, watching as silently as he could, hoped he could see all of these pictures someday. Sam's scarred cheek was in shadow at the moment, but the broken line of his nose was highlighted. His face could have been designed to go with the word Pride. From that shitty awful start in life to an undisputed winner. No wonder he loved this guy.

Andy said, "Any other broken bones?"

"I broke a rib, a collarbone, and a wrist falling off a bike when I was fifteen."

"Did you consider staying with martial arts as a profession?"

"Oh, sure. But I didn't want to teach. Wanted something a little easier. More peaceful."

111

"Okay, tell me about your love life."

Sam laughed loud and long, surprising both Andy and Mateo. "The second-most-obvious way for people to get beat up in life, right?" He sat up, shed his pants, and started a series of balancing poses, body glistening under the lights. "I knew I was gay pretty early. Didn't try to do anything about it till I was out of school. Never felt quite that safe. On the fight circuit everybody's in the closet. There were hookups. Always on the down-low. My first time was with another fighter. I used to think of him as a boyfriend but that isn't really what it was. I didn't have a steady boyfriend till I quit fighting. He was…well, it didn't last long."

Andy didn't push on that. "Okay. We're almost done. Tell me one thing you haven't done in life that you really want to do or would have liked to do."

"Whoa." Sam shed his tank top and folded up into lotus position facing Andy, taking a few deep breaths. The lights highlighting his sleek musculature struck the cheekbone scar unforgivingly. "I guess I would have liked to compete at the national level. Going into MMA might not've been a smart move. I might have been a national champion in tae kwon do, if I'd really focused on it."

"Why didn't you?"

"Money." An older fighter who didn't mind helping others up the ladder gave him some advice about that. "A guy who trained at the dojo said, you could fight for a few years and make some bank, and then you can decide what you really want to do. He helped me a lot."

That was good to hear. There had been mentors in Mateo's life, too. He needed to get in touch and thank them.

"One last thing. Can you give me a handstand?"

Sam didn't answer, just tipped forward onto his hands, levitated his hips and then straightened his legs. His braid fell directly over his head, continuing the straight line of his spine, framed by the broad wings of his back.

Andy said, "Beautiful. Thanks."

Sam dropped his feet to the floor and stood straight, looking not into the camera but at Mateo. His face was serene.

"Hold it right there for a second. Thanks. That's all." Andy straightened up from the camera.

"My God, you are gorgeous," said Mateo, wiping his wet eyes.

"You're most comfortable expressing yourself physically, aren't you, Sam?"

"I guess." He was still looking at Mateo.

"Did you realize you were doing bound postures when you talked about your family in Berkeley? And then the big heart opener when you mentioned Thanksgiving. What you said was terrific. I wish I were a filmmaker sometimes." The video camera was still running, because something told Andy this session wasn't completely finished.

Sam said to Mateo, "Are you okay?"

"I'm great. You're great. This was great."

"I'm going to go through all this over the next week and then I'll give you a call to come and review. Okay?"

"That's fine." Sam looked at Andy now. "Thanks for this. I needed to say some of that. Um, would it be possible to get a couple pictures of me and Mateo together?"

"Sure, no problem."

Mateo fluttered a bit. "Oh crap, let me go wash my face!"

Sam smiled. "Get up here, little diva." Mateo went over to the box and stepped up onto the platform, diving into Sam's arms and resting his head on Sam's shoulder.

"Fuck, that's perfect," said Andy. "Hold it. Okay, give me a three-quarter position, both looking at the camera. Good. Now kiss him, Sam."

Sam did. A few times. Then Mateo squeezed him tight and lifted him off the floor. "Whoa!"

Mateo said fiercely, "*Mine.*"

***

On the way home, the men didn't talk much. Mateo was driving, and Sam was thoughtful. As they got into WeHo, Sam glanced over and spoke. "I can't get over how quiet you were."

"I can't either. Andy asked me to react as little as I could. He didn't want you distracted by me."

"Hmm. It was kind of interesting. Saying all that stuff. Almost like you were in another room."

"Like a confessional."

"Yeah, maybe. You know, when we were leaving you went a little ahead of me. Andy said to me, that guy really loves you."

"Well, I do."

"I know. It's just…I've never had that before."

"I know you haven't. Never knew why until now." Mateo glanced over. "Your last family. They sent you that picture." And Sam had immediately found a frame for it, hanging it in the kitchen.

"I asked for it. I finally realized I've made a home here, and I wanted a picture of them because they

114

were important. I'm in touch with the Mendozas, too. My first sensei and his wife. She's been in remission all this time, they're starting to think the cancer won't come back."

"That's good."

"I sent them a Christmas card and told them about you. Never really came out to them before. Had to leave their house before I was out to anybody. I was afraid," he admitted.

"But they wrote back to you. I saw the card." The card that said, we're so happy for you. Mateo hadn't realized how big that must have been for Sam. Then he remembered how huge it was for him, that his parents' card was addressed to both of them. "We're kind of in the same place, aren't we? Both still figuring this out."

"Maybe that's one reason we fit so well."

"Yeah, maybe so." Mateo couldn't help smiling. Someday soon, he'd bring up that thing Sam said about competing. But today was a lot; he'd let it settle.

***

A couple days later, on the phone with Kristine, Mateo said, "You would not *believe* what that photographer got out of him. Like, without even trying! I never knew he'd been in foster care."

"How much do you guys talk about the past?"

"Not that much, I guess. We tend to talk more about what we're doing now and what to do, like, next week or next month." And there was always so much of that to talk about; they were *busy*.

"But that's natural. I don't go all reminiscey with Justin, either."

"How's that going, anyway?" Mateo had his own thoughts on the subject.

"Oh, you know." Kristine sounded like her thoughts might be running in the same direction. "We'll both be graduating in June and it's been fun, but I don't know."

"How do the 'rents feel about him?"

"They like him. Mom wants us to get married."

Mateo wasn't surprised. No way were the mothers not in cahoots. "But you don't want to?"

"He still hasn't asked me!"

"What the fuck?!"

"Right? Anyway I guess I love him, but I have this feeling he's got a very different picture of the future than I have. Like, he really loves this area and I know he wants to stay here forever."

"And you don't." He was sure of it.

"And I don't."

"Well, good luck. Big brother says don't commit to shit just to make somebody else happy."

"Eh," she said, voice full of trepidation. "It's hard knowing other people want you to do something. Like, *all* the other people. I don't know if I'm as brave as you."

"Sure you are. And I for one don't want you to marry that dude and get stuck in Pomona unless you absolutely positively want to. You can always come crash with us again if things get weird."

"Two guys, one girl, and one bathroom?"

"Hey, I'm getting all Martha Stewart up in here."

"Does that mean you keep things clean?"

"Hey, no fair, last time I'd just moved in." Mateo looked around the apartment with satisfaction, sinking his fingers into Pachuco's fur. "This is a *home*, Kris.

116

It's not big but we treat it right." And he never wanted
to leave. Plus: "I'm learning to cook."

"Mateo!"

"I know!"

Chapter 13

February 2013

The routine of living together seemed to suit both of them. Mateo found he had plenty of time to work out, to fool around in the kitchen, to do things at the dance studio. His employers, having recently added another engineer to the staff, sent him a slightly higher volume of work, but he didn't have any trouble turning it around. His occasional trips out to Santa Monica for meetings felt almost like fun now.

Sam's life, of course, had hardly changed at all. The addition of Mateo seemed to make everything easier. It wasn't only the fact of having someone else contributing to the rent, or the time and money saved by eating at home more often. It was a sense of comfort. He had a hard time defining it.

He was thinking about it one morning, on a day he didn't have to go to the store until midafternoon. They'd had breakfast together, and now Mateo was working at his computer. Sam was reading on the bed with Pachuco, because he wanted to be in the same room as his lover. He wanted to say something, but he didn't want to interrupt. Eventually Mateo pushed away from the desk with a satisfied grunt and stood up, stretching his back. "There. Enough of that for a while."

"Why are you like this?"

Mateo turned, startled. "What do you mean?"

"It's not a bad thing. I mean you're so domestic. I didn't expect that."

Mateo leaned against the desk, uneasy. "You're domestic. You made a home. That's what I wanted.

That's why when I spent that day with you and saw the way you live, and you were the way you are." He stalled.

Sam's voice was soft. "The way I am?"

"Peaceful. Kind. You took care of me when you didn't have to." He could tell that wasn't enough. Sam wasn't trying to put him on the defensive, obviously. He was only trying to figure something out. This conversation was probably a little past due. Mateo flung open the Growing Up Experience door. "I don't know how this might relate to your experience. You met my family. I was the third of four kids in a home where gender roles were really by the book, and I knew I was this way when I was, like, eight. So from then till I came out, thirteen years, I was always afraid. If they knew, would they still love me. Because I knew they loved me but I never felt like it was unconditional. We had a lot of hoops to jump through. Always this family thing and that church thing and what the neighbors expect. Behave this way, talk this way, do fucking cotillion and take a girl to the homecoming dance. Not for a minute of those thirteen years did I feel like I belonged in that house. I was not who they thought I was. Or who they wanted me to be." He looked away for a second.

Sam didn't want to interrupt. He knew this wasn't easy. This was everything he'd said to Andy, and maybe Mateo could only say it now because of hearing all that from Sam. He had to know it was okay. "I know what you mean."

"I know you do. And I didn't know that at first, but maybe I felt it. You knew who I was, because I wasn't hiding anything from you. I was lonely and a little bit lost, and I wanted someone to hold me and make me feel like I wasn't this huge disappointment."

119

"Baby." Sam held out his hand. Mateo took it. "And then I pushed you away. I'm sorry."

"It might have been necessary, though. For both of us. You told me how you spent that year. You know how I spent it. I worked through a lot of shit, and on the other side I realized that the way I felt about you *wasn't* only because I was lonely. It wasn't only because you're incredibly hot. It was because you're exactly the kind of person I wanted to belong to. Someone strong and physical and active who's also kind and peaceful and smart. You were living a life you'd made for yourself, in a home that was actually a home. You have friends. You value people and you don't judge. And when I was here in your home I didn't want to, like, set it on fire." Sam almost laughed. Mateo was still holding his hand, smiling a little now. "I felt at home here, and that was because of you. So that's why I'm like this. Because I could see a couple of places where I could make your life easier, or better, but all you want from me is *me*."

"I love you."

"I love you too. I'm going to drive you crazy sometimes because I want to do everything in the world with you and you're just going to want to chill out."

Sam did laugh then. "I had some years when nobody wanted to do anything with me. We'll figure it out."

"You know you can tell me anything, right? You can even tell me No." Mateo moved over to the side of the bed, standing between Sam's knees.

"Oh, baby. I couldn't tell you no."

"Rory would *kill* you." Mateo squeaked as Sam pulled him down onto the bed, laughed as he rolled them over, sighed as their lips met.

***

Once Mateo got used to the roughnecks (including Cory) at Sam's gym, he gave as good as he got. They went there for weights days. Sam invited him along to the dojo, but Mateo didn't want to commit to a class. He had a full schedule already. Instead, they took over Dana and Rory's outdoor space once in a while. At first it was only the two of them, practicing yoga or tai chi or another of the martial arts. After a while, whichever of the women was around would join them. Before long, Rory found out that Mateo used to be a gymnast. "No shit," she said delightedly. "Me too, before I got boobinated. I thought you were awfully bouncy in that paso with Richard."

They were all out on beach towels in the yard, stretching. Sam was interested to see where this would go. "He told me his parents put the girls in ballet and the boys in gymnastics."

"It was either that or have the house torn to pieces around them," Mateo said. "Four kids in seven years."

"Good God," Rory said blankly.

Dana said, "You guys should come with us to the aerial gym sometime. They've got all the stuff. Pole, lyra, silk, even a flying trapeze. Plus tumbling mats. Rory's always trying to get me to bounce around with her and I'm all, honey no. I am forty. That ship has sailed."

"You don't look forty," Sam said. He told Mateo, "She only learned pole six years ago."

"Six and a half. Going on seven. Jesus, time flies." Dana wasn't particularly troubled over her upcoming forty-first birthday. She assessed the men.

121

"I'll bet you would kick ass on the silk, or the rope. Either of you. Ever want to fly, Sam?"

"Never gave it a thought. Grip strength isn't my strongest suit." He gestured daintily with his well-kept hand; both women laughed.

"Mine either." Mateo thought it sounded like fun, though. "Want to go sometime?"

"Sure. I'd like to see you on the mats. You and Rory both." They compared calendars and found a few days they could all get to that gym at the same time. The first time, Sam quickly decided to spare his hands, opting to join Rory and Mateo at the mats. They started teaching him some tricks.

Rory had many bitter things to say about how those tricks looked when executed by a body like his. "It is so fucking annoying being this short," she said. "You are literally a foot taller than me. Gaahh." She shot Mateo a narrow-eyed look. "Don't you say a word. Five foot eight is a nice normal adult human height." Mateo performed an elaborate Whatever Honey gesture and she laughed. "You've been watching Dmitri. I swear that man can say more with an eyebrow than most people do in five-minute speeches."

"I love him." Mateo went over to the balance beam, which was temporarily vacant. "Let's see how I do at this. I used to suck." After a few minutes: "Oh, I still suck." Rory snickered. Sam went to spot Mateo. "Thanks honey. Yikes, we need to put one of these in the yard or something."

"Oh we do, do we." Rory could foresee all kinds of mayhem involving the neighborhood wildlife, not to mention the kids that belonged to the renters in the big house. "I think actually no. If you fall off a balance beam, I want you to do it here."

"Yeah, preferably when Sam is here to catch me. Eek! Whoops, yeah, getting down now. You should try this," he told Sam. "I'll bet you'd be good at it."

Sam wasn't averse to trying, so he got up on the beam. "Wow, this didn't seem so high up from the floor." He traversed it cautiously, got to the end, and turned around. Rory swung up in front of him. "Hey girl. Want to do some dirty dancing?"

"Totally!" They played around with it for a few minutes, goofing on the fallen-tree scene from the movie. Then she did a back walkover, and he made an annoyed sound. "You could do the basic," she said, noticing that he was standing there as solidly as if he were on the floor. "I'll be right here if you start to go offline. Mateo, ready to spot him?"

"You're insane," Sam said, smiling. "I haven't even tried to do that turnaround thing you just did."

"Well, try it." He did. Then he did a balancing-stick pose, to see if he could. "See?" Rory backed up a little, without looking. Mateo squeaked with alarm. She looked down at him. "Cutie patootie. I've been doing this for twenty-five years. Set your hands down like this, Sam." She demonstrated. "Then one leg up nice and slow. You don't have to take it over if you don't want to." She straightened up again and watched. He did it to the almost-halfway, not-quite-committed point with each leg. She gave him some pointers on hand placement. "You're coming up super vertical. I'm right here if you want to try going over."

"This is nuts," he said, upside down, then went into a split handstand. Rory caught his leading foot while the trailing foot was still behind him. "Down." He remembered how she placed her foot. She kept her hand lightly on the outside of his shin to keep him in line. He angled his foot on the beam the same way she had.

Rory assessed conditions. His back bend was perfect. The trailing leg was almost vertical in the air. "Okay, you're down. Go the rest of the way if you want or go back where you started. Mateo's right there." Sam returned to the trailing foot, stood up straight, gazed at the beam thoughtfully, and made eye contact with Rory. Then he went for it.

"Holy shit!" Mateo applauded, bouncing a little. "Holy mother fucking son of a bitching shit!" Sam and Rory were both cracking up as they got down off the beam. "I fell off the beam so many times trying to do that, and here you are, first time out, popping a walkover like you've been doing it for years. I am impressed."

"Me too." Rory patted Sam's back. "First time doing a walkover at all, and then half an hour later you're doing it on the beam. Did you see that?" She directed the question to Dana.

"Everybody saw that. I wish I had my phone out, I'd have taken a video."

"Do it again," Mateo begged. "I want to show it to Cory and blow his mind." He went and got his phone, woke it up and gave it to Dana. Sam and Rory looked at each other, shrugged, and got back on the beam. Mateo went to the far side to spot them, not that he expected any trouble.

A couple minutes later Dana said, "Got it. Wow, those legs."

"Right?!" Rory sounded disgusted.

***

They showed the video to Cory the next time they were all at the gym. He watched it twice, making sounds of disbelief, then stared up at Sam. "That is some next-level hotness."

"Right?" Mateo was pleased. In fact, he was smug. "It's great having someone who can do things better than me."

"You don't mind?"

Sam put in, "He's competitive. If I'm better at something, he works harder. If he's better at something, and for the record, baby, you're better at a lot of things," he gave that a dirty little twist just to see Mateo squirm with delight, "then *I* work harder. Don't I?"

"You do." Mateo looked at Cory. "He does. He works *hard*."

"Jesus, fuck you both," Cory said, laughing.

"You wish."

"I really do. Go lift some goddamned weights and quit rubbing it in."

"You wish."

"Fuck off!"

Sam was cracking up. He caught hold of Mateo and towed him into the weight room.

Chapter 14

Valentine's Day had never really been on Sam's radar. It wasn't a thing between men who were only hooking up, and one way or another he'd never been seeing anybody more serious on or around that holiday. But Mateo was serious, and Mateo was forever if Sam had anything to say about it. So he wanted to set a precedent that this was a thing for them. Wanted to make a statement that he understood and valued the importance of recognizing what they had. And he now felt sufficiently confident about doing things right that he didn't mention it to Vince, or to Rory, before making his plan.

When he ran into Rory at the coffee shop on the thirteenth, she said, "Hey big guy. How's the kid?"

"He's perfect. How's Dana?"

"She's perfect. You guys doing anything for V Day?"

"Yes we are. Mateo doesn't know it yet."

"Ooh, something sneaky. Give me a hint."

"We're going out to dinner someplace nice. He has a new suit to wear. I'm getting him flowers. Is that good?"

Rory was speechless for a second. She'd been ready to give him shit about doing some lame guy thing. She latched onto one part of it: "A new suit?"

"We went and picked it out last month. I told him I'd go get it when they finished the tailoring, and that's done."

"Excellent work, my friend. Where are you taking him?"

"The Four Seasons. I heard they do it nice there." Sam was enjoying Rory's expression. "How about you?"

"Well I thought I had it all worked out but now I feel like I forgot something." Sam laughed. Rory stared at him over her coffee cup. "So you gave yourself the night off? Didn't Benny pitch a fit?"

"Benny did pitch a fit. I reminded him how I usually work holidays, asked if maybe he'd like to work on his anniversary night, and he shut up." Sam rolled his eyes. His assistant manager was a good guy, but he'd gotten a little spoiled by Single Sam.

"Like a boss," Rory said admiringly. "Be sure to take a selfie tomorrow night when you're both all dressed up."

"I'll get the server to take a picture. We can send it to all our people." On that note they parted, Rory to go home and level up her own V Day plans, and Sam to head to the gym for a quick workout before his shift.

***

Sam was at work the next day when the flowers were delivered. Mateo answered the door and almost didn't know what to do. The delivery person said, "Mateo de la Cruz?"

"Uh-huh."

"These are for you. Happy Valentine's Day."

Mateo took the flowers, a dozen roses in mixed colors in a round ceramic vase, said something appreciative, and closed the door. "Pachuco, can you believe this? Do not eat these." He carried them into the bedroom, set them on the desk, and found the attached card. Sam's note read:

I NEVER HAD A VALENTINE BEFORE. SO HAPPY YOU'RE MINE. I LOVE YOU.

Mateo cried a little, then stuck the open note in the plastic prong thing, took a picture of it with the flowers in the background, and sent it to Kristine. He had no idea what she was supposed to be doing just then, but she replied immediately: *OMG Mateo I'm crying*

Me too

What did you get him?

I got him a tree

WTF

LOL he told me about going to this state park full of redwood trees and I found out you can donate to plant new ones. So I did that in his name

Wow Mateo that's good. Something that basically lives forever

EXACTLY. What plans?

Dinner with Justin what else

Don't sound so thrilled about it

I promise I'll thank him nicely. Are you going out?

Yes we are don't know where but we're dressing up. Gotta get some shit done first. Love you

Love you too!

Mateo did have work to do, but he didn't put the phone down until he'd sent a text to Sam: **Thank you for the beautiful flowers. I never had a Valentine before either. You're the BEST. I love you XOX**

***

Sam read the text within fifteen minutes of receiving it. He'd been busy helping someone who came in to pick up a tux for a special dinner that was

128

apparently going to include a proposal. It was his favorite kind of transaction; the guy was really excited. He'd come in the month before to make his selection and get fitted. After trying on the sleek black suit and choosing his accessories, he shook Sam's hand. "She can't say no to this, can she?"

Sam said, "Of course not," hoping she didn't. Then he packed everything up to go and sent the guy on his way, taking the next minute to check his phone. He sent back *I love you too XOX* and started counting down till Benny would get there and he could leave.

Mateo was half dressed when Sam got home. "Hey lover. Are you wearing that one?"

"No, I'm going to change." Sam came in and kissed Mateo. "You liked the flowers."

"No one ever got me flowers before. Did you like your card?"

"You know I did." Sam kissed him again. He'd found it on the driver's seat when he left that morning. "You got me a tree."

"I'll get you another one next year."

Sam smiled. Mateo did that all the time, made references to things they'd do in the future. Sam loved it. "We can go visit them sometime. You'd like that park."

"Mom and Dad took us all to Yosemite once. Was it like that?"

"Little bit." Sam was shedding clothing, eyes on his lover. Mateo's new suit was dark gray, a lightweight silk blend. He had a new pair of black wingtip shoes, and a fresh white dress shirt. "Want me to get your tie for you?"

"God, yes. I've been practicing with that old one I got at the thrift shop but you do it better." Mateo stood still while Sam knotted his striped pink tie, then slid

129

the matching silk square into the chest pocket of the jacket. "How do I look?"

"Like a fashion model. People are going to stop and stare when we walk in."

"They'll be staring at you. Especially if you don't put some pants on." He patted Sam's ass, then went to check himself out in the full-length mirror on the back of the bedroom door. "Hey! Not bad!" Sam laughed. He finished getting dressed while Mateo had a word with Pachuco. When he walked out to the living room Mateo whistled. "Is that new?"

Sam was wearing a black-and-silver houndstooth jacket over a white shirt, with black pants and spectator shoes. "No, I got it a while ago. Which tie?" He was holding two. Mateo chose the solid magenta raw silk instead of the black one with thin silver chevrons. Sam nodded, returned to the bedroom briefly, then came out ready to go. "You are such a knockout."

"You are." Mateo checked to make sure his pants were free of cat hair. "Let's go paint the town, honey." He still had no clue where they were going. The Four Seasons was barely on his radar, even though it was within a few minutes of the apartment, so when they pulled up to the valet stand he was surprised. Then they went in and were treated like celebrities, and he said softly, "Have you been here before?"

"No." Sam was holding Mateo's hand. "I heard about what it's like though. Vince brought Kelli here last year."

They both knew it was partly the artificial significance of the date, plus the fun of being all dressed up, but this did feel special. Live music, excellent service, a spacious and quiet room, real flowers on the table. Mateo told Sam about texting Kristine a picture of the roses; Sam told Mateo about the guy picking up the tux. Mateo managed not to make any hints about future occasions when one or the other of them might want a tux. "We're going to get a picture tonight, right? My parents have never seen me in a real suit."

"Before we go, I promise." Their table was in an alcove, semi-private, framed with drapery. It was a great place to get a picture. Sam told the server they wanted one. "I know it's not your job and it's probably annoying, but this is kind of a big night for us. We'd appreciate it."

"I'd be delighted. Will you be ordering dessert?"

They didn't usually, because Mateo was always watching his weight, but tonight they decided to share one. It came out with a dendrobium orchid blossom on top. Once that was on the table, with two dessert forks and two flutes of champagne, they stood up for their picture. The server took several. They flipped through all of them as they ate the dessert, deciding which one they'd send to Mateo's parents, and which to the Lees and the Mendozas. Sam's favorite was the one where they were looking at each other, instead of smiling at the camera. He sent that one to Rory and Dana, then to Kristine. Their glasses were empty. Neither of them wanted coffee. He left a huge tip. As they stood again to go, he said, "I wouldn't mind doing this every year."

Mateo leaned against him as they waited at the valet stand. "That would be nice. My treat next time."

Then it was the short drive home, undressing with care, having a moment with Pachuco, getting ready for bed. Logic said it was a work night, so make it fast; all the romance of the flowers and the card and

131

the evening out argued in favor of making this last. Mateo wanted more romance. He lit a couple of candles and told Sam to lie down. "Someday I'm going to get Andy to take some full-color pictures of you. Like this, with candlelight, naked. God, you're gorgeous." He straddled Sam's hips, leaned down for a kiss, felt those hands sweeping up his sides, over his chest, and up his neck into his hair. They kissed like that for some time, until they heated up and started to grind, thoroughly aroused. Sam reached over to the nightstand, getting the lube out. Mateo sat up. "What's it going to be, honey?"

"What do you want?"

"I want you in." He was expecting Sam to say On Your Back or On Your Knees. Either one would have been fine.

"Stay right there." Mateo made an interested sound. Sam put his hands on Mateo's ribs and lifted him a little. Then he had the lube, one hand on himself and the other between Mateo's legs.

"Oh my Lord." Mateo was getting the idea. He'd seen pictures of this. He was still close enough to kiss Sam, so he did that, making faint noises as Sam got him ready. "Now? Please. God. Yes." Sam let him push back. "Oh my Jesus." He had to raise up to take that cock. Arched his back, eyes closed, feeling Sam's hand on his chest and hearing the low sound he made as Mateo took him deeper. Quivering with tension, trying not to surge up, letting Mateo set the pace. Mateo was panting, almost frowning. Then he changed his angle a bit and said, "Fuck *yes* oh my God almighty."

Sam choked back a laugh or a groan, he wasn't sure which. Mateo looked magnificent, the candlelight outlining the curves of his muscles under that golden skin. Sam was sure this was the most beautiful thing he would ever see in his life. His phone was on the nightstand. He got hold of it and opened the photo app. Mateo was moving now. It was going to be over soon, Sam couldn't hold back his climax, and Mateo was about to come. Sam took a picture and dropped the phone, clamping one hand on Mateo's hip and wrapping the other around his cock. "Go, baby. Now, you're killing me, give it to me. Oh fuck please Mateo *yes*."

Mateo's body jerked as he climaxed. "Jesus!" Sam held him tight and surged up once. "God!"

They didn't move for a few seconds, both breathing hard. Mateo opened his eyes and looked down. Sam's eyes were closed and his lips were parted. I did that, Mateo thought, pleased. He put a hand on Sam's chest, drawing a finger through the wetness on his belly. Sam smiled. "That was you."

"I know. Mmm." Mateo disengaged carefully.

"Okay?"

"Oh yeah." He leaned down for one more kiss. "Did you take a picture?" Sam nodded. "Let me see."

Chapter 15

April 2013

Being grown-ups and having a home, Mateo decided, meant inviting people over. Sure, there were a hundred great places to meet people in and around WeHo, but he wanted to show off some of his new domestic skills. If part of him also wanted to show off this thing called Mateo And Sam, he thought he could be forgiven.

A good excuse to host something came after 'Cut Open' closed. They invited the photographer over, with Rory and Dana to help celebrate since they were already friends with the guy. The first thing the women noticed was the framed 16x24 print of a black and white photo of Mateo lifting Sam off the floor. "Well, wow," Rory said. "I don't need to ask where you got that."

"Andy brought it." Sam was smiling. "Wasn't that nice?"

The photographer shrugged it off. "Call it a thank you. Those images of you anchored the exhibit."

"The whole thing was really good. Very different for you," Dana said to Andy.

"You know I like trying new things, but yeah, it really was. The next collection's gotta be a pivot, I'm done with trauma for a while. Anyway, I hear the kid is cooking today so this should be interesting."

"I heard that," Mateo said from the kitchen. It was only a few feet away from the living room, so there was no way he *couldn't* have heard it.

Sam had rearranged the living area, pushing the couch against the far wall so they could all sit on cushions around the large coffee table. Dana flopped down comfortably. "We should do something like this."

Rory flopped down beside her. "You're right. We always eat in front of the TV. I can't remember the last time we had a party where people actually sat down at the table."

"Because the chairs are a pain in the ass."

Sam laughed. "All this is, is an old door from Liz's Antique Hardware on some blocks." He was so excited to be hosting for the first time, but he'd been a little worried about his limitations. Should have known better.

"I like it," Rory decided. "When you want space, you can prop it up against the wall."

"So tell us what we're getting here, Mateo." Dana looked over at the chef, in the kitchen.

"My mom tried to teach me all this Filipino stuff but to be honest, it's all either fried or it's really complicated, so hell no. I took a class down at the culinary school on Melrose."

"I know the one."

Mateo brought over the first tray. "So you're getting beef tournedos with mushroom risotto."

"Wow!" Rory looked impressed.

Sam looked smug. "Our eating-out bill has gone way down lately."

"And the grocery bill has gone way up!" Mateo served everyone. Sam poured the wine, killing the first bottle.

Dana lifted her glass; they all put theirs in for a clink. "Cheers. So, you went to see the exhibit, right?" She gave Andy a sideways look.

"Oh my God, we walked in and Sam got mobbed," Mateo said proudly.

Andy nodded. "Every one of those prints is sold."

"People wanted autographs. It was a trip." Sam smiled, shaking his head.

"Pretty much every artist in the building wants to use you." Andy was smiling too. "And a lot of people were asking for a book, so I'm getting one printed. You'll get the same royalty on that."

"Doing books is so easy now," said Dana. "I did one for my folks the last time we redecorated."

Rory said, "We're thinking about doing a book for the Underground Cabaret. The videos keep selling, so, you know. Why not."

"Happy to put one together for you," Andy said. "How's it all been working since the grand reopening?" He glanced at Dana.

"Pretty well, really," she said. "We've got a lot of regulars. There are open auditions for each show, but the cabaret group is regular, the kickline is pretty regular. We're looking for new circus-arts talent."

Rory shrugged. "But we may be going back to every other month."

"Why the change?" Sam set down his glass.

"Michelle's doing all this ballroom stuff with Dmitri now, plus two of our principals are knocked up. We don't want to change the mix too much. It's been rolling really smooth."

"So instead of changing the way the Cabaret shows are set up, Michelle and Dmitri are developing a ballroom show for alternate months," Dana said. "Tyrone said they can give it a try. The partner dance numbers have been popular all along, ever since Vince."

"Jesus yes, Vince." Rory gave Sam a look. "I still can't believe you never came to see any of his shit till last fall. Have you looked at it online?"

"Yeah, I got caught up. Mateo was giving me crap about it."

"Yes I was," said the chef. "I went down the rabbit hole when I was prepping that thing with Richard. Must have watched Vince's first thing about a hundred times. You know we don't miss those shows now." Rory nodded approvingly.

"They keep getting better," said Andy. "I don't know of any other company that's been able to manage itself so well over such a long period of time. I mean, a company where all the principals are basically volunteers."

"Tyrone giving us that deal at Chrome was a big, big part of making it work," said Rory. "Also, I gotta say, Marcy and Anne leaving helped. A lot." She drank some wine, with an air of relief.

Mateo perked up. "Juicy back story?"

Rory said, "We had us a couple of bitches."

Dana elaborated. "They were good at what they did, and they played a big part in putting the company together, but trying to run things with them was like being in a bag of mad cats all the time."

Sam looked around. "Speaking of cats, where's Pachuco?"

"I gave him his very own little steak so he would bug off. He should be passed out in a beef coma right about now." Mateo added, "I swear, he gets his tail in the plates deliberately."

"Thanks for sparing us the cat-hair garnish. This is really good," said Andy.

Rory nodded. "Yeah, it is. What class was that? I could stand to expand my repertoire."

"It's called Man Food," Mateo said apologetically.

She gave him an incredulous look. "Well, fuck it then." Dana and Andy both laughed.

"Who'd like some more wine?" said Sam. Four hands went up.

***

Their first lesson was right around the corner, so Mateo and Sam met at Shall We Dance to talk about what to work on. Mateo had a lot of ideas (and enthusiasm), but Sam was nervous. Learning ballroom dancing sounded reasonable until you found out there were four different styles. Mateo was looking at him hopefully. Sam made an apologetic face. "I can't contribute much. I don't know enough."

"You know more than you think you do. Anyway, there's no right or wrong here. I'm going to ask Dmitri what he thinks." Mateo went over to the office and poked his head in. "Hey boss?"

"Yes?"

"What style should Sam and I do?"

"International Latin."

Oh shit. "Not Rhythm?"

Dmitri looked stern. "Definitely Latin."

"Shit," he said incautiously. "I suck at Latin."

There was something very close to a laugh from Dmitri. "Julia is excellent coach. Also, next month we have party here for Vince and Kelli. You two should come."

"Thanks!" He went back to Sam and gave him the news. "For today, you want to mess around with some rumba? I can show you the basic syllabus." Sam nodded, so they got to work. It was good that they were already used to communicating how-to. Good that Sam didn't mind taking direction from someone younger. As they walked home, Mateo was buzzing, high on dancing. He could've babbled about it for hours. But Sam had clearly had enough for the day, and it was much too early to suggest any of the wild ideas he'd had, so he changed the subject. "I didn't expect to see Andy at the studio. Anybody drop any hints?"

"No." Sam was curious about that too. "Let's see if Vince and Kelli know anything." They had a dinner date, the last time they would see their friends before the East Coast wedding.

***

Kelli was buzzing with energy when they met up at the Italian restaurant. "First of all, our wedding dance is going to knock your socks off at the party. Second of all, my God you two looked so good together the other night. You're doing Latin, right?"

"Right." Sam gave Mateo a sideways look. "This one tells me once I get rumba, the rest of them will fall into place. Is that true?"

"I don't know," Kelli said guiltily. "We dance American style." Mateo made an aggravated face; she made an apologetic face.

Vince said, "I recommend assuming it's true. Has anybody tried to draft you into the Cabaret yet?"

"Not yet." Mateo patted Sam's leg under the table. "I don't want to freak the big guy out so I've been dodging Rory on that subject."

"You don't need to." Sam was smiling at him now. "She's been bugging me since the second she heard we were taking lessons together. She's like, oh my God paso." Kelli laughed. "And I'm like, what the fuck, I don't know *anything* yet, give me a minute." Now Vince laughed.

"But it seems like there's an awful lot going on in there!" Mateo drank some wine. "We saw Andy, the photographer guy, when we got to the studio today. He was doing something with Dmitri that was not photography." The two men had only been talking, but there was no camera in sight, and Andy had dance shoes on.

Vince and Kelli gave each other a querying look. Kelli said, "No idea. We see him around, he's always at the Cabaret shows, but nope. Did it look like he was taking lessons? Maybe he got tired of sitting on the sidelines."

"Eh." Mateo dismissed the photographer. "Dmitri and Michelle are winning the Smooth events all over the place, she and Julia are gearing up with this new ballroom show concept, he's got a new girl coming in to manage the studio, the place is a madhouse. It's awesome."

"That new show could be interesting. I love doing the Cabaret but something a little more strictly ballroom is going to be easier to work into." Kelli finished her Caesar salad. That seemed to be the cue for the server to come and clear the first course. A few minutes later they all had their entrées, and conversation languished. As soon as she set down her fork, Kelli picked up the thread. "Do you want to, honey? We don't have much else on the schedule. We're missing the 'On Safari' reprise." She looked at Mateo. "Not really. We're doing that same 'I Wanna Be Like You' mambo at the D.C. Salsa Challenge. My mother was like, you're getting married *and* you're doing a competition? What is wrong with you?"

Mateo laughed into his wineglass. Kelli now made big hopeful eyes at Vince. "You think we should do something for the ballroom show in September?"

"I think you should." Everybody looked at Sam. "The August show too."

Vince made an incredulous face. "We already talked about Halloween. That would be three shows in a row. Three new performances in three months."

"We've done it before," Kelli pointed out. "Recently." She clearly wanted to do it; there might as well have been a neon sign over her head flashing YES YES YES. Mateo giggled.

Vince stared at Sam, eyes narrowed. "If we do that, you have to do something." Sam's eyebrows went up. "Do salsa, do paso doble, do fucking tai chi for all I care."

Mateo put both hands on the table, grinning, delighted that somebody else said it so he didn't have to. "When? We seriously just started."

"It's May. Give it six months." Sam started to say something; Vince pointed a fork at him. "Kelli and I did our first performance barely six months after we started dating."

Sam was clearly regretting starting this. "Yeah, but you were both already dancers!"

"*You're* already a dancer!" Mateo and Kelli were both having hysterics. Vince was on the verge of cracking up too. He gave Sam a warning look. "November. It'll be one of the ballroom shows. Get Michelle or Julia on your side. You'll be fine."

Chapter 16

A few weeks into their dance lessons, Sam was not sure about this. Dmitri's colleague Julia had given them a sequence of basic figures in rumba, and it was too different from salsa. "Maybe I just don't hear the music the way you do."

"I can tell." Mateo had his hand on Sam's back. "I don't want you to get frustrated, but I feel so *sure* that you can get this."

"Sam, try to think of the figures as a kata," Julia suggested. "They don't change. These figures are the foundation of rumba. Everything every dancer does builds on these. The music isn't actually important. It's more the rhythm."

"But there's so much going on in the music, it's like I can't even *hear* the rhythm." He gave Mateo a helpless look. "And we've got this thing we have to do."

"We don't *have* to do it, baby." Mateo patted him. They'd told Julia everything, all about Vince's challenge, and she'd promised to help them. He really didn't want to force this on Sam, though.

"Let me try something." Julia went over to the music system, scrolling through the playlist. "Here it is, I knew it was in here. Just listen for a minute." She cued a track. Nothing but drums, a complex layered arrangement with a strong quick-quick-slow beat under syncopated accents. "Mateo, could you do the leader's part for Sam to see?"

Mateo started the routine, dancing as if he were doing tai chi. No extra flourishes; simple, strong lines. Sam got it. "Oh!"

"Do it alongside Mateo, Sam." Mateo started the routine again and Sam moved with him. This time it was working. "There you go," Julia said, satisfied.

"It's starting to make sense."

"Why don't you practice to this till next week. I'll email the track to you."

"Thanks, Julia! This is great." Mateo was relieved. "Once he gets the rhythms, then we'll worry about shit like hip action."

Julia laughed. "Whatever works. Hey, you could do me a favor. Can you join the beginners' social class? I need an extra leader. Who's not a beginner. I need a ringer, in other words."

Mateo glanced at his lover. "That okay, Sam?"

"Sure. Benny's been whining about working so many nights, anyway."

"He whines no matter what you do. Yeah, I could come."

Julia nodded, pleased. "You guys coming to the party this weekend?"

Mateo gave her a look. "Honey, you should know we do not miss parties." They talked about that most of the way home. After dinner and some relaxation, he sat on Sam's lap and said, "You can say no. We do not have to do a show. You can tell Vince to go fuck himself."

Sam laughed softly. "I don't want to do that. I might freak out a little here and there but you say we can do it, and I believe you. Maybe it would help if I knew what music we would have."

"We've still got a lot of time. Julia will tell us the second they decide what the November show is going to be based around. Or we could push it to December.

143

That's always a holiday show, we could pick music right away. Decide what dance you want to do."

Sam realized he was feeling a little stubborn about it. He didn': like backing away from a challenge. "Let's get me up to speed on all five of these dances. At least off the starting line." He kissed Mateo. "I know I won't be as good as that Richard guy was last year. But I'll do my best."

"I know you will, honey. And your best is awfully good." Mateo kissed him again. A few minutes later he stood up, stripped, helped Sam out of his pants, and got back on his lap. Facing him this time, straddling his thighs, pulling his shirt off and pressing close. "God I love you."

Sam stroked a hand down Mateo's back and then around in between them. "Mmm, baby. I love you too."

***

The following Sunday evening the studio was closed to lessons, but plenty of people were there, and everybody was dressed to kill. Dmitri was hosting a celebration for Vince and Kelli, back from their wedding and another Salsa Challenge win. After several performances from friends, the guests of honor took their positions in the center of the dance floor.

Vince wore charcoal pinstripe trousers and vest with a black-on-white pinstripe shirt, bow tie, and fedora. Kelli had changed into an ivory confection that looked like a can-can dress. The music, The Jive Aces' 'Bring Me Sunshine,' started slow. She and Vince danced a sweet old-fashioned foxtrot for a minute, and then the music changed up to a swinging Lindy Hop.

Kelli did a fast turn away from Vince and the long skirt of her dress peeled off in his hand, exposing her fishnet-covered legs and hot-pink shoes. Vince tossed the skirt to Sam and his hat to Vicky. The crowd hooted, whistled, and laughed as the newlyweds threw themselves into a crazy swing routine, finishing to raucous applause.

"I love that song," Sam said, looking at Mateo. That's what his lover did, bring the sunshine.

"That was some killer swing," Mateo said. "I love that they did that for a wedding dance."

"The dress is based on one Kelli wore for the Salsa Challenge last year," their new friend Sharon said.

Mateo looked up at Sam, thinking out loud. "Hmm, the Salsa Challenge. They have a same-sex division, I hear."

Sam gave him a half-serious warning look. "Oh no you don't."

"I feel ya, Sam," said Sharon. "This one has me prepping for the Gay Games next year." She pointed to her girlfriend.

"Oh, like you couldn't have said no," Vicky objected.

"How often do I say no?"

"Exactly!" Sam looked at Mateo, who had his scheming face on, and laughed. "Quit that! I've learned *one* dance so far." One that he was comfortable with, anyway.

Vicky said, "You and me, Mateo. We'll keep this train on the track."

Sam appealed to Sharon. "I'm in trouble, aren't I?" She nodded soberly. Mateo was still grinning, but Sam wanted to make sure he hadn't misread things.

On their walk home he said, "You know I love doing all this crazy shit with you, right? Me moaning about it doesn't mean anything."

Mateo looked up at him, then took his hand. "Thanks for saying that. I do wonder sometimes if I'm driving you nuts. I know I can be a little much." Next thing he knew Sam had him wrapped in those strong arms. "Mmph?"

"I love you. It makes me so *happy* that you want to do things with me. You want to go places and see people, with me. You want to be with me. It means so much." Sam gave him a little space then, but only so he could go in for a kiss. He forgot all about them being out in public until they separated again and he realized there was applause. "Uh, maybe we should get ourselves home."

"Yeah you know honey, maybe so." Mateo took hold of his hand again and they started walking. "You realize I want to do all those things with you because I love you."

"Uh-huh. So happy," Sam said softly.

Mateo squeezed his hand. "Me too. Uh, what Sharon said?"

"Yeah?"

"I found out about that last year. The Gay Games having Dance Sport. Figured I'd wait a minute before I mentioned it, just like I was gonna wait to mention doing something with the Cabaret."

Sam huffed out a laugh. "Are you saying the whole world is conspiring to get me into a show? Or doing competition?"

"Seems like it." Still a couple blocks from home. Mateo weighed his options and chose to continue the conversation. "I know you like dancing socially. But I can't help thinking you'd get a helluva charge out of competition."

"Mmm. I thought about it too."

"You did?"

"Way back last Thanksgiving, when I had to work and you went to the California Star Ball. Vince and Kelli were up in San Francisco competing, and I thought, you know, that might be cool. 'Cause I *am* competitive."

"Mmm, yeah, I noticed." They both snickered. "Then there's the show. I know Vince basically big-dogged you, but it seemed like the very idea didn't freak you out. He wouldn't't've given you any real shit about saying no, and neither would I."

Sam glanced over. "If we get close to the point where we have to really commit and I don't think I'm ready, I'll say so. Fair enough?"

"More than." Mateo squeezed his hand.

***

The following week, Mateo and Sam walked down to Rory and Dana's place for dinner. Sam was carrying a couple of bottles of wine in an over-the-shoulder cooler bag; Mateo was loving life. It seemed like they passed someone they knew on every block, exchanging greetings and smiles. "This neighborhood is so much friendlier than where I was before."

Sam glanced over. "When I asked people where I should live in L.A., they all said WeHo. They said, get in someplace and hang onto it." Which was exactly what he'd done.

Mateo approved. The apartment was small, but you couldn't beat the location. There were whole weeks when the only reason he got in his car was to move it for street cleaning. "Can't wait to see what the girls have done with the place."

"Me too. It was nice before but I thought it could use a little more color here and there."

"That's something I liked about your place right off. It seemed like a real home. I never thought about how generic white walls are. I never see the finished products of what my guys do. You know when we do the renderings, we hardly ever add color."

Sam was smiling. "I hate white walls. People say they look clean. To me they just look temporary. Anyway I've been there a long time. The landlord didn't mind when I said I wanted to paint. Wants me to prime it white if I ever leave, but otherwise he doesn't care." They walked up the block, then up the driveway and past the big house to the cottage in back. Window boxes full of flowers flanked the bright pink door; a rainbow banner hung alongside.

Mateo liked it. "That's so cute." He leaned over to sniff a geranium as Sam knocked. Dana opened the door and a mouthwatering aroma of spices wafted out.

"Hey guys, come on in! Andy's going to be here in about a half hour, and look who else is here." They walked in to greet another Cabaret artist. "We met Paula last year during the 'Haunted' show. You might remember her, Mateo."

"Sure do. That was a great number. You did those two trapeze things this year! How the hell do you go from striptease to trapeze?"

Paula said, "My old dance teachers have the same question. I love working with the Cabaret, it's like here's the theme, do something whack."

"With Kim and Stacey out it's been great to have her on the line. There aren't that many stray aerialists running around Los Angeles," Dana said, smiling. "Rory's putting the finishing touches on the dining room."

"This looks like the beach," said Mateo, admiring the effect of warm mid-brown wood floors with freshly painted blue walls. "What's that color called?"

Dana said, "It's called Voyage. Really changes the space, doesn't it? But come see the dining room." She led them down the short hall.

Mateo's reaction was "Whoa!"

The back half of the cottage was all one room, now painted a deep plum that made the walls seem to disappear. A wall of windows looked out to a thick stand of bamboo. The windows were framed with silk panels in bright vertical stripes, trimmed with layers of tassel and pom-pom fringe. The ceiling was painted hot pink and hung with an array of small chandeliers, all painted scarlet and strung with colorful beads. A table occupied most of one side of the room.

Rory looked up from the opposite corner, where she was lighting a group of candles in brass holders on an Indian brass tray table next to a carved wooden room-divider screen. "Hey guys!"

"Rory, the place looks terrific," said Sam, going over to give her a kiss.

Mateo did that too. "It's so *sexy*."

Dana laughed. "Well, *we* thought so."

"I love it," Paula said enviously. "I'm going to steal the whole scheme for my place."

"Feel free, we stole it from Tony Duquette."

Mateo checked out the table, a double-pedestal rectangle (now with considerately beveled corners) fitted into a U-shaped continuous bench seat. "So, I remember somebody hating on the chairs. Does the bench work better?"

"So much better," said Dana. "We can fit more people, we can store shit in there, and there's no ten thousand legs to trip over."

"We cut off the corners so people can scoot around without getting skewered." Rory patted the tabletop. "And our carpenter guy did the backrest."

"It's great. All this glass wasn't here before, was it?" Sam asked, indicating the back wall. "I can't even remember what it looked like."

"There were a couple of double-hungs," said Rory. "We wanted to really see the bamboo, so we carved out the wall and plugged in this whole raft of vintage windows. You're among the first people to see this, by the way. What a fucking process."

"It looks awesome," said Paula. "How cool that the landlord let you do that."

Dana smiled. "Well, actually I *am* the landlord. I own the house in front, it's rented out."

"Beautiful *and* smart," Mateo said to Rory. "It's no wonder you like her."

Rory looked smug. "Right?"

The doorbell rang. "That'll be Andy." Dana went to let him in.

When she brought him to the back he took one look and pretended to swoon. "I just had an idea for a whole 'nother show, ladies." He turned around and left the room again.

Paula looked at Dana; Dana looked at Rory; Rory said, "Going to get his camera, I'll bet."

Mateo made an irritated noise. "But my shirt clashes with these colors."

"Take it off," Sam suggested, which made all three women laugh. "Maybe after dinner."

"But honestly. There is no possible way to clash with these colors," Dana said. "These are *all* the colors." Between the bamboo, the paint, and the drapery, she had a point. Mateo ended up taking off his shirt anyway.

"That was totes ridiculous," he said as they ambled home, much later, still buzzed and exhausted from laughter. "I mean, *completely*."

Sam, arm around his lover's shoulders, grinned to himself. He couldn't wait to see the pictures. "Ever played that game before?"

"Never have I ever played a drinking game before," Mateo said, full of regrets. "And never again. Those girls know way too much about my sex life now."

Chapter 17

A couple weeks later, Sam woke to the sound of Pachuco meowing. "What?"

Mateo opened an eye and listened. "Cat?"

"He doesn't do that."

"What's he doing?"

Sam sat up, turned the bedside lamp's dimmer switch to low and flipped on the light. Pachuco was still yowling. "He's kind of clawing at the back door."

Mateo sat up too. "You're right, he doesn't do that."

"Something outside must have set him off." Sam slid out of bed, pulled on a pair of shorts, and walked over to the door, bending down to pet the agitated cat. "What's up, buddy?"

Mateo joined him. "You want to check it out?"

"Yeah, hold onto him, would you?"

"Sure." Mateo picked up Pachuco as Sam opened the door. They didn't see anything obviously off in the alley. "Dude, quit squirming. This little fucker is strong."

"Hang on." Sam stepped outside and looked both ways. "There's a box on the ground by the dumpster. I'm going to take a look."

"Watch your step."

Sam slid his feet into flip-flops, then walked a short way down the alley. He bent down and peeked under the crossed top flaps of the cardboard box. "Oh, damn it."

"What is it?"

"Kittens."

"You are *shitting* me."

"Nope."

"Well, they're just coyote bait out there. Better bring 'em inside before, ow! Stop it, bitch! Pachuco's digging a hole in my chest."

Sam picked up the box and carried it in. There was a chorus of squeaking from inside. He set the box down on the kitchen counter as Mateo closed the door, then let Pachuco jump down. "You're like a cat Lassie, huh? Oh no, kittens in a box!" Pachuco ignored him, jumping up on the counter, where he was not (technically) allowed. Neither of the men told him to get down.

Sam opened the flaps of the box to reveal five kittens. Four, in a frightened huddle, had gone quiet; one, all black, was climbing up the side of the box and yelling. "That one's got some nerve," said Mateo.

"Bet it's got some fleas, too."

"Towels and shampoo coming right up." Sam had the kittens corralled in the sink when Mateo returned; he took the box back outside and pitched it into the dumpster, hoping that any fleas went with it. There followed a wet, splashy, squeaky interval as the kittens got washed. Pachuco crouched on the counter and supervised until Mateo toweled off the first newcomer and set it on the floor. Then the big cat jumped down to sit and stare at the kitten. Mateo glanced at him and laughed. "He's like, what did I get myself into. Think these guys are old enough to be litter-trained?"

"Yeah, I'd say they're about two months. At least whoever the asshole was waited until they were old enough to wean." Sam dried the last kitten and set it on the floor beside its siblings. They were all bobble-

153

heading around, taking occasional cautious steps one direction or another, occasionally squeaking.

"I hate people sometimes."

"Me too."

"Let's see if they'll eat." Mateo got a can of Spot's Stew, emptied it onto a plate, added a little dry milk and water. He offered it first to Pachuco, who sampled it and seemed to approve. The kittens were now huddled under the coffee table, but the black one detached itself right away and headed for the plate. Before long all the others joined it.

Sam looked at Mateo. "Guess we can go back to bed."

"Guess we need to hold an adoption fair. I'll take 'em to the vet tomorrow and get them checked out."

***

Pachuco wasn't on the bed with them as usual when Sam woke up in the morning. He went out to the living space and saw the big cat on the couch, with all the kittens piled up around him. He blinked contentedly at Sam, who reached down to pet his head. He was purring. "If I'd known you wanted a kitten, I would have gotten you one before." This was too damn cute. Sam went to get his phone so he could take some pictures.

That night, he got home from work to find Mateo on the couch, watching TV; Pachuco on the table, looking far more alert than usual at this time of day; and five kittens rampaging around the room. "I take it they're healthy?"

"*Exhaustingly* healthy. I haven't done a thing today except be a kitten wrangler. The orange one was a little bit anemic, probably from fleas, but the vet says he should be okay."

"When can they get neutered?"

"About another month or so." Mateo reorganized himself to look at Sam, fixing them drinks in the kitchen. "Know anybody who wants a bunch of kittens?"

They'd both seen pet-adoption notices in the neighborhood coffee shops plenty of times. "No, but I'll bet we can find five people who want one apiece."

"Four. I'm in love with the black one. Surprise." Sam came over and put a glass in Mateo's hand, then leaned over and kissed him. Mateo smiled up at him. "It's a girl, by the way. I've named her Frida. Pachuco likes her, too. You should have seen him after I brought them home. They all ran over to him and he started washing them, like ew, oh my God, let me get the vet stank off of you." Sam laughed. "I took some pictures because it was so damn cute. And I made a flyer to put up in the neighborhood. It's on the counter."

Sam went over and picked it up. It read:

> To the worthless sack of sh!t
> who dumped these kittens:
> [photo]
> Spay your cat.
> We recommend this vet.
> [address]
> Sincerely, your neighbors.

"That's perfect," he said. "Like everything else you do."

Mateo's toes curled with delight. "Aw honey. Come over here and kiss me again. A lot."

***

155

The next weekend, they left their half-dozen cats alone and went to Chrome for the new show 'Mating Dance.' It was only six numbers, which seemed really short after the last Cabaret production. Maybe it was a strategy: most of the audience was yelling for more. "I love them so much," Mateo said, after the curtain closed and he had a fresh drink in hand. "Julia and Dmitri."

Sam leaned on the table and gazed at him, smiling. "I knew that's who you meant."

"I totally adopted both of them. Or forced them to adopt me, either way. Did you know Ray is sixteen years younger than Julia?" Their coach and her boyfriend-slash-partner had opened the show with a sexy rumba set to 'Dancing in the Dark.'

"No." Sam sounded like he didn't quite believe it. "She looks amazing."

"Her daughter is at Santa Monica College."

"No!" Sam swallowed some of his cocktail. "God, she's in great shape."

Mateo nodded, mouth full of rum and Coke. He swallowed with an orgasmic sound. "I'm going to regret all this sugar later but damn it tastes good. She didn't even start dancing till she was thirty-something. What did you think of this show format?"

"I liked all the dances. Liked the last one best, that disco number. The story kind of worked but are they planning to do the same thing every time? I don't see how they could really do stories that were fresh." Sam drank some more of his Cape Cod, wondering with amusement when he started thinking so seriously about dance. Probably had something to do with the pretty boy next to him, having a sexual experience with his rum and Coke.

Mateo didn't notice the way Sam was grinning into his cocktail glass. "Yeah, me too. I'm not sure if the story idea was Dmitri's or Michelle's or Julia's. I'll bet they re-think it. You don't need a story to have a great ballroom show." Not when they had Dmitri dancing in it. He still had a little crush on the studio boss, even after all this time. It was mixed in with that be-my-daddy thing that was so embarrassing he never told anyone except Sam. "Maybe they'll go with themes, like the rest of the Cabaret shows."

Sam perked up. "God, I hope they do. Then we could choose our own music, right?"

"Jesus, yes. That would be great. I'll give Julia a nudge. You're doing so fantastic, though. No matter what, you're going to kick ass in November." Sam got a hold of his upper arm and pulled him close for a kiss. "Mmm. You want to dance a little before we go home?" The house music tonight was, no surprise, a very danceable mix.

"Maybe a little." Sam slid off the barstool and stood between Mateo's knees. Kissed him again, felt his body light up the same way Sam's had. Felt him open his legs, shifting forward on the seat so they were tight together. Couldn't help pushing against him, hearing the soft sound Mateo made, a bit more vocal than a gasp. "Jesus."

"Maybe that was enough dancing," Mateo said, breathless. "If we do much more of that I'm going to come right here."

"Oh God." Sam stood away, almost laughing at how profoundly aroused he was and how completely indiscreet this was. Fortunately, nobody seemed to be paying attention. Or maybe he simply couldn't see anyone but Mateo. "Finish your drink, baby. Let's go home."

"Fuck the drink. Get me out of here." Mateo wound a hand into Sam's shirt and dragged him close again, murmuring, "Take me home and fuck me."

***

August 2013

"I was never so surprised in my life. And was I annoyed? He didn't say *anything*!" Kelli looked completely done-out-of-a-party. They were at the Mexican restaurant for a change, giant margaritas on the table along with a dish of queso con chorizo and two baskets of tortilla chips. She scooped up some dip and ate it before saying, "I still wouldn't know if I hadn't noticed the ring and asked him. He blushed! Dmitri *blushed*!" Vince was giggling, no other word for it. She glared at him, then appealed to Mateo. "Did you know they were doing that?"

"Nobody knew. We knew they were going out of town but not why. Then when they actually closed the studio for that weekend, Julia was like what the what. Elena said thank God, now I can catch up on this paperwork." Mateo slurped some of his drink. "Michelle had to break it to Julia. I don't know how she didn't notice the ring. Well, maybe I do. She's been re-doing her house, working off some frustration now that Ray got so busy." He ate a chip. "I'm not surprised Dmitri didn't tell anybody."

Vince swallowed some of his margarita. "He and Patrick have been together a long time. Ten years, I think. Their thing belongs to them, not us."

"Maybe that's why they got married out of state. Or maybe they didn't trust that all those Prop 8 motherfuckers wouldn't rev up again." Only a couple of months before, same-sex marriage had finally been ruled legal in California. Mateo dipped another chip and crunched it down.

158

Sam swirled a chip in the dip until he got a chunk of chorizo. He ate it with enjoyment, then sipped his drink, watching his friends and Mateo gossip. He didn't have to ask Vince if he was happy to be married; it was plain as day. They hadn't seen much of each other since June.

Mateo ate another chip and said, "We saw Andy at the studio again today. He was definitely doing some kind of lesson. Michelle and Julia are in on it somehow." Everybody associated with the Cabaret was getting interested. Mateo was interested because of the way the guy had pulled all that history out of Sam. Also he was freaking *hot*. Mateo hadn't noticed so much at the photo session, he'd been too focused on Sam, but the guy really came alive when he danced.

"Oh my God!" Kelli looked excited. She set her glass down. "He's going to dance in 'Milonga' in September. Michelle told me. She said don't tell anybody so don't tell anybody. He's dancing with *mmph*." Vince had his hand over her mouth, shaking his head. She made big eyes; he took his hand away. "Okay. It's a secret till the posters go up. Anyway he's getting some Argentine tango coaching from Dmitri."

Sam changed the subject, sort of, pointing a chip at Vince. "What are *you* doing for that one? How about that gorgeous thing from last December? You could dance that again."

"Maybe." Vince glanced at Kelli. "There's a lot of great tango music in the world, though. And a lot of great music you can dance tango to."

Kelli swallowed another chip. "God, we need some burritos, stat. The margarita is way ahead of this dip. This man comes up with some wild stuff

159

sometimes, you guys. Have you decided what *you're* dancing to?"

"Well," Sam began, then stalled.

Mateo rescued him. "Julia gave us the theme for November, which I know you know is 'Tourists.' And neither of us could really come up with anything right off the bat so we got online and Googled, you know, songs about traveling. And we found this really pretty acoustic song by the Red Hot Chili Peppers called 'Road Trippin.'' Two guitars, bass, and strings. It's a rumba. So that's what we're doing."

"And it's kicking *my ass* because I only even got rumba when Julia played me this all-drums track, and this damn thing doesn't have any damn drums." Sam was exasperated, but he was laughing.

"But are you enjoying it?" Kelli nudged Sam.

"Oh yeah. It's the hardest thing I've ever done, but Julia's pulling me along, and Mateo is always right there to remind me why it's worth doing."

"Aww." Kelli leaned against Vince for a second. "I always loved to dance, but it's a lot of work if you want to be good at it. Finding someone who loved it as much as me was like winning the lottery."

Mateo lifted his glass. "I'll drink to that."

Chapter 18

The next time Sam and Mateo went to the dance studio they got permission from Dmitri to put up an adoption notice. Michelle came over as they taped it up on the bathroom door, studying the four kittens pictured in little mug shots. "What's this?"

Mateo said, "Somebody dumped these kittens in our alley a few weeks ago. They're old enough to be neutered now and they all have a clean bill of health."

"Hmm. Kenji and I have been talking about getting a cat." She stepped away, digging in her bag for her phone.

Vicky said, "What's this about a cat?" and came over with Sharon.

"Hi girls. Want a kitten? Healthy, friendly, active, cute as hell?"

"That tuxedo one looks like Prospero," said Sharon.

"It's like a Prospero Mini-Me."

"He needs to get more exercise." Sharon glanced at Vicky.

Vicky smiled at her. "Running away from a kitten ought to do it."

Sam was smiling too. "Free to good homes."

"If you could take it to the vet for neutering, we'll pick it up and pay the bill," said Sharon.

"Great, thanks. That one's a girl."

"We could call her Miranda," Vicky suggested. "If it's not too obvious."

"It's perfect, honey." Sharon patted her back as they returned to the dance floor.

Michelle came back over. "Kenji says we should take two."

"Wow, really? That would be great," said Mateo. "Would you like to come and meet them?"

"No, I told him what they look like and he says he wants the tabby and the calico. We could come over on Sunday to get them. We'll take them to a vet near us."

"That's terrific, thanks," Sam said. "I know they'll have a great home with you."

Michelle smiled. "We'll need an extra hand vac, but whatever."

Mateo marked up the notice, writing TOO LATE!, I'M TAKEN!, and YOU MISSED OUT! below the tuxedo, tabby, and calico mug shots. "Aw, poor little orange guy."

"I think I know someone who's going to want him," said Sam.

"That's good." Michelle eyed them. "So how are you guys doing?"

"We're good. Our rumba for November is coming along, and I've got the others kind of halfway digested." Sam was playing it down a little.

"He's doing great," Mateo corrected, heroically not bragging that their first bronze-silver syllabus routines had recently been upgraded to silver-gold.

"That's what Julia said. I can't wait to see what you do, especially with paso doble. Oh, Mateo, Dmitri wanted to ask you something."

"Oh yeah? Thanks." He went over to the office, tapped on the open door, and leaned in. "Hi boss, you wanted to talk to me? Thanks about the kittens, by the way, three are already claimed."

"Is good. Yes. We begin a social Rhythm class here in the fall. I invite you to teach."

Mateo blinked, astonished. He still felt like a total beginner compared to some of the other dancers he'd seen over the past sixteen months, and now he'd get to lead his own class? No chance he'd say no, even if it meant learning on the job. "Really? Wow, thanks! What night and what time?" They discussed the details for a few minutes. Then Mateo bounced back over to Sam, who'd packed up their gear for the walk home. As they cleared the studio door, Mateo's news burst out. "Dmitri just asked me to teach a group class in the fall!"

"Hey, that's great. I remember you said you kind of wanted to get into teaching." Sam glanced over. "He's been watching you for a while now, I guess. Must have read your mind."

Mateo laughed. "Yeah, maybe."

"I can schedule myself to work on the nights you're teaching."

"Aw, you don't want to take my class?" He pouted a little, more for effect than anything else. It wasn't like they didn't spend enough time together.

"I don't want to dance with anybody but you." Sam gave him a sideways smile. He didn't mind dancing with their instructor Julia, but that was different.

Mateo smiled, crowding close to bounce a shoulder off of Sam. "Well, in that case. The social students would be all over you anyway and I'd have to throw a tantrum. You know, hmm."

"Oh lord, that's your scheming voice."

"Shut up! Remember at Vince and Kelli's party, when Sharon talked about the Gay Games? And we kinda sorta talked about whether you hated the idea of competition?"

"No." Mateo laughed again, nudging him. Sam nudged back. "Yeah, of course I remember. You're talking about us doing the Gay Games."

Mateo mentally crossed his fingers. "I'd like to discuss it."

Sam cut to the chase. "How do you qualify?"

"There aren't any official qualifying events. Vicky said they found out about a thing, up in Oakland in April, that's like the unofficial same-sex ballroom championships. People can just sign up and go. They have the Games all over, every four years like the real Olympics. Next year it's in Cleveland. This would be a chance for me to compete someplace with *you*." He let that settle for a minute. "Most Dance Sport, it's a man and a woman. I would so love to compete with you, and it's a big deal. Competitors from all over the world. And it's not, like, tomorrow, but it's not so far out that we'd be like, ugh, when will we get there, and it's in the U.S. this time." Sam looked thoughtful. Mateo went on. "Speaking from experience, having a definite goal helps people focus on learning. And since you're learning Latin *anyway*." He trailed off suggestively.

"So it's for my own good as a student, right?"

"Right!"

Sam laughed under his breath. "We can give it a try. But if I'm not getting it at a certain point, let's be real about it."

Mateo nodded seriously. He didn't want to go out and fail any more than Sam did. "Let's be real."

"Are you seriously going to be able to fit in all of this around your job?"

"Amazingly, yes," said Mateo. "Because I'm not coming up with the stuff, you know. They send me their crappy back-of-a-napkin sketches and I turn it all into nice, clean, to-scale machine drawings. It never did take forty hours to do a week's work. And they love that I don't bitch about after-hours requests anymore."

"Well, as long as it's working for you."

"Baby, I'm having the time of my life."

***

The following weekend, three of the kittens went to their new homes. The orange one and Frida, both of whom showed signs of developing long coats, cried for their siblings for an afternoon, but recovered by morning. Sam gave them some extra cuddles anyway. "They're tough little characters, aren't they?"

"I'm sure it helps that Papa Pachuco is here."

"So funny how he adopted them."

"Who was it you think will want the orange one?"

"Rory. Could we feed them tonight?"

"Sure. I've got stuff for spaghetti."

Sam got on the phone, catching Rory on the first try. "Hey girl. You and Dana free tonight? Want to come over for dinner and meet somebody? Spaghetti. Well of course, homemade sauce, you know I've got Bobby Flay up in here. Sure, that's good." He disconnected. "They'll be here around eight."

"Bobby Flay, huh?"

"Well, you're actually a lot cuter." He put his arms around Mateo, nuzzling his neck. "You're the cutest."

"Hmm. Spaghetti sauce doesn't take very long, you know," said Mateo against Sam's mouth. "Are there any cats on the couch?"

"There are cats everywhere. They'll move."

***

The apartment was redolent of tomato and garlic by the time Rory and Dana arrived. They brought two bottles of Chianti and a tub of grated fresh Parmesan, which Dana handed off to Mateo. "Hi girls! Ooh, thanks! Hey, you both like Italian sausage, right?"

"You bet."

"Good, 'cause it's already in the sauce." He made an oops face and both women laughed.

"So who are we supposed to be meeting?" said Rory.

Sam said, "We wanted to introduce you to our new kitten, Frida. And her brother."

Dana's eyes got big. "Uh-oh."

"Pachuco woke us up a few weeks ago, yowling at the back door. Sam went outside to see what he was yelling about and found this box of kittens," Mateo explained.

"Where are they?"

"Probably on the bed. Oh, nope, here they come," said Sam. "Gotta see what's happening."

"Ooh, Rory."

Rory studied the orange kitten. "He looks like Simba, doesn't he?"

"Was Simba your cat?" Mateo asked.

"No, he was a long-haired guinea pig."

"So he only looks a *little* like Simba," said Sam, who had met the late lamented guinea pig.

Mateo said, "The black one is Frida. She kind of moved in on me the very first day."

"Something about the way she was making a speech the second we opened the box," Sam said.

166

Rory smiled. "She's cute, too. But I've always had a soft spot for blonde animals. We had a Golden Retriever when I was a kid."

"I haven't had a kitten since I was, I don't know, ten?" said Dana.

Sam said, "This one's practically a teenager."

"He's awesome." Rory sat cross-legged on the floor. The orange kitten inspected her, long and incipiently-fluffy tail waving, tufted ears pricked forward. After a moment he placed a cautious paw on Rory's knee and looked up at her. She held still.

The kitten looked over his shoulder as if to check with Frida. She gave the cat equivalent of a shrug, moseying off to the kitchen with a twitch of her own soon-to-be-plumey tail. The orange kitten turned back to Rory and stepped up on her lap. He turned around a couple of times, looked at her again, then plopped down.

"And there you have it," said Dana. "Looks like we have a cat. Well played, gentlemen."

Sam laughed. "If you want, we can get him neutered at the same time we take Frida in, and you can pick him up."

"You'll be the good guys then for sure." Mateo was watching from the kitchen.

"Sounds like a plan." Rory looked down at the kitten. "What should we call him?"

"How about Spike?" Dana suggested. Mateo and Rory gave her a thumbs-up. Sam, now that business was concluded, opened a bottle of wine.

Rory carefully transferred the kitten as they went over to the table for dinner. He complained once, then settled back down in her lap. Sam poured the wine and they all dug in. "So how did you girls and Sam meet, anyway?" said Mateo. "I've been meaning to ask."

"Oh, wow." Sam thought back. "It's been a while. I'd quit the fights. Five years ago?"

"Sam and I were both at the Starbucks at Santa Monica and Robertson when there was an accident right outside," said Rory. "I was sitting by the window, hogging up a table, saw the whole thing. Couple of cars, one turning left, misjudged how fast the other guy was coming. And the other guy didn't brake. Then somebody *else* comes along and crashes into *both* of them."

"I'd just gotten my coffee, and I saw what was going on. Well, I heard it."

"And he came over to look out the window and I told him to go ahead and sit down."

"And she started doing commentary on it like it was a boxing match."

"Because I recognized him. I'd seen a clip of his last fight during this cable show about MMA."

"And she was so *funny*."

"That's my girl," said Dana.

"It was this colossal clusterfuck," Rory said cheerfully. "Nobody was hurt and there were all these people standing around yelling at each other, there's three cars blocking the westbound lanes, and then *another* idiot comes along and tries to make a left turn! Across the wreckage!"

Sam laughed. "And then he tries to *back up* into the eastbound through lane."

"Because he's an idiot. And of course, somebody hits *him*, so now the whole intersection is FUBAR."

"It took, like, two hours to get it cleaned up."

"You could hear the honking from our place," said Dana. "I called Rory to find out where the hell she was, and she said she had picked up a stray, and could she bring him home."

"So then we spent the next, what, three years trying to fix Sam up with various nice boys we knew."

"And finally we hear this story about the beautiful guy from the club, and find out he didn't call you back."

"And we had a little come to Jesus."

"Which didn't work."

"But you sorted things out yourselves," Rory concluded. "Eventually."

Mateo smiled. "He called me a pit bull once."

"Honey, you're a pit bull in the best possible way."

***

After the girls were gone and Mateo had the kitchen cleaned up, he flopped down on the couch, stretching out sideways. All three cats landed on him shortly after. Sam was at the other end, feet up on the coffee table, sort-of watching a kung fu movie. "So you thought I was beautiful, huh." Mateo knew he had; there had been that moment, sometime in the middle of their first night together. He'd heard it a couple times since then, along with other nice words, but he was a needy little fuck.

Sam turned his head and smiled. "I still think you're beautiful. You know I do. Want me to say so more often?"

"Oh, maybe once in a while." Mateo wriggled down so he could put his toes on Sam's thigh. "Now that I'm a housewife."

"You're the cutest housewife I ever did see." Sam was petting Mateo's feet. "Even your little dancing feet are cute." He looked up. "I'm so glad you like Rory and Dana. They're my best friends, aside from you. I mean, Vince is great, and I love Kelli too, but Rory and Dana are my family here."

"They love you. I'm glad you have them. My family," he rolled his eyes, blowing out a breath. "Kristine is fine. The others are okay. Dad's almost over it. Mom's over it. They still don't really get it, though."

"Why you had to leave?"

"Yeah. I'm so lucky I found you."

"We're both lucky." Sam regarded him. "What happens if you dump those cats so you can get over here and cuddle with me?"

"Let's find out."

***

The following week, Sam and Mateo took Frida and Spike to the vet. After passing the cat carrier to a nurse, the receptionist handed them a card. Sam said, "What's this?"

"Some girl who was in with her cat asked us to give it to the people who saved the kittens."

"Huh." He opened the card. Mateo leaned over to see. It read *Thank you so much. I have spayed my cat and kicked out my asshole EX boyfriend who stole those kittens and threw them away. You are good people.*

"Well, what do you know," said Mateo. They turned the card around so the receptionist could see.

She smiled. "You are good people. You can pick these guys up at the end of the day."

170

They went out, discussing their schedules for the next few days. Sam shook his head. "All this dance shit. If it weren't for that, you'd be coasting."

"I'd be a fat housewife. But if I weren't a dancer we'd never have rocked that first salsa, and I wouldn't have had to stalk you." Into the car, both snickering. "You know what, I'm just not going to worry about it. Unless it's bugging you."

"We've got enough flexibility, it's not like either of us is home alone all the time. I like being home in the mornings with you on the days I work the late shift. And the days that you're not at the studio it's just, you know, normal."

"Lucy and Desi. If Desi puts Lucy face-down on the couch."

Sam laughed and leaned over to kiss him. "He probably did. I had this idea."

"What's that?"

"You remember that wine-tasting class we took?"

"How could I forget! You had to pour me into the car!"

"Maybe we could take a little trip, go to some wineries. We haven't really gone anywhere together, like on vacation."

"Oh my God, I *love* that idea." Mateo realized he hadn't ever been on a vacation at all, not as an adult.

Sam detected genuine excitement, which meant he was doing it right again. "Want to go before your class starts at the studio?"

"Think Rory would cat-sit for us?"

"I'll bet she would. Let's give her a call and find out." They got home a few minutes later. Sam parked the car and got his phone out.

Just as he was about to dial, Mateo's phone buzzed. "It's Kristine. Hey sis, what's up?"

"I have a big, huge favor to ask."

This sounded serious. He glanced at Sam. "Whatcha need?"

"Could I couch-surf for a little while?"

Definitely serious. "What happened?"

"Justin asked me to marry him and I said no. We broke up. Mom had this totally unexpected fit and Dad is giving me the silent treatment. Things are weird."

"Tell her of course," said Sam, who could hear everything.

"On one condition," Mateo told his sister, smiling at Sam.

"What?"

"Cat-sit for us while we're on vacation."

"Absolutely."

"Let me call you back in a minute after we look at the calendars and sort some shit out."

"Okay. Thanks! And thanks, Sam!"

Mateo disconnected. "Poor little sister. She's always been the good kid."

"Played by the rules, huh."

"And how. She's never been on the receiving end of parental disapproval like me."

"You weren't exactly a troublemaker, were you?"

"No, I was just a pain in the ass." After consulting the calendars, Mateo sent a quick email to Julia to postpone their next round of lessons, another to his employers to let them know he'd be out of town (but still available), then finally called Kristine back to tell her when to come. "We'll have a welcome party. Get some friends from the neighborhood over so you don't feel stranded here."

"You're so awesome!"

"That was Sam's idea, actually, and yes he is awesome. You think you might want to move into town? 'Cause we can introduce you to some people. The owner of the dance studio, his competition partner is married to a designer. Bring your portfolio." He disconnected, and looked at Sam. "I just thought of something."

"What?"

"We need to get that couch shampooed."

Sam got out of the car, suppressing a smile. Followed Mateo into the apartment. Locked the door, then steered his lover toward the couch. Might as well get it dirtier first.

Chapter 19

September 2013

"Oh my God," Mateo said, staring at his phone.

Sam looked over from the driver's seat. "What's the matter?"

"Nothing. I just realized in one month it'll be our anniversary." He glanced up at Sam. "One year from when I walked into your shop and told you I thought I was in love with you."

Sam was smiling. "And you were."

"God, was I ever. I still am. This has been *such* a good year. Eleven months. Whatever, there's no way the next month isn't going to be awesome." Mateo was absolutely sure of that.

"And now your sister's in town. She was so cute yesterday." Kristine had clearly not believed Mateo was a domesticated man until she actually walked into the apartment. The siblings' conversation on that subject had Sam laughing so hard it hurt. Then she apologized for cluttering up their uncluttered, well-organized, maturely decorated place with all her college-girl crap. "We'll have people over when we get back. Make sure she meets Michelle. It's good she and Dmitri aren't out of town this month."

"Or next month. They're doing that comp in Burbank. The whole studio is going to go and make noise."

Sam didn't pay as much attention to the studio calendar as Mateo did, but he knew that competition was toward the end of the month. "Is their event going to conflict with the Cabaret?"

"Don't know yet. If it's the same weekend, it'll still only be one night. We can go to the Cabaret on the Monday. Or, shit, maybe you have to work."

"I'll make a deal with Benny."

Mateo was turned toward Sam in the seat, trying to interpret his expression. "You look sneaky." Sam laughed. Mateo narrowed his eyes. "What have you got up your sleeve?"

"I don't even have any sleeves."

That was true, and those bare muscular arms were very distracting. "Are you going to tell me where we're going?"

"Not till we drive through the gate."

"Give me a hint. What county?"

"Nope." Mateo made an irritated sound and Sam laughed again. He fended off all inquiries until they reached Santa Barbara County and exited Highway 101.

Then Mateo was too busy looking around to ask questions until they drove through the gate of the Cheshire Cat Inn. "Oh my Lord. We're staying here? This is so cute! Sam!"

Sam parked the car in the first available space because he couldn't wait one more minute to kiss his lover. "Mmm," he said after a few minutes. "I love you. Get a good look at the garden now, because you're not gonna see it again till sometime tomorrow." Mateo laughed against his mouth. Sam dove in again.

***

A few hours later, Mateo located his phone and sent a text to Kristine. Actually, he sent a picture of their in-room spa tub. She texted back almost immediately: *NO WAY*

Yes way

175

Have you already been in it?

What do you think?

Bahaha splish splash

LOL for real. There's a fireplace too but it's too hot to turn it on

So when do you actually go wine-tasting?

The big guy hooked us up with a limo. It's coming for us after breakfast

I need to find me one like Sam

Yes you do! Everybody does! How many times has Mom called you?

Only twice. I sent her a picture of your apartment and she said is that a hotel

LMAO she did not

Okay no she didn't but only because of the cats

Are they behaving?

They are suspicious. Why are you texting me instead of fooling around with Sam?

Duh already did that. He drove the whole way, he's napping

Oh okay. Then I guess you should be checking your email

Jeez what a nag

You know you won't get anything done tomorrow. You'll be out on the Wino Tour

You have a point. Guess I'll fire up the laptop. Text me if you want though

Multitasker. Have a great time and don't worry about me. OXO

Back at ya. Mateo set down the phone and opened up his laptop, where he found a couple of hours' worth of work. The ideal amount. By the time he sent off the drawings, Sam was up and ready for dinner.

They stayed three nights in Santa Barbara, and drove home with two cartons of wine, a lot of stories, and a mutual feeling of significance. Mateo would have called that trip a honeymoon, if he weren't afraid of freaking Sam out. He knew, without a doubt, that he wanted to marry this man someday. It wasn't necessary. It wasn't urgent. But they could now, and he thought they should, and one day he would say so.

***

Sam suspected Mateo had ideas and feelings about their vacation, possibly but not necessarily the same ones Sam had. He found a time to meet Vince for coffee, just the two of them, hoping for a reality check. "Got you this in Santa Barbara," he said, handing over a bottle of wine in a gift bag.

Vince pulled out the bottle. "Hey, nice, thanks. What's the occasion?"

"Just saying thanks. Got one for Dana and Rory too. This trip with Mateo was just, you know, fucking wow. And I might not have ever had that experience if not for my friends showing me the way. So thanks."

Bottle stashed away again, Vince sipped coffee and studied Sam. "First trip together, right?"

"First time ever going on a trip with a boyfriend. Lover. Whatever we are."

Vince gave him a look. "Ever consider getting married?"

Sam laughed into his coffee. "Oh, it's come to mind all right." He glanced up. "When was the first time you went somewhere with Kelli?"

"Oh, man, we did it the *hard* way." Vince snickered. "Hadn't been on any kind of trip together,

177

then up and went to Baltimore for Thanksgiving with her family. The very first year, remember? Barely four months after we met!"

"Oh shit, that's right! And I was all pouty because the year before, you and me and your buddy Elliott went to your Mom's house."

"The holiday in a box thing, because we were all working crazy hours," Vince said. "And then we ran off to San Francisco last year, but fortunately you had Pomona."

"Pomona was a little bit weird," Sam admitted. "You asked Keli to marry you right after House of Blues. Six months in."

"Yep. No regrets. Perfect timing." They stared at each other. "You're thinking about it?"

Sam wriggled, uncomfortable. "I don't know many gay guys who are married. Dmitri and Patrick, basically. And they're twenty-plus years older than us."

"Meaning what's the rush?"

"Meaning, huh." Sam thought about it. After a minute, he said, "I feel like I'm supposed to want to. Like now that it's legal, I should automatically want that. But, you know, I don't want kids. Mateo doesn't want kids. Neither of us is religious. We could get the same legal benefits from a registered partnership. I looked into it," he added. "Because once he moved in, I figured it was only a matter of time."

"But you haven't done it yet."

"Haven't even started the conversation. Neither has he." Which seemed significant.

Vince finished his coffee. "It's not a requirement. You're allowed to be together in your own way. And if someday one of you says you'd like to change your way, you're getting pretty good at talking."

Sam smiled. "Yeah. Getting better, anyway."

***

Kristine's introduction to Los Angeles was a complete success. Sam and Mateo invited people over the weekend after they got back from Santa Barbara. Since those people included Dana, Rory, Vince, and Kelli, it was only a matter of time before Kristine had a social life of her own. She reminded Mateo that she needed to get a job, and find her own place to live, not necessarily in that order. But they were both having such fun living together again that they didn't want to rush it.

"This only works because you're unemployed and I work from home," Mateo admitted one day. Sam was at work, Mateo had wrapped up an assignment, and Kristine was fresh out of the shower.

"Oh, I know. If we were all fighting over the shower, my God. Do you guys ever shower together?" She sat on their bed cross-legged to towel her hair dry.

"We get in the shower together," he said airily. "Not necessarily to get ready for work."

Kristine cackled. "I know I'm cramping your style. I promise I'll be out of here soon. How much do you love him?"

It sounded as though the question escaped her. Mateo took it seriously. "More than I thought it was possible to love someone. If I had known this existed, it would've been what I wanted all along. All I wanted was someone who accepted me. And then I literally crashed into Sam, and he's everything, and he loves me."

"Oh Mateo." She reached for his hand.

179

He squeezed her fingers. "What's amazing is, everything he needed is something I can give him. He fills the empty places I have, and I fill the ones he has. Which is not a sexual innuendo, thank you very much. He tells me all the time how much better his life is now."

"Do you have to think about it?"

He shrugged. "Not really. There are things I want to do, or he wants to do, and we talk about them. But day to day, it's like I see what he needs, and he sees what I need. We compromise sometimes. We don't always want exactly the same thing at exactly the same time. It's okay though. We want each other to be happy. You didn't feel that way with Justin." It was sort of a question.

"I, huh. I honestly don't think we got to that point. The first year, I thought he probably was the one. But it wasn't perfect. He wasn't everything. I always had that doubt, you know, was I going to be okay with this forever. And then the pressure started, and the assumptions. It started making me mad."

"I know it did. Assumptions are the worst."

"The worst! Especially when one of them is that I'm going to start having babies right away, and doesn't everybody know what that means? It means I don't get to have a career. Nobody takes you seriously if you go in and say well I have to be out of here at three because the daycare closes at four. They're like, well, good luck with that but we need you here till five, or maybe six, or maybe nine. We need you when we need you, and if you can't be here then we need someone else." That all spilled out in a rush, telling Mateo it was, and had been, a major concern.

"You want kids someday."

"I really do. I love kids, I want some of my own. Besides, I have to make up for you not having any." He snorted out a laugh. "No, but really. You know how Justin proposed?"

"I'm assuming he fucked it up, because you didn't just say no. You broke up with him."

"So very right. He said, I want you to be my wife and the mother of my children. And he said it like I should be thrilled. Like it never even occurred to him that I went to college for a fucking *reason*. Like being his wife was the greatest thing he could imagine for me. Like it was a fucking *gift*." She was crying. Mateo moved over to the bed and put his arms around her. After a minute she wiped her face with the towel and sniffed. "God, I didn't even know I was still so mad about it."

Hurt, too. Mateo squeezed her. "What's he do, anyway? He was a year ahead of you, right?"

"Right." Kristine sniffed again, then sighed. "Hospitality management. Has a job at a hotel. He'll do fine."

"He's going to have to move to move up. Did he realize that?"

"I don't think he did." She shrugged. She didn't care what Justin did now that she didn't have to do it with him. "What would you do if Sam said he wanted to leave Los Angeles?"

"I'd say okay, where do you want to go?" She gave him a disbelieving look. He made a Yes Really face. "We've got great friends here. We have fun things to do. But we could make new friends and find other things to do. There are other cities with communities like this."

"It wouldn't be the same."

"No, of course not. It would be hard to leave all this. But nothing stays the same. Or at least, it's not supposed to. Santa Monica and WeHo may be separate cities but it's all Los Angeles, right? So I've only ever lived in two places. No burning desire to go explore the world, but if he wanted to, I'd be up for it. I've changed Sam's life, he's changed mine. Five years from now, who knows what'll be happening with us."

Kristine leaned against him. "I'll bet I know one thing. Bet you'll still be in love." He kissed her forehead.

***

It wasn't long before Kristine was introduced to Michelle, and shortly after that she had a meeting with Michelle's husband Kenji. She came back to West Hollywood half excited and half terrified. "He kept my portfolio," she told Mateo, clutching a glass of wine. "Said he wanted to take his time looking at it because it was so thorough."

"Well, that's a good thing, right?" Mateo sipped his wine, then set it down so he could get on with the thing he was cooking. "Did you like him?"

"Oh, he's dreamy. He's so polite. And they're so well-organized over there, I mean aside from the kittens, but they really need me. It was all I could do not to say, look, Mr. Matsumoto, you need someone in here who can sew *and* operate a computer, and that's me. If he doesn't offer me the job the second I walk through the door I swear I'm going to say that."

Mateo grinned at his cutting board, concentrating on garlic. "You should. You'd be great at it and I would totally love it if you got settled here. For more reasons than just to freak out our parents. When does he want you to come back over?"

"Day after tomorrow. He said, we have orders from Embassy Ball and some of them are due before California Star. Like I know what those are." Mateo started to say something and she cut him off. "Yes, I'm going to look them up as soon as I finish drinking this wine. God I want that job. The fabrics he had in there, *ungh*, I want to cut them." Mateo snickered. "He showed me this ballgown he made for Michelle, it's for her show dance with Dmitri. He said it was 'Cry Me a River,' and it's online. Did you see it?"

"Yeah, we saw it. They tried it out at this show in July. She didn't have a ballgown for it then, though. What's the dress look like?" Kristine didn't answer, but a minute later she held her phone where he could see it. He studied the photo. "So you know how to make shit like that?"

"Of course I do. I need to meet Dmitri, don't I?"

"Yes you do. He's the best. He's my L.A. daddy." Kristine laughed. Mateo smiled as he diced a bell pepper. It was easier to make that a joke now that he was back on speaking terms with his real father. "We're taking you to the next show this weekend. Vince and Kelli are dancing. And there's a celebrity. This actor from a series called 'L.A. Vice' is dancing with the guy who took that picture." He pointed his knife at the photo of him and Sam.

"If he's a celebrity, are we going to be able to get tickets?"

Mateo set the knife down and gave her a long-suffering look. "Girl, please. The show runner is our coach." She inhaled some wine, coughed, and laughed again. "I told her we'd need three tickets as soon as I knew you were going to be here. Get out of my kitchen and go do your homework."

"Yes sir." Kristine drank the rest of her wine, set the glass on the counter, and went to fire up her laptop.

Chapter 20

The next Monday night, they were all prepared for Hollywood nonsense. The grapevine said that the photographer Andy Martin and his dance partner Victor Garcia were excellent. Sam said loyally, "I'll bet they weren't better than Vince and Kelli."

"I don't know," Mateo said, stirring up trouble. "I read that article. Andy used to be a Broadway dancer. And Dmitri did their choreography. Did you talk to Vince?" Sam made a sound of assent. "He must have seen them at dress rehearsal. What did he say?"

"He said they were really good."

"I'm sure they weren't better than Vince and Kelli," Kristine said, poking Mateo. "Jeez, until a week ago I barely knew what Argentine tango was. If I don't hear from Matsumoto-san tomorrow my head is going to explode." He hadn't offered the job when she went back for her portfolio. She had managed to say she thought he needed her. He said he'd call by Tuesday. Kristine was trying not to completely obsess about the situation.

"He was busy," Mateo said, not for the first time. He'd heard about both meetings once too often. "Michelle said there was a movie-studio wardrobe emergency. Soon that will be your life."

"Light a candle." They pulled up at the club, or rather at the end of the queue of cars waiting for the club's parking valets. "Wow. Is it always like this?"

"No. This is the celebrity factor." Sam sounded annoyed. Mateo suppressed a laugh. Kristine poked him again, starting some nonsense about maybe they should've dressed up more for the paparazzi.

When they finally got inside it was only ten minutes to showtime. Mateo showed Kristine where the restroom was, asked what she wanted to drink, and sat down with Sam at their lounge table. Kristine joined them a few seconds before their drinks were delivered, less than a minute before the lights flickered. "They're starting on time," Mateo said. "I hope you like this."

Kristine said, "I hope I do too. It would be awful to get a job making ballgowns and not like to watch dancing. How many of the performers do you know?"

"Vince and Kelli, obviously. But Dmitri and Michelle are dancing too. It's their competition tango, switched up a little. You're in for a treat."

"Oh wow. Okay." Kristine sucked down some of her drink as the lights went down. She noticed that Mateo and Sam were holding hands.

Sam nudged Mateo when the lights came up at intermission. Mateo looked at his sister, whose expression was orgasmic. "Uh, Kris?"

"Oh my *Jesus*. Okay. I saw you guys dance and thought, huh, okay, they're having fun. But I need to learn how, like, *immediately*." Sam and Mateo both laughed. "And none of your people have even danced yet! That whole first half was all like whoever!" Mateo was cracking up as a server arrived to get their second drink order. The men took turns visiting the bathroom and listening to Kristine. They both knew things were going to be even better in the second half.

Because of the celebrity factor, Andy and Victor were closing the show. Vince and Kelli opened Act 2 with 'Violentango.' It was a sexy interpretation of traditional milonga style. "I don't know where he even gets that," Mateo muttered to Sam. "He's never been to Argentina."

"Yet." Sam was thoroughly enjoying the show. The only tango he'd seen had been here at Chrome, as part of the Cabaret. This program really celebrated it. The second couple finished, and then Dmitri and Michelle danced to 'Libertango.' Kristine actually whimpered a little. Mateo was holding one of her hands and one of Sam's until their friends finished. Then they joined in the roar of applause. There was a slight delay, giving the commotion time to die down before the next couple took the stage. Mateo felt a little sorry for them, having to go on between Michelle and Dmitri and the big draw. They were good, but nobody was going to remember them.

Then there was another brief delay. The stage was black; two men took positions at center; a spotlight came on and their music started. Mateo heard Kristine say "Holy shit" under her breath. He wanted to look at Sam but didn't want to look away from the stage. He hadn't heard that Andy and this actor guy were involved, but they were incredibly hot together. The choreography was perfect (thanks to Dmitri) and the performance rightfully received a standing ovation.

Sam leaned against Mateo and spoke close to his face. "Baby, we may need to learn Argentine tango."

"Oh thank God you said that." Mateo looked up, smiling, irresistible. Sam kissed him.

***

October 2013

By the middle of October, Kristine had a job with Matsumoto Costume & Couture and an apartment in West L.A. Mateo was teaching his second six-week series at Shall We Dance. He and Sam had ironed out all five Latin dances, their routine for the November show was solid, and Mateo was looking ahead. "Okay, we have ten months yet till the Games. I think we're in good shape." Sam looked doubtful; Mateo patted him. "No, really. I'm happy. I know you don't love it like I do, and all I want to do is get up there and have fun with you. So I think we should just keep practicing what we've got and not pressure ourselves. We'll be up against some professionals. If we go thinking we've got to try to win, it's going to be a downer when we don't."

"Are you sure? You're pretty competitive."

"If our goal is just to have fun, we are guaranteed to have a great experience. That works for me." Sam still seemed unconvinced, so Mateo said, "Really. We've got the November thing coming up and I think we should focus on that because performing together is big for us. It's big for me!" He leaned close for a kiss.

"It's big for me too, obviously." Sam wasn't sorry he'd committed to it, not when it made his lover this happy. "What else is on your mind?"

Mateo told him about a young woman named Yolanda who'd come to the studio, looking for a professional partner in the American Rhythm style. "It would be good exposure for me as a teacher. Want to go to a competition next weekend in the OC? It'll give you a taste of what the Games will be like."

Once he thought about it, Sam agreed it was high time he saw what Dance Sport actually was. He swapped a shift and they drove down to Irvine, entering the hotel ballroom just as the announcer was calling a new event. "Now, welcome to the floor your competitors in the first round of tonight's Amateur International Latin Championship. Make some noise for your favorite couples!"

"That's no joke," said Mateo. "In ballroom, you cheer everything you like. Yell out their names, yell out their number, whatever. It helps keep competitors' energy up, because sometimes, like these guys, they're dancing in three or four rounds before they even get to the final."

"Wow." Sam watched with interest as the various events played out. He and Mateo did their part to make noise when they spotted couples who trained at Dmitri's. "How does the judging work, anyway? I mean, how do the judges choose?"

"At the amateur levels, there are usually clear differences in technical proficiency. It's pretty easy to pick out the best and worst in the group, and then the judge fills in the other places. For professionals, well, it helps to already be known. If the judges have seen a couple a bunch of times and they're consistently good, they're pretty much guaranteed going into the final as long as they don't obviously fuck something up."

"So it's kind of political?"

"A little bit. Even with amateurs, there's a little of that. The judges want to see commitment to the sport, which means you show up and compete. You don't go to one competition a year and expect to make the final, much less win."

"Not like a fight."

"Not at all. I mean, even if nobody ever heard of you, if you put somebody down it's pretty clear you're the winner."

"Can't do that here, I guess."

Mateo shook his head, big-eyed. "There was kind of a famous crash one time in a Standard event. One couple was turning too close to another and somebody got hit in the head with an elbow. Like, actual concussion. That is not the kind of contact sport we

189

want here. No, for the pros it comes down to tiny little details. Sometimes even to the costume."

Sam knew he wasn't going absorb everything from one night; there were too many different styles, too many people on the floor, too much going on. But it was exciting to see so many people doing what he was learning to do and treating it as a sport. Toward the end of the evening, he could really appreciate the athletic rigor of the competition. "I see what you mean about all the different rounds."

"Yeah. And you have to dance full-out each time, because if you slack off and that's the moment a judge is looking at you," Mateo made a slash-across-the-throat gesture, "it's all over."

"Pretty intense. So, the Gay Games will be like this?"

"Yep. The International Latin Championship? Just like that. Except, you know, in our event it's all guys. So it's going to be testosterone soup, and things are probably going to be really big and really fast."

"We better start doing more cardio." Mateo made a face. Sam laughed. "Yeah, me too."

***

"Speaking of costume," which they hadn't been, but Sam was on his knees beside the bed with Mateo's legs over his shoulders and they both needed to pause for breath, "do the men have to wear all black in competition?"

Sweating, half-delirious, and aroused almost beyond bearing, Mateo broke up laughing. "My fashion guru have some other ideas?"

"Yeah, like not all black." Sam was laughing too, right up until he got Mateo's dick in his mouth again. "Mmm."

"Oh yeah, Jesus yeah, *baby*." Mateo tried to think. "Uh. Um. It's not a rule. Black. Oh God. At the Games. We could wear. Colors," he gasped out, abs clenching as his climax crested. "Jeeeeesus!"

Sam held on till the waves of orgasm faded and Mateo began to soften, then crawled up on the bed. Cock hard and high and drooling, waiting for Mateo to scoot back against the headboard. His gorgeous golden boy, lips parted, eyes avid, waiting. He wanted colors, all right, colors that would make people look twice to see if they were really naked on the floor. He rubbed the head of his cock across Mateo's mouth, watched that pink tongue sweep out to lick up precome, then slid inside.

Half an hour later, they were in the shower. An hour after that, they were on the road back to Los Angeles, and Sam had another question. "Are all ballroom events so white?"

Mateo winced. "Yeah. Pretty much. I mean there are a lot of Asian dancers, but not a lot of Latinos and hardly any black people. The American Rhythm division is a little more diverse. There have been Latino and black champions. But outside the collegiate circuit, yeah."

"Will that be a problem at the Gay Games?"

"I can't imagine that it would be." After a second, he glanced over. Sam's hands were relaxed on the steering wheel and he hadn't dropped any hints, but: "Did someone do or say something shitty?"

Sam shook his head. "No. Honestly no. We got some side-eye but I think it was because we're gay, not because I'm black."

Another wince, followed by a sigh. "Ugh. Yeah. It's also a very don't ask, don't tell sport."

"Aren't they all?"

"Unfortunately. Well, at least *that* won't be an issue at the Games. I mean, *definitely*." They both snickered. Mateo patted Sam's thigh, left his hand there, and ran the mental movie again. The one with them in a room full of other gay men, dancing their asses off for a medal. He knew Sam pretty well by now. The idea that people might think they didn't belong, because of their skin color or anything else, would only make the guy more determined to win.

Chapter 21

A few days after their OC excursion, Sam was rehearsing their rumba at home. Mateo was, as usual, caught between wanting to get up and join Sam and wanting to simply sit and admire him. On the couch with Pachuco and Frida, sort-of-reading one of Sam's books about martial arts. The couch was pushed all the way up to the back wall, table top hidden behind it, block legs stacked in the corner.

Earbuds in, eyes unfocused, Sam knew Mateo was watching. He knew it was a challenge sometimes for his lover to keep quiet and let Sam work things through in his own way, at his own pace. This time, Sam particularly appreciated that forbearance. He knew the routine, and by now he understood the mechanics of the rumba. He gave Mateo some shit about the fact that each of the five Latin dances had different mechanics. But with Julia and Dmitri helping him along, he'd leveled up unusually fast. He'd have known even if Julia didn't tell him so, from the reactions of others in the studio. It was deeply satisfying, much more so than he would have expected. Now he was working on finding the connection with their music.

The audition process wasn't a formality. The Cabaret people were friends now, but that didn't mean they'd automatically take this submission. Mateo teaching at Shall We Dance was an advantage; having Julia—the Mating Dance show runner—as their coach was huge. But Sam knew they had to look professional. Both of them. So he'd been living with this music. Talked it through with Vince, who everyone said was better with music than anyone they knew who wasn't actually a musician. Sam really liked the song, and had from the start, even though the thought of dancing to it scared the crap out of him at first. He could hear the rhythm in it now. It was so slow, so quiet, softer than most of the music they heard at the studio. Sam wanted to look smooth. He wanted to be sexy, but not in an obvious, exaggerated way. More like that pop slogan: dance like no one is watching. Like it was for him and Mateo alone. But not a seduction, maybe not even foreplay. Maybe that quiet time after lovemaking, when they both still wanted to kiss, still wanted to hold onto each other and say all those mushy things.

Mateo watched the smooth and slinky execution of the dance, Sam's hot eyes and half-smile. Something had changed. Clicked. Evolved. He was so excited.

***

"Holy crickets, Sam." Julia stopped the video playback, glancing up at her students, who both looked awfully smug. "This is beautiful."

"He's been working on it nonstop," said Mateo proudly.

"Good job, both of you. I'll show it to Michelle next time she's in. Better decide what you're going to wear."

"Really?!" Mateo was delighted. He knew it was good, but that wasn't enough. People paid to see these shows. They'd get paid (a little) for *doing* the show. It wasn't the same as performing at a social, or even a showcase, at a dance studio.

Julia nodded. "I might suggest opening the show with this number. It'll get the audience into the right mood, settle them down."

Mateo and Sam made eye contact. The best thing about going first: you were done first. That thought stopped Sam from immediately asking her not to have them open. Plus, she might be right. This was a romantic number. People on dates would draw close; people there alone would be thrown into a state of pleasant melancholy that would get them ordering drinks and looking for someone to talk to at intermission. They'd be primed for the rest of the show. Then there'd be Julia and Ray doing their cha-cha to 'One Night in Bangkok,' and the other couple he'd seen practicing 'Have Love, Will Travel.' Eight numbers in all. "Well," he said slowly, "if I screw it up, there's the whole rest of the show for people to forget about it."

"You won't screw it up, no way" Mateo said firmly. "You're gonna smash it. Really? You'd be okay with opening?"

Sam checked in with himself. "If Dmitri likes it. If Michelle and the others agree. I won't say no." Mateo seized him, squeezing, lifting him off the floor a little the way he did at the photo shoot with Andy. Sam laughed, just like he had then. They'd come a long way in the past ten months.

***

November 2013

The week before 'Tourists,' Sam and Mateo met up with Vince and Kelli, who gave them some minor bullshit about how these rank beginners were opening the show. If Mateo didn't know how much Sam was enjoying it, he would have been annoyed. Since he did know, all he did was serve up some bullshit of his own. "Yeah, you know, when Julia said you weren't submitting anything I almost texted you to ask if

195

everything was okay. I mean, missing a show. Should we be worried?" He made a *tsk* noise. Kelli giggled.

Vince gave him a look. "We can't carry the whole company."

Everybody else said "Oh!" and Vince cracked up. Mateo said, "I am totally telling Michelle you said that."

"You should," Kelli said. "If you can pin her down for a second. Their big thing is the weekend after your thing. I wish we could go, but." She did a little chair dance. "Buenos Aires!"

"Where are they going?" Sam probably should have known. He had a tendency to let Mateo keep track of all their social and dance business.

"To a thing called the Ohio Star Ball." Vince knew Sam would appreciate this. "It's the biggest ballroom competition in the country and it hosts the World Championship of the American Smooth style. All last year they were doing the prep event, Rising Star. This year the buzz says they win the championship."

"Mateo told me a little about how the championship stuff works for amateurs. What do they get if they win?"

"Coaching business. Private lessons. Performance engagements. Everything they do now, but more of it, and they can charge more." Kelli knocked on the table. "They should win. And we're going to have to see it on video, because all our money is going to Argentina."

"We could have done both." Vince was leaning back in his chair, smiling at her.

"Well, okay, but this way we can do all the tango shit in the world. God, I'm so excited."

Sam raised his glass toward Vince. "Once we get done with the Games, we want you to teach us tango." Mateo looked excited; that hadn't been a sure thing. Every time Sam did something like that he felt more secure, more seen, more listened-to. Appreciated, understood, and loved. He put a hand on Sam's leg under the table. Sam gave him a quick smile. "After the show in September, we both thought, that's next."

Kelli got hold of Mateo's other hand and squeezed it. "You are going to *love* it."

***

Show night. Adrenaline bomb. Mateo almost asked Sam if he was nervous, but then he realized that would be counterproductive. If he was nervous, he was hiding it really well. If he wasn't, great. Mateo was, a little bit. He'd never been troubled by stage fright before, but then he'd hardly ever been on an actual stage before. It helped that so many of the dancers in the lineup were people they knew. After dress rehearsal, they were at least acquainted with everybody.

They were the only same-sex couple performing. Mateo had been hoping Vicky and Sharon would submit something, but at least this audience wasn't likely to start a riot over it. After the thing in September, when Andy danced with that actor, the social media about Chrome and the Cabaret went nuts. But it seemed to have more to do with the actor's personal story than with some cisgender agenda issue. He pulled his mind back on track so he could finish doing his makeup.

"You don't need that," Sam said, amused.

"*You* don't need it. I want people to notice my eyes." He put down the eyeliner pencil, satisfied with the effect. First that little bit of extra length to his

197

eyebrows, then the thin line above and below his lashes. He fluttered them at Sam, who leaned over to kiss him. "Ready for this, honey?"

"I'm ready." Sam didn't know why he wasn't nervous. Maybe because this wasn't a competition. There was no way to lose. Nobody was going to get hurt. They'd go out on stage and dance this thing they could do in their sleep, and then they were done for the night. Nothing else to do but wait for intermission, when they could go out in the house to watch the second act. "Let's stretch for a minute."

The green room (also the dressing room) had a wall of mirror over the makeup counter, and a barre across half of the opposite wall. The end wall was occupied by a long clothes-hanging rod under a shelf. With all the first-act performers in there, the room was pretty tight. But people made space for the men at the barre. Sam had never used one before starting lessons at Shall We Dance; he and Mateo both had a how-to session with Dmitri back at the beginning.

They heard Rory on the intercom. "Five minutes to Act One." That meant they had a couple more minutes, in case either of them wanted a mouthful of water or a dash to the bathroom. Neither of them did. They checked each other out, confirming that they were ready. They were both dancing in jeans, with white tank tops under unbuttoned flannel shirts. Casual and comfortable, only their Cuban-heeled Latin shoes betraying what they were there for. When they went to Worldtone, Sam had looked at those and put on such a resigned expression that Mateo had laughed for about five minutes.

Rory spoke again. "Two minutes to Act One. Act One beginners, please." That was their cue. They went out to the wing, followed by the couple who would dance the second number. The working light went off, leaving only the dim gooseneck lamp on Rory's station at the control board. Sam and Mateo went out on stage and took their position as Rory said, "Welcome to Chrome. Take your seats, park your drinks, and get ready for tonight's presentation of Mating Dance: Tourists. Buckle up and enjoy the ride." The curtains opened, the spotlight came on, and their music started.

Sam liked the spotlight: it made the audience hard to see. He could pretend he and Mateo really were dancing with no one watching. Except Mateo so obviously knew. He was a flirt when he danced with Sam, always all Come And Get It, which always worked. He played it different tonight, though. This time he was following Sam's mood as well as his lead. Showing the world that he would follow Sam anywhere. It was breathtaking.

He felt like he'd been underwater when they took their bows. Bent to pick up the shirt he'd stripped off of his lover toward the end of the dance. Still holding hands as they left the stage, only then hearing the applause. As soon as they were in the wing he pulled Mateo in for a kiss. "You're so perfect."

"I'm so turned *on* right now. When you took my shirt off I was like, oh yes honey. Let's do it right here." Mateo was more than half serious. "When did you decide to do that?"

"I don't know. Did I decide?" They were both snickering as they went in the green room, horny as hell, wishing there weren't so many people around. It got funnier every time they looked at each other, but they couldn't seem to keep their hands to themselves.

"You two are an outrage," Julia said as they returned from the Act One curtain call. "What did you do different? We need a monitor in here." They busted up laughing.

Once out in the noisy club, drinks in hand, they started talking about their performance. How they felt about it, more than how they thought they'd performed it. Mateo was completely jazzed. "That was so much fun. I hope you didn't hate it."

Sam shook his head, smiling. "I didn't hate it. I was afraid I would. I didn't know how it would feel. But the energy in the room, it was almost like a fight. They told us, you know, in the UFC. These are real fights, this isn't the WWE, but you're still putting on a show. Give them what they want. Feed the beast."

"So you had to get in character?"

"Yeah, a little bit. I had to put on Mean Sam."

"Tonight you put on Sexy Sam. I'm so lucky I get to go home with you." Mateo put his free hand on Sam's thigh and leaned close to say, "You know, we don't have to stay. We can see Act Two tomorrow, do some dancing at the after-party. We could go home right now and you could take the rest of my clothes off."

That suddenly seemed like a great idea. Sam finished his drink, leaned in for another kiss, and lifted Mateo off his barstool. "Let's get out of here before they start." Mateo didn't even bother finishing his cocktail.

Chapter 22

Sam and Benny did rock-paper-scissors to see who would get the day after Thanksgiving off. Mateo was still snickering about it when he and Sam caught their flight to Oakland. They were flying at ungodly hours so they wouldn't have to spend an unpredictable number of hours driving. Holiday traffic on the I-5 freeway was always a nightmare; driving had never been an option. "It's one lousy day. It's not like you won't be back on Saturday. And it's not like he's holding the fort all alone the way you do sometimes."

"I don't do it that often. You told Kristine thank you from me, right?"

"Yeah, I did." Kristine had promised to check on Pachuco and Frida after she got back to L.A. from Pomona. She said it would be a good excuse not to spend the night with her parents, who were still mad about the whole Justin thing. "She said she didn't think there would be a roast pig this year," Mateo said. "I told her she could blame it on me."

"Big brother." It made Sam smile.

"Hey, I'll take the rap for being a bad influence. It doesn't bother me. God I can't wait to meet all your people. Anita was so cute in her email."

"I never thought they'd invite the Mendozas. It's going to be a lot of people. Even more than last year." But this year everybody seemed cool about it. Sam and Mateo were a done deal, an established couple. Sam couldn't wait to show his lover off to the people who'd helped shape his life.

Predictably, everyone loved him. Predictably, he talked about dancing. Then everyone wanted to see the video of 'Road Trippin,'' so they got online for that. And then everyone wanted to know about the other Latin dances Sam was learning. Mateo offered to teach everybody cha-cha, and it turned into a dance party.

When the house was finally quiet, Anita Lee said, "I think this is the first Thanksgiving we've had that I'm not going to bed regretting everything I ate. When are you two dancing again?"

Mateo glanced at Sam. "We haven't decided yet. But there's a good chance we'll be doing a thing up here next April. We'll keep in touch."

"It's pretty much a sure thing," Sam said, giving in to what had probably always been inevitable. "It's a sort of qualifying event for the Gay Games. We'll tell you all about it in the morning."

There was a moment of hilarious weirdness when they went to bed. It was the first time they'd stayed overnight in someone else's house. They both wore pajama pants instead of getting naked as usual. And they both snort-laughed as quietly as they could when they were under the covers. "I'm afraid to kiss you," Sam said after a minute. "I can't get busy in my mom's house." It was the first time he'd called her that out loud.

Mateo kissed his nose, said, "I love you. Good night," and turned his back. He felt Sam laughing.

Sam's good intentions went to hell the next morning. He woke up in the nearly-dark room, with Mateo still asleep but pressed against him, clearly having some kind of sexy dream. His own body must have picked up on it; he was ferociously aroused. There was no way Sam could go down the hall in this condition. He thought it was early enough that if they made any noise, the Lees wouldn't hear. He slid a hand inside Mateo's pants and put his mouth on that smooth neck. "Are you awake? Or do you want me to do this in your sleep." He felt Mateo wake up. Heard the soft sound. "You're awake now. What were you dreaming of?"

"You. Oh my God, Sam." He pushed himself into Sam's hand.

"I want your mouth." Mateo whimpered. Sam moved away enough to get his pants off. Mateo was doing the same thing. Then he went for Sam, getting his mouth full with a hungry sound. Sam tugged on a knee, pulling Mateo's hips close so he could get his own mouthful. They were as quiet as possible, and it didn't take long at all. Mateo held Sam in his mouth for a few extra seconds after swallowing, then pulled away with his mouth still tight. "Jesus!" A stifled laugh, then his tongue across the tip of Sam's cock. "Damn, baby."

Mateo levered himself up, satisfied. "Good morning." Sam was smiling up at him. He scrubbed a hand through his hair. "What time is it?"

"I don't know." Sam propped himself on an elbow, reached for his phone on the nightstand, and woke it up. "Oh, it's only six." Twelve hours before they needed to leave for the airport. Way too early to assume the Lees were awake, much less sociable. But he felt wide awake. Mateo, on the other hand, still looked sleepy. "You should go back to sleep."

"What are you going to do?"

"Go in the backyard, do some tai chi."

"Okay." Mateo looked around for his pants. "Going to the bathroom." Sam watched him go, got dressed while waiting for him to return, kissed him back into bed, and pulled the quilt up. Then he went down the hall himself before going quietly out the back door. He'd always loved this garden. The Lees had owned the house for a long time. Over the seventeen years since Sam had first gone to live with them, their classic Chinese landscape had settled into a pleasing illusion of age. The mature cypress tree in one corner balanced a group of Japanese maples around a small pond. Pebble-mosaic paths wound through a seemingly random collection of dwarf rhododendrons and camellias.

Near the house, a broad patio bordered with ferns and moss provided plenty of space for Sam to do his practice. He was prepared for this, with yoga socks and gloves. He'd moved on from tai chi to yoga and was standing in tree pose with his eyes closed when he heard a soft step and smelled green tea. "Good morning," he said, opening his eyes. He set his foot down, bent to touch his toes, then stretched up as tall as he could. "God, what a gorgeous day."

Anita laughed softly. It was overcast, almost foggy, and none too warm. She was curled up on the cushioned settee by the back door, a crocheted afghan over her shoulders, two handmade ceramic mugs on the table in front of her. Each had a lid to keep the heat in. "I don't need to ask how you are."

"I'm great." He came over, pulling off his gloves, and sat beside her. After a moment's hesitation, he leaned close and kissed her cheek. "I called you 'mom' last night when Mateo and I were talking. Do you mind?"

"Oh, Sam, of course not." She reached for her mug, setting the lid aside. "Rosario and I talked about that. After I got in touch to invite them to dinner, we met up for coffee. She told me what you were like when you lived with them. How you changed in those five years. She said, if I hadn't gotten sick, we were going to try to adopt him. Did they ever tell you that?"

"No." Sam picked up his mug, set aside the lid, concentrated on the hot tea to hide his eyes. "That's nice. That's good to know."

She answered the hovering question. "They never told you because they thought it would hurt you more. That they had to give you up. And then when you came to us, you were so close to being a man already. An old soul in a fourteen-year-old body. Feihung thought it was better to treat you as a student, an honored guest, than to try to pretend we were your parents. Did we do right?"

"Yes. You were right. I was confused then." He sipped his tea, gazing at the garden. "It was a little strange here at first, after the last place with all those kids. It was good to be in a quiet place. I could tell you wanted me to learn. The university scared me, though. The thought of trying to do that, trying to choose something to study that would be my whole life." He glanced at her, faintly smiling. "Of course I ended up doing that anyway. Your kids did too."

"Our son did," Anita corrected. "Jason always wanted to be a doctor. Faith struggled a little. She wanted to be an entertainer. A real job felt like prison to her."

"She likes what she does now, though."

"Oh, she loves it." The Lees' daughter was a manager for a civic auditorium in Santa Rosa. "She says one day she expects to see you and Mateo on her stage."

Sam laughed, hastily stifling it because it sounded so loud in that quiet garden. "I've been in one show, in the basement of a bar. I seriously doubt we'll ever need a stage that big," he said, smiling. "Faith was with her wife's family yesterday?"

"Yes, they'll be here Sunday. She said to say hi to you and Mateo."

Sam could tell Anita wanted to ask him something. Probably something about Mateo. Maybe something that came to mind because he mentioned Faith and her wife. "I don't know." She didn't ask what he meant. After a moment he went on. "When I asked him to live with me, we weren't sure he could keep his same job. I said my job would cover him, my insurance, if." He stopped.

"If." Last year, that could mean only one thing. "You haven't talked about it since?" They were still new, after all, and Mateo was only twenty-five.

Sam might have been thinking the same things. "Well, he kept his job. He likes it. They like him. We haven't talked about that, any of that. We've been so busy."

Anita shook her head, laughing softly. "I suppose there's no hurry."

"Not now. They can't take it away again now." Sam sipped his tea. "I love him so much."

"He loves you too. As long as you both feel sure of that, you'll be fine."

***

When Sam returned to their room, Mateo was more or less awake, happy to stay in bed until it was his turn to shower. They both packed their bags before joining the Lees for breakfast. The day's conversations had mostly to do with Feihung's upcoming sabbatical, Mateo and Sam's plans regarding the Gay Games, and Anita's problematic teaching assistant.

"That was completely different from last year," Mateo said, once they were at the airport and waiting to board. "It was great. Was it enough time with everybody?"

"It was fine. It would have been nice if Faith and Emily were there, but it was good. Anita said she was joking about seeing us on her stage sometime."

Mateo noted that he didn't call her 'mom' this time, but then the circumstances were different. "What did you say?"

"I said I've been on stage once." Sam was smiling. "Do you want to do that again? It was fun." He added that because he wanted to be clear he was up for it.

"You know I'd love to." Mateo was instantly excited. "Not December, that's not enough time. I'll see if they have all the themes posted when I check in with Julia. You're sure?"

Sam leaned over to kiss him. "Yes, baby, I'm sure." Sure about everything, except when to suggest the next step, and which version it should be. Maybe after the Games. Maybe after doing something that big, there would be no doubt it was the right time.

***

December 2013

Sam had been feeling more competitive ever since Irvine, where he saw Dance Sport for real. With 'Tourists' out of the way, after they got back from Berkeley, he asked Julia to gradually level up their routines. She was happy to oblige. Meanwhile, Mateo also started practicing with Yolanda, intending to debut as professional partners in January.

"That's not a lot of time," said Sam, one evening at home. The cats were on the couch, Mateo was in the kitchen, and Sam was hanging out watching as dinner prep proceeded.

"It's just about getting a set of routines ready. We can fine-tune them as we go."

"How do you like her?"

"She's cute, I guess. She picks up choreo fast. But I'm not sure she's getting the technique. Her background is in ballet and man, that turnout is wrong, wrong, wrong. You do *not* turn out from the hip in ballroom!"

"Has she been doing this long?"

"No, she's a newbie like me. Thank God we're in a studio with people like Dmitri and Julia. They are giving us the beat down."

Sam laughed. "I'm going to do a private with Dmitri next week. Get him to teach me how to do that jump that the winning guy did in the paso doble."

"The tour jetée? For real?" Mateo grabbed Sam and danced him around the kitchen for a minute. "Kitties, did you hear that? They don't care," he said to Sam, who was laughing. "Maybe we should have dogs. Dogs are ready to party all the time. Get with the program, cats."

* * *

On a Saturday morning later that month, Sam left Mateo at home working on a drafting project and met with Julia to talk about a new round of private lessons. "I feel pretty solid in these routines now. But you know, Mateo took me down to a competition in October." He hesitated.

Julia wasn't sure where this was going. "Problem?"

"He says he just wants to go to the Games and have fun. But I want to give him more than that. He

208

gives me so much. You remember that song Vince and Kelli danced to?"

"It's one of the favorites at our studio parties. 'Bring Me Sunshine.'"

"That's what Mateo does. And I, I want to get more serious about this. I don't want us to get cut in the first round."

Julia was surprised but pleased. "You're making me very happy right now."

"Dmitri showed me that tour jetée thing. And the tour en l'air. So we put those into the paso doble, and the butterflies, and Mateo put in his flip. I think it's our best dance."

"You're right, it is. Yours is more like martial arts than flamenco, it's going to stand out. Plus, a paired tour of any kind is not something a lot of people try, and you guys do them well."

"Well, thanks. But I've been watching some of the competitions on YouTube, and paso is the fourth dance. The judges might have already written us off."

Julia nodded. "That's true."

"So I want to use these private sessions with you to learn how I can do better in the other dances. I don't want to hold him back."

"Your technique is actually quite good. As to performance, can I show you something?" Julia took him into the office, where the manager was working. "Hey, Elena, can we borrow the screen for a few minutes?"

"Sure. I was about to run around the corner for a cappuccino. Want something?"

"Latte?"

"Chai would be great, thanks," said Sam.

"Okay, see you in a few." Elena went out and Julia sat down at the computer, opening YouTube to run a quick search. "Okay. This is actually a paso doble. Take a look at how he moves." It was a clip from the 2012 season of 'So You Think You Can Dance.' The leader was a martial artist, and it showed in the performance. "Look at his speed. You've got that, even though you're so much taller." She pulled up another clip featuring the same performer, his original audition for the show. "Look at those spins, and the way he drops right down. His transitions are like lightning. You can't look away."

"I could work on that."

"We could put that into the samba, the changes in elevation. For the rumba, we can really showcase the flexibility and strength you two bring, and your great extension. Counterbalance and intertwining."

Sam nodded, pleased that he understood what she meant. "How about the cha-cha?"

"Let's use your legs. Cover some ground, really travel. Mateo could work a lot of syncopation. For jive, let's tighten up your kicks and flicks sequences. Maybe add some solo spins?"

"Anything. 'Cause really, whatever you wish I could do? Throw it at me. Let's see if I can catch it."

"Better be careful what you say."

Sam didn't blame her for being skeptical. Up to now he'd been, if not exactly humoring Mateo, at least not fully committed. "I've been thinking about this a lot, and I'm serious. I want to show up for you and Dmitri and myself. This is a new way for me to compete. I want to win if we possibly can. Plus, you know, my boy commits. Whatever he does, he's there for it, a hundred percent. He gives till it hurts. How

210

can I possibly deserve that if I won't do the same for him?"

Julia bit her lip and took a moment, eyes glistening. "Sam, you're killing me here."

"I'm in," he said emphatically. "Break me if you have to."

"I'll give you everything I've got. Look, you're going to show up on the floor. You'll be one of the tallest men there, you're a beautiful couple, and you're a *real* couple. People are going to notice you. If you give them the kind of movement you're capable of, with the great connection you already have, and the passion you just showed me, you could do really well."

Sam nodded. "Mateo says we can't do lifts at all."

"That's right. Strict rules. But as long as he's got one foot on the floor, or you're both generating your own movement, all bets are off."

"Let's get to work." Elena came back then, and they took a minute to chat over their drinks. Before he and Julia got down to business, Sam sent a text to Mateo: **Gonna have some new shit to work on**.

Mateo's reply came almost immediately: *What are you up to?*

Told Julia to throw the book at me
???
Going for the gold, baby. You deserve it
!!!!!! I love you
I love you too

***

Mateo and Yolanda competed three times in January and early February, and it wasn't going so well. Sam got home from work to find Mateo taking

211

out his frustration on some chicken breasts. "What are you doing in here, karate kid?"

"Chicken marsala. But also, sublimation."

"Last weekend was kind of a disappointment, huh. It almost seemed like she was dancing by herself." A few months ago, Sam realized, he wouldn't have noticed.

Mateo pointed the mallet at him. "That's *exactly* what it's like."

"Is it the ballet thing?"

"Maybe. In ballet partnering, the guy is basically just a prop. Ugh, let's not talk about her. If I pound these any more we'll be able to read through them." He dropped the mallet. "Let's talk about *you* and how awesome *you* are!"

Sam smiled. "Dmitri says I should cut my hair."

"What?! No fucking way!"

"Not to cut it short, but just not quite this long."

Mateo asked suspiciously, "How long?"

"Like, to here." He indicated a line below his shoulders.

"Well. Hmm. I guess you could still get a good ponytail going." Mateo loved the long hair. He was not at all convinced about this idea. But Dmitri knew his shit.

"Like Jackie Chan after his queue gets cut off in 'Shanghai Noon,'" Sam suggested.

Mateo thought about it. "I could live with that."

"And another thing." Sam gave him a sideways look. "Julia suggested I do some pro-am with her."

"That would be smart. Get used to being on the floor with a bunch of other people."

"Get used to chasing them out of my way."

"Damn right. Unleash your natural aggression again. She certainly knows the routines."

"She can't do the big tricks, though."

"You're gonna have to be careful not to outrun her," Mateo pointed out.

"I'll probably get stage fright and freeze up."

"All the more reason to start doing it now. 'Cause you're not allowed to freeze up in Cleveland. You stop for a second and I'll back-lead you so hard you won't know what hit you."

"Bossy little shit."

"I'll show *you* bossy." Mateo stepped into his space. Sam yielded, laughing, backing toward the newly slipcovered couch.

Chapter 23

The next time Mateo and Yolanda competed, Sam and Julia were entered for pro-am. As they waited in the on-deck area, Sam did some deep breathing and tried to ignore the other five men in the event. Told himself it didn't matter that all six of them were wearing all black; he looked nothing like the others. Sam was taller and dark-skinned and he had long hair. He was himself, dressed for his new sport, ready to make his mark.

Julia asked if he was okay. He looked down at her. "I'm good. I'm pretending it's a fight." Julia laughed. "But don't worry, I won't hit anybody."

"Just don't even think about anyone but me. And listen for the beat."

The announcer said, "And now, welcome to the floor our competitors in the Pro-Am Adult International Latin Novice Scholarship."

"Here we go! Wait till they call your number."

Sam panicked. "Wait, what's my number?"

Julia laughed. "Three oh six. Don't worry, Sam, I'm here for you."

He took her hand. "Right. Thanks." It was nice to have a partner going into this.

***

Mateo watched from the sidelines as Sam and Julia walked onto the floor. Along with the other five men, there were a dozen women with their male instructors. "Your first dance is cha-cha," said the announcer. "Music, please." Some dancers began moving immediately. Sam briefly waited, head up, listening. Then he started to move, perfectly on time.

"Go, baby, go!" Mateo yelled. Sam appeared unfazed by the crowd on the floor. He saw empty space and took Julia into it. They traveled twice as much as any of the others, punctuating their chassé and locking actions with syncopated crossovers, spins, and swivels. As the music faded, Sam gave Julia a final spin into a crossover check and finally smiled. Mateo was ecstatic. "Three oh six! Woo-hoo!"

"Competitors, take your places please for your next dance. And...samba." Julia began moving in a sinuous circle of volta actions. Sam moved around her, shaping her into a traveling sequence of samba rolls.

"Do it!" yelled Mateo. "Three oh six!!" He saw Julia grin. She and Sam separated for a sequence of crossing actions. Then he spun and dropped to one knee, in what Mateo thought of as his super-hero landing, and she fan-kicked over his head. As her foot came down, Sam's hands went to her thigh and hip, and he gave her an invisibly-fast three-quarter turn, taking her down across his knee. One arm supported her shoulders, and his face was close to hers.

A passing dancer stopped beside Mateo. "Damn, that's hot."

Sam was back up on his feet in a second, lifting Julia with him and spinning her into a shadow position for another series of rolls, which segued into an extended chassé, which led into a series of weaving actions. There was one more position change, and Sam and Julia were in a sequence of promenade runs when the music faded. They'd circled the entire floor.

Mateo and the passing dancer both yelled, "Three oh six!!" She turned to him and added, "They let that track run long."

"I think they wanted to see more," he said. "So did I."

"I can't even look at anyone else out there. Do you know him?"

"I sure do," Mateo said, grinning, smug as fuck. "We live together. Training for the Gay Games next summer."

"Rock on!" They did a fist bump.

The announcer said, "Please take your positions for your third and final dance…the rumba. Music, please."

Sam found a position at the very center of the floor. As the music began, he was very still, focused on Julia, who had her back to him. She danced some side breaks, then a forward check and rondé to a solo spin. Sam reached out to catch her hand, stepping up to her. He let her stretch forward into a backbend, then closed with her, whipped around her, and spun her down the floor before going into a deep lunge. Julia had an arm across his shoulders, and went into a split, almost fully on the floor. Her other hand was on his chest and her face was turned up to his. Mateo swallowed, thinking holy fuck, I get to do that with him.

The passing dancer said, "Wow. Which one is the pro?"

"The girl," said Mateo, a little breathless.

"That guy is good."

"Yes. Yes, he is. THREE OH SIX!!" he screamed. Then, "It's his first competition."

"No way! THREE OH SIX!"

The rest of the rumba used enhanced versions of basic figures. Sam's reach and his core strength let Julia stretch and melt into movements, shading the timing. It seemed a foregone conclusion that they would dance in the final round, but they anxiously checked the call-back sheet regardless. Sam exhaled with relief when he saw their number. By then, Mateo was beside him, totally unsurprised. "Told you. I've got to go get warmed up, our thing is right after your final."

"Will you be able to watch?"

"Not sure. You ordered the video, right?"

"Shit, no. Let me go do that."

"Yes! Pictures, too!" said Julia, laughing as Sam loped off to the vendors' table. "He is doing so great."

"It looked amazing." Mateo was glad he was wearing a dance belt; he'd had a hard-on for the past ten minutes.

"Only one of the other guys made the final."

"I think he had the rest of them beat before they even got on the floor. He's in full I Will Stomp You mode."

"I've never seen that before, it's kind of a thrill. He doesn't push, but people get out of his way. If he dances like this at the Games, you guys are going to rock it." She gave him a sideways glance. "It's really something being handled by someone that strong."

"You ought to know." Julia's boyfriend Ray was physically very much like Sam. She was cracking up as Mateo headed for the practice room.

***

Sam's second-place trophy stood on the desk, glinting in the morning light as they waited for room service to deliver their breakfast. Mateo stretched lazily. "So, did you have fun?"

"I really did. Julia was great."

"This girl was standing by me during your semifinal and asked me which one of you was the pro."

217

"No way." Sam was delighted.

"Yes way. You'd have won if it wasn't your first time out."

"I want to do it again. I didn't think I would dig it so much. It's that adrenaline thing, I guess."

"Like a martial-arts competition?"

"Yeah, without the getting beat on part."

Mateo laughed. "I was totally turned on, watching you. That's why I couldn't watch the final. That sheer shirt was working for me. Not to mention the hip action."

Sam leaned over to kiss him. "I thought you seemed a little worked up last night."

"I seriously considered jerking off before my event. I was like, *ngh*."

"Yolanda did better this time."

"Yeah, she did. I don't think we'll keep going, though. Probably call it quits after the Emerald Ball."

"Are you going to try to find a new partner?"

"Maybe. We'll see. I know it's making me a better dancer. And a better teacher." He'd already had a thought, and this seemed like a good time to share it. "Elena used to compete. I might talk to her." When their food arrived, they turned the TV on to watch the Food Network, to give themselves a break from all the dance talk.

But as they drove back to L.A., the conversation returned to dancing. Now that Sam had one trophy, he kind of wanted another. He wanted to study that video with Julia and figure out how to improve. "Think I should plan on doing pro-am every time you and Yolanda are dancing somewhere?"

"If Julia's up for it, I'm sure it would be good for you." Mateo giggled as a thought occurred to him. "Dmitri's going to have a plague of girls."

218

"What are you talking about?"

"Once they find out where you train, amateur girls who want a partner will be lining up. There aren't enough good Latin men, especially not tall ones."

"Would that be good for me to do?"

Mateo glanced over from the driver's seat. "If you *want* to do it, then it would be good for you. More practice, more exposure, more exercise. Oh, and the chance to be a national champion. You could end up going to the World Games."

Sam looked over, surprised. "No kidding?"

"Dance Sport's not in the Olympics yet, but it's been in the World Games for years."

"Man, I just keep learning. Okay, so what are the downsides?"

"A bitterly jealous me." He was mostly kidding, but Sam was concerned.

"Well, I don't want that."

"Look, if you wanted to, I'd be the last person to say don't do it. The Gay Games is the highest I can go with you. And even if I wanted to go back to amateur status, which I don't, I'd still want to stick with American style and that's not in competition worldwide. So seriously. Would I be jealous? Yeah, a little. But would I be thrilled? Definitely."

"I don't know."

"Just let whatever happens, happen. We'll deal with it. I think you've missed competition."

Sam grinned. "Yeah, maybe."

"But don't mention it at the studio until you make up your mind, because you will be swarmed, *swarmed*, by women." He wasn't kidding at all. Sam laughed anyway.

At home, after greeting the cats and doing penance for being away, Mateo got on the Internet and looked up the World Games. "Okay, so the last one was last year, next one's in 2017."

"Hey, look at that," said Sam. "Salsa was in it last year, along with ballroom."

"No shit! Used to be Rock N Roll."

"What the heck is that?"

"Like swing dance only with a shitload of lifts and tricks. Really athletic. This level of salsa is like that too, it's mind-blowing." He found a video.

Sam watched in disbelief. The event made International Latin look as calm as tai chi. "Okay, that's a no." Mateo laughed. Sam tugged a lock of his hair. "I want to focus on our thing first, the Gay Games, but tell me how I would qualify for this. If I wanted to try. In Latin, not that gymnastic ghost pepper salsa."

Another laugh, then Mateo said, "Well, you'd want to check me on this because I haven't looked it up since college, right? The amateur adult champions, or like the top three most highly-ranked amateur couples nationally, make up the U.S. teams for Standard and Latin."

"What's adult?"

"Age nineteen to thirty-five."

"I'd be too old by 2017," Sam said, disappointed.

"But both partners don't have to be the same age. If your partner is under thirty-five you'd still be in the adult category." Sam made a confused sound; Mateo made it worse. "A Senior can dance down into Adult, but an Adult can't dance up into Senior."

"Wait a minute, *senior*? Shut your mouth!"

"Right? Once you're over thirty-five, you're senior."

"That is fucked up." Sam was appalled.

Mateo tried not to crack up. "It's because most people over thirty-five turn into a tub of goo. But that's not going to happen to you. And even if you're in the Senior division, there are still world championship events you could go to."

Sam shook his head. It was too much to take in. "Okay, let's sit on all this for a while. This spring, it's all about getting ready for the Games." He leaned against Mateo for a second. "I'm really glad you got me into this. I love you."

"I love you too, honey." He didn't really want to ask, but he really needed to. "Straight talk. Did anyone give you any shit at the comp?"

Sam knew what he meant. "A couple of dirty looks in the men's room, but I choose to believe it's because I made the final and they didn't."

"Nobody said anything?"

"Nope."

"Well, good."

***

What with their Games prep and planning two Cabaret performances, Sam was finding it a challenge to keep up with both his non-dancing workouts and his friends. After missing each other several times, he and Vince arranged to meet up at the gym. Vince's gym, because he'd heard all about Sam's gym from Mateo.

"You are not noticeably out of shape," he told Sam when they'd progressed to barbells, and thus to spotting each other. Sam huffed out a laugh and set down the weight. Vince took Sam's place on the bench. "It's amazing how effective a workout it is, slinging a dance partner around."

"Truth." Sam wiped his face. "I had to drop my regular class at the dojo. It was taking too big a bite out of the schedule. Mateo and I go over to Rory and Dana's and do stuff there, in the yard."

"You've been doing that for a while. Still going to the aerial gym?"

"We get there about once a month. So how was Valentine's Day now that you're a married man?" He caught the satisfied expression on his friend's face. "Oh, I see." Vince laughed. "We went to the Four Seasons again."

"He doesn't mind doing the same thing twice, huh." Vince set down the weight.

"No. He likes a routine, same as I do. Where'd you go with Kelli this year?"

"Went to a milonga out in the Valley. Your turn." Sam added some weight. Vince gave him a hateful look, watched the reps, took his turn with a lot of bitching. "That's my limit."

"Pretty good for a short guy."

"Oh, eat me." Vince glared at his cackling friend. "You've been hanging around those muscleheads too long."

"You should hear Mateo in there. I can't believe some of the things that come out of his mouth." He also couldn't believe what a turn-on it was to see Mateo in action, sleek and golden and almost-androgynously beautiful, and hear him throwing down some fearlessly filthy smack talk. His lover had quite a fan club at the gym. Nobody followed them into the shower room. It was a matter of plausible deniability.

Vince probably detected how Sam's mind was wandering. He wiped down the bench, they racked the weight, and then went to the next room to stretch.

"Vicky says you're going up to Oakland together for that April Follies thing. Once you get done with the Games this summer, you ever think about doing a salsa comp?"

"We might do it if you do it again. Be fun to go together, I think. We'd need a lot of prep time, though."

"Jesus, us too. Every time I turn around there's something new to do." Vince didn't sound as if he minded this at all.

Sam smiled. "I know. Isn't it great?"

Chapter 24

The next new thing they were doing was turning their paso doble routine into a show dance. When they talked to Julia in December, she gave them the Underground Cabaret's schedule for the new year. Neither of them was inclined to put anything together for the first two shows of 2014. Sam opted to concentrate on his Latin pro-am events, and Mateo kept busy with Yolanda. But the March show title was 'Carnivale,' and Vince threw them a song called 'Cirque dans la Rue.' They listened to it half a dozen times; Sam sent Vince a text saying *how do you come up with this shit?*; Julia said "Yeah baby," and they got to work. She borrowed material from half a dozen 'So You Think You Can Dance' routines, Michelle and Dmitri coached them on some tricks, and their audition video was accepted. The next thing was a visit to Kristine to get some costumes rolling, because flannel shirts wouldn't cut it and they were determined not to wear basic black.

Then Mateo found Sam frowning at the video and said, "What? Did you decide you hate it?"

Sam looked up and shook his head. "No, but is it too late to change a couple of things?"

"Show me." They watched it through again. Sam pointed at the third repetition of the chorus. "Oh fuck, yeah. It's too much, isn't it? Too much of the same thing. Well, that's the problem with taking a ninety-second routine and turning it into a three-and-a-half-minute dance. What do you want to do?"

"Go full circus. Gymnastics, but like slow motion. We could shadow each other. Do tricks off each other." Sam wasn't even sure what he meant, but he knew they had the capability.

"We could chop that whole piece out," Mateo said, thinking out loud. "From 'make us laugh' to 'just like me.' Really easy to resolve it before going into completely different movement. Let's do the counts." They listened to the track, noting down the number of bars and where the hits in the music landed. "God you're a genius. When can we get to the gym?" Now they compared schedules. They didn't have much time to make the changes, not if they wanted to be able to run the whole thing at the studio a few times before dress rehearsal. Mateo mercilessly jettisoned some rehearsal hours with Yolanda. "We're not getting anywhere anyway," he told Sam. "It won't matter if we leave those routines alone for a week."

With a few other adjustments they were able to get to the gym. Rory came along the first time, because she hadn't been there for a while, and gave them some feedback after they told her what they were doing. "Oh that is sick as *fuck*," she said after they did a thing where Mateo climbed up Sam. "Jesus you guys are strong."

"You could do it," Sam said, smiling. "Get on over here."

"No way, you're too tall. I'll climb up Mateo." He put his hands on her waist and braced himself in a second-position plié. She put her hands on his shoulders, set one foot on his thigh above his knee, they pushed and pulled, and she got the other foot on his opposite thigh below his hip. She said, "I'm going over your head to get on this shoulder. Spot me, Sam?" He was right there. She did a quarter turn, lifting her leg over Mateo's head to sit with his shoulder between her legs. "How kinky did that look?" Sam laughed. "Okay where do we go from here." She was looking at their position in the mirror. Mateo's face said Make Up Your Mind, but he was out of plié and steady. "Um. Hooking back leg to the outside of your ribs here. Front leg in attitude for a second, hmm, that's a pretty line if I do say so myself. Front leg coming across. I'm going to dive back behind your head and hook my arm over your shoulder, wrist to your ribs. Arms out? Don't worry about my free leg. Here I go." A second later she was stretched across his shoulders, top arm extended to match the line of her front leg.

"Oh, *nice*," said Mateo. "Now how the hell are you getting out of that?"

"Like I know? Sam, what do I do? Pretend this is Mateo on you, how are you going to get him down from there?"

Mateo stared into the mirror, wondering the same thing. This was far beyond anything they'd tried so far. He wasn't sure Rory even meant for them to try it; she might have been simply playing around. It wouldn't be the first time.

Sam walked around. "You're not even holding her. This is crazy. Get your hand to the inside of her front knee. Yeah, right above the joint. Rory, drop your back foot and Mateo, lower a little. There you go, she's down." Rory flicked her top foot, lifting that leg out of Mateo's hand again, relaxed her other arm and stepped through as he slid out from under.

"Ow, motherfucker." Mateo was rubbing his side where Rory's heel had dug in. "Now if only someone was taking video."

"I was." They all turned to look; it was Paula. "I was in here working on my trapeze thing till I saw you come in. I thought you guys were doing a paso!"

226

"Well," Sam said. "Shit happened?" Rory and Mateo both cackled. "That's kind of beyond what we were thinking of. He's going to have Latin shoes on."

"God, yes, ouch." Mateo was imagining how much more sore his ribs would be right now. "But you know there's no law that says we have to wear shoes. If we were barefoot the whole thing would be more martial arts."

"And also more circus," Paula said. "Why don't you look at this." They all gathered around and she played the phone video. "It's a great trick."

"Especially if we could do it really fast." Mateo made eye contact with Sam. "You've got to admit it takes our version up about a dozen notches. But I'm a lot heavier than Rory."

"Well, I'm a lot heavier than you," Sam pointed out. "I'm having a really sick idea."

"How sick?" Paula and Rory said it together.

"Like if instead of setting that back foot down behind he kicks it up and over, does a flip to land in front of me."

"Are you *high*?" Mateo giggled. "I'd have to pike it. Both legs."

"You can do that."

"It'd put a hell of a lot of force on your shoulders."

Sam was already imagining how it would work. When he would need to lower and retreat, where his hands should be to stabilize the dismount. If they landed it on 'just like me' they'd be in position to connect with the paso choreography again. "Want to try it?"

"Are you serious?" Clearly he was. Mateo said, "God, I love you. Okay, ladies, stand back." The first time was kind of a mess. The second time was smoother. The third time Paula took video, and the fourth time they did it in two counts of eight, leaving plenty of time for Mateo to do a malevolently graceful piece of styling up on Sam's shoulder. They landed it perfectly, then stood there huffing and puffing and grinning at each other.

"My God, you guys." Rory could hardly believe it. "The Cabaret has *never* had anything like this, not even Michelle's adagio craziness with Dmitri. I can't wait to hear what he has to say about it."

***

They picked up some Dance Paws to swap in for their Latin shoes on the way home. Finished blending in all the new material two days later. Then they found a time to run it at the studio when Dmitri wasn't there, taking video, in costume (deep purple dance pants with psychedelic stretch shirts, the kind that snapped between the legs, which seemed like a really wise choice now that they'd gone full circus). After watching it at home and making a copy, Mateo left the SD card on the office desk and asked Elena to have Dmitri look at it the next time he was in. He got a text the next day, while he and Sam were having dinner at home, and laughed so hard Sam had to take the phone out of his hand: *Mateo I don't know what he said because it was all in Ukrainian but I think it boils down to what is wrong with those crazy @%#$&! Or maybe that's what I was thinking*

Sam sent a reply: **Hi Elena this is Sam. Think Tony will want that clip for his project?** Elena's husband worked on documentary series called 'Live Work Dance.'

OMG he totally will. Can I take it home?

Absolutely. See you soon. Sam handed the phone to Mateo. "Who should we invite to this show?"

228

"Let's ask Cory." Mateo produced an evil grin. "I can't wait to see his face."

"Torturing the poor guy." Sam was smiling.

"Poor guy, my hairy ass. You know he gets off on watching us. He's been wanting to get with you for ages. He'll be all, goddamn, why couldn't he be throwing me around like that." He watched Sam laugh, moved his wineglass out of the danger zone, and momentarily regretted the presence of cats. If those two little bandits weren't lurking around, he could put Sam on the couch and come back to dinner later.

Sam took a breath and said, "You don't have a hairy ass. At least the last time I checked."

"Seems like forever." Mateo drank some wine, giving his lover a suggestive look over the top of the glass. "Seems like you might want to make sure nothing's changed."

A couple minutes later, they were on the couch, and the cats were on the coffee table, investigating the abandoned dinner plates.

***

April 2014

Mateo lurked around the studio for a few days after 'Carnivale,' waiting for an opportunity to speak privately with Dmitri. It took some patience because the place was so busy. Finally there was a time when Dmitri wasn't with a student or Julia or Michelle, and Elena was out of the office. Mateo skidded over to the boss and said, "Could I have a minute?"

Dmitri had noticed his youngest teacher hovering, and thought he knew what this was about. "In the office." It was not quite a question.

"Yes please." Mateo followed him in, closed the door, and wasted no time. "You know this thing with

Yolanda isn't really working out. If we don't have a breakthrough at Emerald Ball, we're going to call it." Dmitri nodded, unsurprised, but his eyebrows went up when Mateo added, "I talked to Elena. We thought we'd practice those same routines and then we'd like to do a tryout for you. But if you hate this idea tell me now, please." He was a little worried about it. Elena couldn't hide her excitement at the thought of competing again, but she had a full-time job as the manager. Dmitri needed her.

"No," said Dmitri. Mateo could tell he meant he didn't hate the idea. He wasn't smiling, but then he hardly ever did. "Elena mentioned, last year, she might wish to teach part time. I knew she would wish to compete again."

"She told me about her season with you. She said she was awful. I see her dance now and I don't quite buy it." They'd been competing in the Smooth style, and Elena was eight inches shorter than Dmitri, which was a challenge, but they definitely hadn't been awful.

Something much closer to a smile. "Not awful. Only too young."

"I'm pretty young." Dmitri shook his head as if to say he was not that young. On impulse, Mateo asked, "Why did you bring me in? I mean I'm still totally thrilled that you did, but I *am* so young, and I had no teaching experience, and what the hell."

"Everyone must begin," Dmitri said after a moment. "Was new class, social class. You were right for it." He leaned forward, elbows on the desk, very serious. "Everyone is attracted to you. They smile, they enjoy, they are energized. Is perfect for social class. But you have excellent knowledge. And you have beginner's mind. You speak to them as a friend, you say not 'do this' but 'let us try.' They feel, this is possible." Mateo was staring at him; Dmitri never said so much. I love you, he thought. It might have shown on his face. Dmitri's eyes grew warm. He didn't say anything else.

Mateo blinked, swallowed, and said, "You know you are never going to get me out of here. I'm going to be an incessant pest till the end of time."

Dmitri nodded gravely. "Is good."

Chapter 25

By the time they left for Oakland, Sam felt ready. He knew their routines, he had a feel for the competition dance floor now, and Mateo's excitement was contagious. Julia claimed they were as well-prepared as they could possibly be for an event no one at the studio had ever done before.

Going by themselves would have been fine. Going with Vicky and Sharon made it fun. They drove this time, borrowing Sharon's father's SUV so there was plenty of leg room and cargo space. Anita Lee insisted all four of them should stay at the house in Berkeley, an easy distance from the competition venue. "We want to meet your friends," she told Sam. "Faith and Emily are coming for brunch before you have to leave on Sunday. Jason says he'll be here too."

Sam's foster brother was doing his residency in Sacramento, so he got home fairly often. It was nice to think he'd make the effort for this occasion. He'd been there briefly at Thanksgiving, able to get off the hospital schedule for only a few hours. "I haven't really talked to him for a long time."

Mateo noticed he didn't seem at all nervous about it. "When was the last time?"

"After I retired from the UFC. The scar was still fresh. He tried to tell me it looked cool." Sam could laugh about it now. "I've always had a soft spot for him since then. I wonder if he's seeing anybody."

"I guess we'll find out."

They barely had any time to interrogate Jason, though; there was so much to say about the April

Follies. Not least, an explanation for the purple and psychedelic outfits. "We're doing a different color scheme for the big one," Sam said. "But we had these."

"And I'm thinking seriously about stealing the look," Vicky said.

"We could do full psychedelic jumpsuits someday," Sharon suggested. "If the Cabaret ever does a 'Tripping Balls' theme." Mateo and Jason both cracked up.

The news that did top the Follies came from Faith and Emily, who were going to have a baby. Anita got so excited about that, nobody but Sam noticed the significant glance that passed between Vicky and Sharon. He waited until they were on the road home before bringing it up. "You don't have to tell us anything. But it seemed Faith and Emily's news struck a chord."

"You could say that," Vicky hedged. "We have no announcements to make, however."

"Right. No comment at the present time." Sharon sounded amused. "Or maybe we could say negotiations are ongoing."

"Jesus, Sharon, if you're going to say that you might as well tell them everything." Vicky sounded exasperated, but also amused.

Mateo could guess by now, as could Sam. They both claimed they didn't require any further data. Mateo couldn't resist saying, "All I want to know is, are you still going to fit in that ballgown Kris is making for you."

"Oh my fucking God." Sharon smacked him, and then Vicky, who was laughing. "Why do you assume it's going to be me?"

Mateo looked over his shoulder at her. "Seriously?" Vicky laughed harder. Then, because of course he wanted to know more, he asked, "Does Dmitri know?" Both women suddenly got quiet. "Oh no you *didn't*. Oh no he *isn't*. Really?! Oh my God!" The idea that Dmitri might be the father, or at least the planned father, gave Mateo a curious mixture of delight and jealousy. "Okay, Jesus. I'm assuming that's in the vault. It is officially none of my business and I have no idea what we've been talking about and I won't remember a word of this tomorrow. Sam, you too."

Sam was quietly cracking up in the driver's seat. "Already forgotten. So how's Miranda behaving?"

"She's great." Vicky gratefully latched onto the subject change. "She's the boss of the house. Prospero has lost twenty-two ounces from his max pudge."

Sharon was also grateful. They were both dying to talk about their plans but were trying to keep a lid on it at the studio. "The only thing wrong with Miranda is, there is apparently nowhere she would rather sleep than on top of rhinestone-encrusted Spandex."

***

Mateo thought he deserved some kind of award for not letting on that he knew about Vicky and Sharon and Dmitri. Not that he actually knew. It was only an unverified suspicion. He was positive he was right, though. The way those women were with the studio boss was definitely different, now that he was looking for it. But he had plenty of stuff to keep his mind occupied, and before long he barely thought about it. He very deliberately did not think about it when he met with Julia and Dmitri, at their request, to discuss the April Follies experience. They met in the studio office with drinks from the coffee shop. "Really well done, all of you. We're so proud," Julia said. "Were you happy with the results?"

"Third place? Hell yeah we were happy. I was especially happy after I looked at the video and saw what the winners were doing."

"Ah. You noticed." Dmitri sounded satisfied.

"Did the others catch it?" Julia hadn't herself, at first.

"Pretty sure not. I'm not going to say anything to Sam about it." Mateo drank some of his coffee and then made eye contact with each of them. "We've got a good thing going. We're dancing well, there's a good chance we'll make the final anyway, and I want him to have fun. If he has fun, he'll want to do it again. A year would be plenty of time to teach him the follower's part and rework the routines. Four months is not."

Julia nodded. "I agree with you. About all of that."

"I too. You are wise," Dmitri told Mateo. "Those others, they were all professionals?"

"The gold and silver couples, definitely. And the top couple, at least, they're *not* a couple off the floor. Switching leads might open up some baggage." Mateo wriggled uncomfortably. "I'm hoping not. It's going to be tricky enough making it work with the height difference."

"If he says he wants to do it again, we can approach the routines differently." Julia was thinking out loud. "You're so strong, and so well-proportioned, you really don't dance small. You're *not* small," she hastened to add.

Mateo almost laughed at that. "A bunch of people up there were shorter than me. Yeah, it's a matter of shape, I think. Which parts I lead. It's a cool challenge really. Actually, that reminds me! I wanted to ask you about that routine in September. Andy and the actor." He directed that at Dmitri. "They switched leads. Did they already know how to do that?"

Dmitri shook his head. "Victor learned at milongas. Andy is my friend, long time. For this routine, I taught them both."

"Was there any weirdness?"

"None. They both wished to succeed with it. You will see." He meant, and Mateo understood, that he and Sam would have no trouble. Then he looked interested. "Will you and Sam learn Argentine tango?"

"After the Games." Mateo was grinning, the whole switching-leads thing dismissed until it was time for action. "Vince said he would teach us. Both of us, at that show, were like yes please. But one thing at a time." He remembered saying that, later.

***

May 2014

Mateo was only at Shall We Dance to talk to Dmitri about the social Rhythm class. When he left the office, he was expecting to go straight home. But a deep voice said, "Mr. de la Cruz?"

Mateo looked over and up. The voice belonged to a tall, serious-looking red-headed man. If it weren't for the long ponytail, he would have looked like a cop. "Am I in trouble?"

The big guy smiled. "I don't think so. If you have a minute, I'd like to talk to you about a show I'm producing. My name is Red Warner."

Didn't ring any bells. "Uh, hi?" The guy gestured toward a row of empty chairs. Mateo followed, shook

236

his hand, and sat down beside him. "What can I do for you?"

"Well, I saw your piece with the Underground Cabaret at Chrome in March. We're casting a troupe for a show there." He told Mateo about the show, a narrative piece set to mostly hard rock. Nothing like it had ever been on the Chrome stage.

After that conversation, Mateo walked home in a state of such distraction that he almost forgot to stop, passing their apartment before some other part of his brain kicked in. He retraced his steps, went through the door, greeted the cats, and wondered how to put this to Sam. Doing a single dance here and there for the Cabaret was one thing. Their routines for the Games were at the Keep Them Fresh stage. This project wouldn't go into full rehearsal until they were back from Cleveland. But if Sam agreed, they'd have an awful lot to learn: five group routines, plus bits and pieces between the ten dance numbers. Red's admission that he could use help casting the troupe was nowhere near as troubling (or exciting). If Sam didn't want to do this, should Mateo even get involved? But when might he get another chance like this?

Red wanted eight dancers. Mateo could think of several right off the bat. Vince, obviously. Julia's boyfriend Ray. Maybe Vicky; she was tall, strong, and fearless. There were five other Latin guys at the studio. Aaron, the oldest, wasn't interested in performing outside of pro-am competition. Julia tried more than once to get him to do something for Mating Dance, and finally gave up. But the other four—Gary, Sean, Michael, and Richard—all knew paso doble. They could all pick up choreography. If it was built around them, they'd be fine.

237

On second thought, maybe not Richard. They'd never been quite easy together after Sam came on the scene. Mateo didn't think it was his fault, or Sam's. It was something on Richard's side. And the guy seemed kind of fragile lately. He'd always been thin. Red said "battles." Mateo wouldn't want to put anyone in a position where they could get hurt. He needed to talk to Sam. Put it out of his mind, took care of the cats, and got busy prepping dinner.

By the time Sam got home, Mateo was out of the kitchen and at the desk working. He heard his lover greet the cats and come through to the bedroom. Sam bent to kiss Mateo. "Hey baby. Good day?"

Mateo swiveled around to face him. "Weird day. Get comfortable, I need to talk to you. It's nothing bad." Sam nodded, accepting that. He went through his usual getting-home ritual, parking his shoes and stripping. He hung up his suit and tie, put his dress shirt in the bag for the cleaners, and pulled on some warm-up pants and a tee shirt. Then he sat cross-legged on the bed and made an I'm Ready face. Mateo said, "You and I have been asked to dance in a show. A real show. Ten numbers. We'd be in five group routines and they're all battles. It's based on 'Beowulf.' The group numbers would be built around paso doble with some jazz, plus fight choreography. It's going to be at Chrome at the end of September." He'd been watching Sam's expressions: surprise, trepidation, interest, relief. "The guy said he could use my help casting the troupe even if you and I decided not to dance in it. I'd like to do it, all of it. If you don't want to, I promise I won't let it get in the way of our stuff. But I'd really love it if you did it too."

Sam thought for a minute. If they hadn't done those performances with the Cabaret, he wouldn't consider it for a second. If he hadn't genuinely enjoyed doing those, the thought of doing a whole show would have been awful. A year ago his knee-jerk reaction would have been Hell No. But now he and Mateo had done so many things he never thought were possible. The experience so far had been nothing but good. He knew the 'Beowulf' story, from a movie he'd seen. Could almost see how it would work to tell that story in dance. "Let me think about it while we eat. Do they have the music already?"

"I think so. I can ask the guy. That would be great, if we could have it first, wouldn't it? Because fuck, what if it's awful music." Sam laughed. Mateo stood up, leaned in for another kiss, and said, "I love you. Come and eat."

After dinner, Mateo sent an email to Red about the music. Half an hour later he got a reply with a link to a Dropbox. He and Sam went to the bedroom to play all the tracks from the computer, comfortably lying on the bed with the cats. A little less than an hour later, they looked at each other. Mateo was totally jazzed, Sam could tell. "It's great music, isn't it? You already see it, don't you." He couldn't help smiling. There was no way he could say no to something that put this look on his lover's beautiful face. "Tell him we're in." Mateo launched himself at Sam.

***

The next day Mateo sent a follow-up to confirm with Red. Then he got busy finding their other six dancers. Everyone he'd thought of was interested, especially when he handed them a printout of the playlist. He'd typed it up with Red's comments about what part of the story was carried by each of the group numbers, the two duets, and the three solos, including a little information about the two stars and about the director. He told everybody, "Red's got a thing all the way through June so this won't really start rolling till July. But from then on, it's full steam ahead to learn it and rehearse. Have to lock the cast by June fifteenth." Everybody seemed to understand; they all said they'd let him know as soon as possible.

A week after committing, Mateo's head was so full of how he wanted to dance the first number that he couldn't stand it. He sent Red a text asking if it was all right if he did some work on it. The reply was *Knock yourself out, I could use the help!* Then he asked Sam if they could work it through at the studio. Sam pointed to his next free afternoon, and Mateo checked with Dmitri to make sure they wouldn't be in anyone's way. Once they got rolling, and Sam understood where Mateo was going with it, he started having ideas too. "Will these warriors use weapons?"

Mateo didn't know, so he sent a text to Red. Five minutes later he made an annoyed sound and showed the reply to Sam: *What do you think?*

Sam shook his head, smiling. "I think spears. You think about that. I'll go down to the hardware store and get a couple broom handles to play with. Tell him." He kissed Mateo, changed his shoes, and went out the back door.

Mateo texted to Red: **Spears. Adding something to Dropbox later**. All he got back was a thumbs-up. He uttered a rude word and listened to the track again. When Sam walked in again with the broom handles, Mateo showed him the reply and said, "This guy takes delegation to a whole new place."

"Know what we're doing?"

"I've got some ideas. God this is going to be fun. Come and kiss me." For once, a kiss from Sam didn't change the trajectory of Mateo's excitement.

They worked until Dmitri threw them out. Mateo posted a video of their results on the Dropbox for Red to look at. The next day he got back a very satisfying email. Aside from praising the work, Red mentioned that the director wanted a double for the star, the woman playing Grendel and his mother Kali. Mateo summarized all of that for Sam. "He says when Mary's dancing 'Velvet Green' as Kali, there'll be some kind of interaction with Beowulf but he also wants Grendel to be present as if he's stalking Beowulf. He's wondering if you'd be up for doubling Grendel during that. They're working on a costume now, he says it's going to be easy to get in and out."

"Grendel's some kind of monster, right?" Sam kind of liked the idea of being a monster. "We could talk about it once it's a little farther along."

But first he wanted to talk to Vince again. They still saw a lot of Dana and Rory. Mateo had all kinds of people to consult. Sam occasionally needed to bounce things off someone who wasn't Mateo or female. Fortunately, Vince was happy to meet up at his gym again and talk all things monster. "I think you'd be great," he said, toward the end of their workout. "I mean, I have only the vaguest idea what Mateo's going to turn over for this, but what you guys did with the last paso doble was next level."

"That's what Red Warner said," Sam admitted. "It took a turn after we went to the mats with it."

Vince wiped his face with a towel, laughing. "I'll bet. Still having fun?"

Sam knew exactly what he meant. "Oh my God, he's so much fun. He's all, I'm sorry I keep dragging you into shit and I'm all, you're not dragging me anywhere. What does Kelli say about you being a warrior all summer?"

"You don't want to know. Ask you something?"

"Sure, yeah."

"You did your first performance less than a year ago, then pro-am Latin, another performance, the April Follies, and now this. All on top of training for the Gay Games."

Sam waited for the question. When one didn't come, he said, "And?"

"Are you *insane*?" Sam broke up laughing. Vince sat there on the weight bench, grinning at him. "Is it like being in the UFC again?"

"Pretty much, yeah. All training, all the time. And even though it's just for fun, it feels big. Like, this isn't just us fooling around. We're passing auditions. We're dancing better than other people. I like winning."

Vince, still grinning, said, "Yeah. Me too."

"Plus with Mateo teaching now, even competing as a pro, the better he looks with me, the more people are gonna want to work with him. So this is something I can give him." Sam considered his friend for a moment. "Tell you something else, I liked being the black guy at those comps with Julia. I mean it was uncomfortable, but that gave me something to fight. Helped with the nerves. I'll keep doing that. If we do well enough, maybe other people will see us and think, okay, this sport could be for me."

"Maybe so." Vince got to his feet. Flicked Sam with his towel. "You keep going with Julia, you'll be a champion before you know it."

After they showered and dressed, Sam had another thought. "What's it like for you and Kelli if you don't win? You don't fight about it, do you?" He couldn't imagine those two fighting, but they were only human.

"We slag off the winners for a few minutes, then watch our video to see where we could get better."

"You never argue about who messed up?"

Vince shook his head. "That's the thing about dancing. You can make all kinds of mistakes and as long as you don't make it obvious, nobody knows. Because nobody knows what your choreography is. So if my hand isn't exactly where it needs to be, or if she misses a rock step or whatever, it doesn't matter. We're doing this for fun. The whole process has to be at least seventy-five percent fun, or it's not worth doing."

"You never get frustrated?"

"Oh sure! Both of us! We get tired and sore and aggravated and we're like, just fuck this. But, you know, we rest. We stretch. We walk it through and decide if anything truly needs to change or if someone else was just a little bit better that day. If there's ever something we seriously disagree on, we take it to Dmitri."

Sam nodded. "I'll remember that."

"No disagreements yet?"

"Nothing we couldn't solve between us." After a moment, Sam admitted, "We might both have walked around things instead of plowing through 'em."

Vince patted him on the back as they headed out to their cars. "Use your resources. Keep talking. And make sure you get plenty of rest."

Chapter 26

A serious sit-down over their schedules led to some conscious social planning, because, as Sam pointed out, if they didn't put things on the calendar they'd never see anybody outside the gym or dance studio. Everybody else was hella busy too; seeing several people at once made it easier, like a cookout with their four favorite women in early June. At first Sam and Mateo were banished to the yard, watching Rory work the grill, while Dana had a top-secret conference with Vicky and Sharon inside the cottage. "You probably already know exactly what they're gossiping about," Rory said. "I hear the lid came a little bit unscrewed when you were upstate."

Mateo tried unsuccessfully not to giggle while putting on an oblivious face. Sam wrapped a hand around the back of his lover's neck and shook him gently. "Stop that. We don't know anything. What's the latest with you, bouncy girl? Know what you're doing for the July show?" The Cabaret had posted a 'Going for the Gold' theme in honor of the two couples heading to the Gay Games. "I hear Julia and Ray are doing a paso to 'Gonna Fly Now.'"

Mateo added, "And Michelle and Dmitri are doing a foxtrot to this Paul Anka cover of 'Eye of the Tiger.' It's so cheesy. She played it in the office for me and Elena and we were *crying*." The memory made him laugh all over again.

Rory looked as though she were trying not to hear that. "I think everything else is going to be burlesque and circus arts. Like old times. I can't decide about mine, though. It's going to be a super bendy striptease but should it be to 'Goldfinger,' which frankly always sounds really dirty, or should it be –"

"'Goldfinger,'" both men said.

She blinked. "Well, that was easy. And this shit is done." She moved everything to the edges of the cooking surface. "Let me go make sure the coast is clear." She turned off the burner and closed the lid, then disappeared. A minute later she was back with a platter to transfer the food.

Sam carried it in for her. "Okay ladies. General conversation only from this point. *Is* there any general conversation?"

Dana distributed steaks, sweet potatoes, and salad while Rory poured wine. The men noticed that Sharon was drinking. They deduced that whatever was going to happen, hadn't happened yet. Dana said, "Well we all talk about showbiz all the time, that's kind of tired. We could talk about the state of the cherubim."

"Eh, let's save that," Rory said. "Everybody saw most of me in 'Blue Moon,' and there's nothing new since then." Rory's body was almost entirely covered with tattoos of feathers (and, on her back, wings). "How about we harass the boys a little?"

"About what?" Sam said cautiously.

"Oh, you know," Sharon said. "Stuff."

"Yeah. Stuff." Vicky swallowed a bite of steak, chased it with a mouthful of wine, and said, "Taking a vacation this year?"

"Girl, please." Mateo made an Are You Crazy face. "We barely have time to do everything we're doing right here. Poor Sam, I think this Thanksgiving he'd rather go to work than go somewhere."

"I'll go where you go, baby." Sam leaned against him for a second. "Always."

All four women said "Aww."

Mateo gave Sam a kiss on the cheek. "Maybe I'll cook. How about that? Can you imagine what Pachuco and Frida would do with a turkey in the house? And speaking of cats, Spike, Gee Tee Eff Oh. Humans eating here." He put the big orange cat on the floor. "Damn, cat. I remember when I could pick you up with one hand." He looked over at Sam again. "Maybe I'll see if the hot photographer can take some naughty pictures of us."

Vicky and Sharon laughed. Rory and Dana exchanged a glance. Sam said, "What?"

Dana set her wineglass down. "Andy might be a little tied up for a while." Rory hooted. "Shut up! Figuratively speaking. He's seeing somebody, like all the time."

"He's *fucking* somebody all the time," Rory clarified. Mateo had hysterics for a minute, along with Vicky and Sharon. "There was this really long will we or won't we, and then it was like okay we will, and Jesus." Sam and Dana laughed too. "We've barely heard from him since March. Finally got them over here a few days ago and I thought we were going to have to excuse ourselves."

Vicky and Mateo were still laughing. Sam said, "Is it that actor?"

"Yes," Dana and Rory said together. Dana added, "How'd you guess?"

"That tango last September." There was a chorus of agreement from the women. "I'm happy for them. Andy's a nice guy."

"Yes he is. He's one of my bestest friends from way back." Dana drank some wine. "But yeah. Give him a call. Victor gets sent out on location a lot, so

246

this fall there'll probably be some time when Andy's looking for something to do."

Mateo swallowed some grilled sweet potato. "God, you guys, A1 sauce on these spuds is the bomb. We could do a We Survived the Gay Games thing. That would be cool, right?" Sam seemed to agree. "You girls should too."

"Maybe so." Vicky regarded Sharon for a moment. "That might be a good time to take some photographs."

Dana and Rory said "Ssshh!" and all six of them cracked up.

***

At Shall We Dance again a few days later, Mateo and Sam moved on from dancing rounds of their routines for the Games to working on pieces for 'Green Darkness.' They were in a corner, mildly arguing their way through one of the synchronized phrases in front of the mirror, when the star walked in. Mateo was concentrating, so he didn't notice her until Sam nudged him. "What? Oh! Are you Mary?"

"Hello," she said. "Mateo, isn't it? And Sam?" She shook hands with each of them. She was darker-skinned than Sam, nearly his height, with a short natural haircut and a rich English voice. "Did Red warn you?"

"No." Mateo fluttered a little. "I knew you were tall but he never said oh by the way she's Wonder Woman." Mary laughed. "Oh my God. Are you here to work? Do we get to work with you?"

"Actually no, not today. But soon, I promise. Red asked me to drop in to meet you. He said you've taken on the group numbers and we wondered if we could ask another favor. Of your leggy friend here, specifically." Sam looked startled. Mateo suddenly understood why Red texted to ask if they were in the studio today. Mary put a hand out to each of them and walked them over to a row of empty chairs. Sat between them, still holding their hands. "He'll have told you about my first Kali solo, yeah? The 'Velvet Green?'" Two identically confused nods. "Did he mention we want Grendel on stage in that one too?"

Mateo wracked his brain, trying to remember. They had so much going on, and this was such an unexpected visitation, that he couldn't. He conceded with an apologetic non-word. Sam came to his rescue. "There was something about that."

"Well, the question before us is, would you consider working with me on that number, Sam. Because we looked at the routines you've done with the Underground Cabaret, and we both thought your movement is really quite like mine, and then you're so close to my size. Let me show you the concept for the costume." She let go of them, dug in her cross-body bag for her phone, woke it up, and showed them a picture. "The headpiece is very lightweight. They're working on the color and detail now. What do you think?"

"Is that made of camo net?" Sam stared at it. The headpiece or mask looked a bit like a salamander. The rest of the costume was a sort of coverall that fit close to the insides of the arms and legs, but loose and ragged elsewhere.

"That's it. Quite easy to move in, now Lesley's got the inside trimmed up a bit. She's the designer, she's brilliant."

Now that he saw it, Sam understood how easily he could double Mary onstage. "So the idea is that Grendel is stalking the hero, right?"

"Oh, he's not the hero, darling. He's the sacrifice." She gave him a carnivorous smile. "May I send you a video of the Grendel movement I've got so far? It's for that first number. I saw what you'd put on the Dropbox and went right at it."

"Sure." Sam was enjoying this now, especially Mateo's star-struck expression. He'd have to tease him about that later. "Then would I send you a video, or would we get together?"

"Perhaps we could meet. My apartment has a roof deck, there's loads of space. We'll set a date, shall we? Order in some dinner and the three of us could work a bit?" She put a hand on each of them again. "I know you're in training, I don't mean to take all your time. But once to set the tone, yeah?"

"That's fine. Right, baby?"

"Oh. Yes. Fine." Mateo got a hold of himself. "God I can't wait to see what you do with 'Rock Star.' And the duets." He was dying to ask how she'd landed this role, but now was not the time. After dinner, up on the roof, sounded like a much better opportunity to get the Mary 411. They exchanged contact information and then she left. Mateo gave Sam an epic Wow face.

Sam laughed. "You're so cute. Let's go home. I think we've done enough for the day."

"Yeah. I should probably get some shit done for the real job." He was still keeping up with it, but it made for some long days. Told himself it would smooth out after the Games.

Sam noticed the way Mateo sagged, wondering if the guy even realized how tired he was. Eventually all this was bound to catch up with him. He didn't get eight-hour shifts of doing nothing but minding a shop

249

the way Sam did; even his drafting work took brainpower. He'd burn out if they didn't find him a way to unplug and rest, like Vince said. "Let's save you some time and order dinner tonight. Get your sneakers on."

"Yes sir." They didn't talk much on the way home. Mateo knew Sam had an early start the next day. They both probably needed a couple days off from dancing. He ran through their mutual obligations in his head, reviewed their status, and decided they could actually take a week off if they wanted. He was done with Yolanda, he wouldn't start seriously with Elena till after the Games, he and Sam were in great shape for that, and this other stuff was coming together fast. As Sam unlocked their door, Mateo said, "Let's take a break for a few days."

Sam glanced at him, closed the door, locked up. "I was thinking you need to rest. Well, we both do, but you especially. I still want to get with Julia to work on my shit for Desert Classic, but you're just coming along to spectate, right?"

"Right, Elena and I are going to analyze the pro Rhythm event. I meant to ask, how's your jive?"

"I hate it," Sam said sincerely, which made Mateo laugh. "It's so fucking fast, and Julia's amazing but she's not as strong as you are. Adapting that one's been a bitch."

"Still okay with doing those single-dance events along with your scholarship?"

"Oh yeah." Sam flicked through their collection of takeout menus, putting two favorites on the counter for Mateo to consider. Their first few comps, he and Julia did the three-dance scholarship only, but as they got closer to the Games he'd wanted to get out and compete with the jive and paso doble too. Since most pro-am comps let students compete in just one dance at a time if they wanted, that seemed like the most obvious strategy. After they called in their order, he returned to the subject. "She says after the Games we could consider adding the pre-championship four-dance."

Mateo nodded, pleased. While they waited for the delivery he powered through a big chunk of work due by noon the next day. Feeling somewhat restored and much less stressed, he made another suggestion after they ate. "Let's go to bed early tonight."

Sam noticed his lover said not Go To Sleep but Go To Bed. He thought that was a fine idea. "I'll clean this up. You go get ready." Mateo leaned in for a kiss, then got to his feet and obediently left the room. When Sam had the apartment and the cats squared away, he went through to the bathroom, noting that Mateo was flat on the bed with a tea-light candle burning and no clothes on. His eyes were closed when Sam joined him. "Stay like this," Sam said softly. "Let me do it."

"Mm-hmm." One great thing about living together was that it made spontaneity possible. The flip side was that they sometimes forgot to make a special occasion out of lovemaking. Sam took his time tonight, lavishing kisses and touches on Mateo until they were both desperate. He wanted to get Mateo off first. Wouldn't let him get his hands on anything. "Jesus, Sam, please."

"Don't you move." Still flat on his back, glowing in the candlelight, rampantly erect. "God, I could look at this forever." Except he wanted that climax almost as much as Mateo did. He kissed Mateo again, hard and hungry, then moved down his body to get that cock in his mouth. "Mmm."

"Oh my fucking God. Oh Jesus. Sam, my God, *Sam*." The shudder, the convulsion, the cry. Sam hummed happily, swallowed, absorbed the aftershock as if it were in his own body. He sat up and closed Mateo's legs. Then he slicked himself with the lube he'd set ready, another sound escaping, and pushed between his lover's thighs.

"Holy goodness." Instantly breathless, moving fast, because he was so close already. Mateo had one arm wrapped around his back and the other around his head, straining against him, vocal breaths echoing Sam's.

"Yes, harder, yes, God, *now* oh my *fuck* I love how you come." Mateo managed to keep breathing even with Sam's full weight on him. After a minute Sam moved to the side and pulled Mateo into his arms. Mateo rested his head on Sam's shoulder. "I love you."

"I love you too." They both fell asleep long before the candle burned out.

***

By the middle of June, the 'Green Darkness' troupe was locked and Mateo had the beginnings of the five group routines worked out. All featured sequences for the eight troupe members to dance in synch. Mateo posted videos of those sections. Vince and Vicky took turns being Grendel at the studio, so Mateo and Sam could work out how the troupe dancers would use their weapons and interact with the monster. Ray was in there all the time as soon as his series wrapped for the season. The other three guys joined whenever their work schedules permitted.

Vince had been asked to lend his Argentine tango expertise to another number for the show, so he was working on that with Kelli as soon as they finished their routine for the Underground Cabaret's June show. Dmitri gave the production tons of access; basically anytime he and Michelle weren't dancing rounds (they were on campaign for their second World Championship), or Vicky and Sharon weren't dancing rounds of their Gay Games Standard routines, or Sam and Mateo weren't dancing rounds of their Latin routines, something from the show was on the floor.

"This is nuts," Sharon said toward the end of the month, when she and Vicky finished their practice to see all seven of the other troupe members waiting. "They are not paying you enough for this."

"I'd do it for free," Mateo said. "I love doing the Cabaret things but this is a whole 'nother level."

"I love watching him discover what he's capable of," Sam said to Vicky, a few feet away.

She gave him a sideways look. "He says the same thing about you. The boss loves what you guys are doing."

"He said that?"

"Sam, be serious. This is Dmitri we're talking about."

Chapter 27

July 2014

It was a genuine challenge to keep working their Gay Games routines. Sam and Mateo took turns talking each other off the 'Green Darkness' ledge to ensure they used their time wisely, which meant the week before Desert Classic went entirely to Sam's competition prep. He was again the only black guy in his pro-am Latin events, and people still weren't used to that, but the more he got out there with a gang like their big group from Shall We Dance, the less of a Thing it would be. He was taking it seriously, minding his manners, and putting in the work. In a pay-to-play sport that was all anyone should ask.

When Red Warner returned from his movie shoot, he organized a rehearsal out in Van Nuys. The troupe dancers already knew each other, but this was their chance to meet director Tanith, producer/star Red, and Mary. Mateo led a paso doble refresher to warm up, followed by working through the opening number. Tanith contributed comments about use of the stage. Red threw in a few of the fight elements they'd use repeatedly. Mary demonstrated the Grendel movement she'd invented. Mateo put it all together, then tried to apologize for bossing everyone around.

Red waved that off, saying, "This is a project that needs a fresh perspective. It was going to be a play. Now it's a dance concert. We're all making shit up as we go along. But it's time to take a break, and then Mary will show us her first solo."

Mateo and Sam had seen her 'Velvet Green' before, when they all got together for dinner. Mateo had then arranged to have dinner with Kristine so he could squeal to her about the superhero he got to work with, because Sam shouldn't have to listen to that again; his concern was Mary's body language and how to match it.

This kind of movement was new to all of the ballroom dancers. Serious, professional-level jazz, filtered through an alien character. Mateo knew they had to try to incorporate some of that vocabulary in the group routines, so everything felt like it came from the same mind.

He and Sam talked about it on the way home. "I'm so excited but I'm kind of freaked out," Mateo confessed. "Mary is next level. I felt like what we did in March was this huge jump forward but every single part of this has to be even bigger. I do *not* want the audience looking at the troupe and saying, eh, couldn't they get any professionals."

Sam glanced over from the driver's seat. "She and Red are happy with what you've done so far."

"All the more reason to keep doing better. I'm gonna have to mainline jazz. Thank God I'm done with Yolanda."

"I could help," Sam offered tentatively. "I like working on this stuff with you. Why don't you take the parts that are partnering and jazz, and I'll take the parts that are straight-up combat? We can both work with Ray. He knows all that stuff and he's gung ho. And he's an actor, so where we need the troupe to be telling part of the story, I'll bet he can pitch in."

"Okay." Mateo thought this through. It was a good strategy. "Okay, yeah. Once we can get all five pieces on video, start to finish, I'll calm down. Because then Tanith and Red and Mary can pick them apart and tell us what to add or subtract or fix."

"It's not like doing competition routines," Sam allowed. "I see you throw one of those together in half an hour. But you're doing amazing work."

"If I am, it's because I've got you. The others, too, but mostly you." He blew out a breath, told himself to forget about the production for a while, and thought about what he wanted to do with Sam when they got home.

Sam was also thinking about that. He took a few minutes to call Benny and check in about the store—everything was fine, as usual—then moved Mateo out of the kitchen and said, "We'll order in. You're trying to do too much."

All Mateo really heard was Too Much, and it hit hard. "Oh God. Am I driving you crazy? I am, aren't I. You must be tired of this."

"No." Sam was surprised. "No, not at all. Baby." He pulled Mateo close for a moment and kissed him. "I love you. Go sit with the cats, I'll get dinner rolling." He opened a bottle of wine, too, leaving it on the counter to breathe while he went to the couch, scooped Mateo onto his lap, and kissed him again. "You are such a firecracker," he said into that shiny black hair. "You're so talented. You've taught me so much. I really love it." For once the words came easily. "I was doing my thing and it wasn't boring, you can't be bored with a whole world of movement to study, but this is so much better. It's better because we do it *together*. We're learning together. We fool around at the gym and do something and people say wow, we never saw that before. That's so cool. Then this guy who's been in all these movies comes and says I want the two of you in my show? We're going to be on the same stage with someone like Mary? It's nuts." Mateo was curled against him, soft and pliable and smiling. Sam could feel it. "And that's not even what's best. What's best is *you*, the way you are with me. If all you wanted to do was make graphics and cook, I would still love coming home to you. Living with you, listening to you tell me about what the cats did today, and what Kristine said about making dresses for Kenji, and where we should go next to buy wine. You do not drive me crazy. You taught me how to love somebody. I will *never* be tired of you."

"Oh God, Sam." Mateo sniffed, blinking wet eyes. Lifted his face, wrapping an arm around the back of his lover's neck, pulling them tight together for a deep and passionate kiss. "I love you so much."

Sam stroked a hand over Mateo's cheek. "I love you. You are great. This show is going to be great. You'll make it happen."

"*We'll* make it happen." Mateo kissed him again. If a delivery wasn't on the way, he'd have gone further.

***

As they cleaned up the kitchen, getting the cats and the apartment ready for the next day, Sam noticed his lover wasn't quite calm. "Do I need to put you on that couch again?"

Mateo huffed out a laugh, then sighed. "I need to tell you something."

"Hmm. Bed?"

"Yes please." Half an hour later, washed up and naked, he cuddled up with Sam. "Ugh, I feel like shit about this."

"What? Come on, confession time." How bad could it be, after all. Mateo didn't have time for the kind of fucking around that led to confessions in Sam's past. Not that those other guys thought they owed him one. They just let him find out and expected him to shrug it off. Surely this wasn't about anything like that.

Still, the next sentence was a complete surprise. "You know at the April Follies?"

"Uh, yeah?"

"The two couples who beat us were switching leads."

"Switching." Sam took a moment. "Oh. *Oh.*"

"Yeah."

"And you didn't mention it because why?" Annoyance bled through his tone.

Mateo cringed. "Because we would've had to rework all five routines and come up with a whole new vocabulary to deal with the shapes and the leverage and all that shit, and I thought it wouldn't be fair because you've only been dancing Latin for, you know, not even a year. And then here's the show and we're doing all this other craziness and obviously you could've picked it up just fine and we'd have a better shot at winning in Cleveland and I fucked you over."

Sam breathed through that high-speed babble, still annoyed but coping. Only when he felt a tear drop onto his bare chest did he sigh and let it go. He brushed a kiss across Mateo's hair. Thought through the whole problem, trying to put himself in Mateo's position. Accepting that he hadn't expected to be even half this good so soon in his dance career. He huffed out a laugh at the idea of even *having* a dance career. Nuzzled down to kiss Mateo's forehead. "You were a sneaky little shit. Don't do that again. But I get it. How could you know I'd be so good?"

A shaky laugh against his skin. Sam squeezed gently, feeling Mateo's breath settle, feeling the slight

258

tremble ease off. This boy hated it when they weren't perfectly in tune, and he'd freaked out twice tonight. They needed to sleep on all this.

After a minute, Mateo said, "I'm sorry. Really. You're a pro athlete and by April I already knew how fast you pick shit up. I made an assumption based on *my* experience."

"We might run up against that again."

"Jesus, I hope not. Maybe. Ugh."

"Want to talk about it at dinner tomorrow?" They had plans with Vince and Cory, who was deeply invested in the whole warriors thing.

Mateo produced a sort of squeak. Sam squeezed him again. Another moment, then a sigh. "Yeah. Sure. Put me on trial with those guys."

***

In the end, it wasn't a big deal. Vince told a story about his first Cabaret routine, combining swing and burlesque and Michelle on the dance pole. "I had no idea what I was doing. Then the very next one was 'Blue Angel' with Kelli, and we stole all this content from other things we'd seen, and we had no idea what we were doing. The first time doing *anything* is always a mess, but you have to start somewhere. Speaking from personal experience, unless it's a true life-or-death competency situation, it's a lot better to give someone space to fuck up than to assume they'll fuck up."

"I know," Mateo said penitently.

"I barely even know what you're talking about," Cory said, "but I probably would've done the same as Mateo. Like, we're doing good, let's stick with this till next time. I mean, come on. You both have full-time jobs." He studied Vince. "You do too."

Vince half-laughed, half-shrugged. "Pretty much all we do right now is work, eat, sleep, and dance."

"For real," Mateo said. "The gym is only to support the dancing at this point."

Cory stared at the three other men. "I hope there's some fucking in there somewhere."

They all cackled. "There is fucking," Vince said thoughtfully. "In fact, my wife is probably home from girls' night by now, all liquored up and ready for action, so I'm going to mosey on down the street."

"Tell her we said hi," Mateo offered, giggling.

"Sure will. Thanks for dinner." A round of handshakes and he was gone. The others took a few minutes to tidy up from the meal, then settled down on the couch.

Corey nudged Sam. "So when *is* the next one?"

"Uh, four years from now. In Paris."

"Paris?! Oh my God, you're gonna go, right?"

Sam and Mateo answered simultaneously. "Maybe?"

"For fuck's sake! Think how good you'll be in four years! I mean, if you don't break your necks doing any of that gymnastic bullshit."

Mateo grinned at him, then said to Sam, "You'll be a pro-am champ for sure."

Sam replied, "You'll probably be an American Rhythm champion with Elena."

Corey put in, "And whatever craziness you do with these shows, that's just gravy. Seriously. Paris. Do it for your fans," he added, with a big-eyed pleading expression.

Sam and Mateo broke up in relieved hysterics for a minute, leaning on each other. Sam pulled Cory into a group hug that turned into a tussle of groping and giggling. "You're such a nut."

"Don't talk about nuts. Jesus, you guys. I'm gonna keep making passes," Cory told them. "Maybe you get the seven-year itch and I get lucky."

Mateo sat back, wiping tears of laughter off his face. "You'll be the first to know."

"Not today, though," Sam said. "In fact, I think we'll kick you out now."

Cory made a big production out of standing up, adjusting himself, staring at them with his hands on his hips. Flexing a little, which made Mateo giggle again. "I'll get you, my pretty," Cory warned. "And your big dog too."

"You wish," Mateo said pertly.

***

A week later, Vicky said, "Where the hell is this coming from?" She was sitting on the studio floor, stretching. Vince was on one side of her, Ray on the other. Both men were leaning against the wall, looking as though they wanted to say Ow.

All three were staring at Mateo, who said, "I swear I don't know. I mean, I've been doing these little bits of martial arts with Sam for a year and a half now. He suggested the spears."

"I dig the spears." Vince said that with a rueful glance at his bruised forearm. "In spite of everything."

"You're rocking those jazz phrases that just came in." Ray leaned across Vicky's leg to give Vince a fist bump, then patted Vicky. "You too."

Mateo stretched out on his back. The four of them were alone in the studio, doing a last bit of choreography for 'Green Darkness.' They would run it one more time, on video, before they left.

"Everybody's great. But I'm so lucky you all train here. I can't believe none of you have beaten me to death. Who's this punk kid think he is." Vicky snorted out a laugh.

Vince and Ray exchanged a glance. Ray said, "It was that paso you did in March. That was truly groundbreaking. Coming up with that in the middle of training for the Games? I don't think anybody believes Red was crazy tapping you. However you got here, this is where you belong."

The words landed like hot fudge on a sundae. Mateo told himself he could cherish them later. "That was half Sam, though. I bounce all this off Sam. Dmitri and Julia and Michelle and Rory and Sam." It seemed important to say that, to acknowledge all the great teachers and collaborators he had.

Vicky stretched a little further, taking hold of his foot, shaking it gently. "You're a good communicator. You can execute it, but then you can talk somebody through it. I've never done shit like this before. Well, you know. A pro-am Latin routine does not look like this. God, I can't wait to see how it looks on stage."

"Fuck yeah, for real." Vince grinned. "When everything comes together."

"Full cast run-throughs in two weeks. Everything but costume." Ray was grinning too. "I haven't done something like this since high school. A full program, with a plot and everything."

"Does Sam even know what you guys have accomplished here?" Vicky got her feet under her and stood up. "Ow, *fuck*. He's getting some credit too, right?"

"I hope so. Tanith knows he's contributing." Mateo had only met the show's director the one time.

She seemed to have thrown the production at Red, weighing in mostly via email with notes on the progress videos about pacing, character, or story points. Mateo had no idea if this was normal. "Time to run it again on tape? Before we congeal?"

"God, yes." Vince let Vicky pull him up, then the two of them hoisted Ray to his feet. All three older dancers stared down at Mateo for a second. "Well, come on, choreographer."

"Bite me," he said, and stayed right there until they put him on his feet. Then they started the camera, took their positions, and did it again.

Chapter 28

August 2014

The week before the Games, Mateo finally had a chance to talk to Richard. Between the crazy-busy schedule at the studio and real life, they didn't seem to be there at the same time very often. When they were, too many other people were there as well. But on this day, Dmitri had left early for an appointment. Michelle was at home. Julia and Elena were gone for the day, the troupe wasn't rehearsing, and Mateo had the office to himself until his class started. Ordinarily he would have gotten on the laptop and done a little work for his employers. Now he spotted Richard changing into street shoes and thought he wasn't going to get a better chance.

He approached casually, speaking softly. "Richard. Julia says you're doing great with the teacher training program. Could I talk to you in the office for a minute?"

Richard finished tying a shoelace before looking up, sitting back in his chair, and apparently thinking it over. "Okay." He stood up and followed Mateo across the room. Once in the office, he sat down as if he were exhausted.

Mateo closed the door behind them and perched on the edge of the desk. "You've seen some of what we're doing for this show of Tanith Salazar's." Richard nodded. "I wanted to explain why I didn't ask you to join the troupe. I wanted you to know it's not because I couldn't get you to go out with me two years ago." Richard had been studying his hands; now he looked up. He was so thin. Mateo suddenly

264

recognized it. "It's because I knew the routines were going to be kind of violent. Much worse than what we did in our Frankenstein paso. With eight of us, and those two monsters as the stars, the odds on someone getting hurt are kind of bad. I've noticed, well, I didn't want you to get hurt."

Richard stared at him for a few seconds. "You noticed what, exactly?"

Mateo crossed his fingers behind his back, hoping he was right. "Look, I had a friend in college who was anorexic. I know it can be hard to manage, especially when you're an athlete. Most people think the two things are mutually exclusive, don't they? You work pretty hard in here sometimes." He felt like he should stop talking. This was the most personal they'd ever gotten, and he could be wrong. It could be something even worse.

"I'm twenty-eight years old," Richard said. It sounded like a non sequitur. Mateo knew he reacted; he would have said the other man was older. "I know. I look older, don't I? You're right. I don't like to talk about it. Everyone always has advice and nobody knows what they're talking about."

"Well, I'm not going to give you advice. I just wanted to say, I think you're a really good dancer and you're getting better all the time and I enjoyed doing that thing with you. Someday I hope we can do another thing. When we take *this* thing on stage it's going to be a train wreck." Richard almost laughed. "We all have bruises in places nobody should have bruises. So it was never about my respect for you as a dancer, okay? And it wasn't spite."

After a moment Richard said, "Thank you. I wondered for a minute. I know I gave you the brush-off before."

265

"I figured that was because we were both dug in here. It could get awkward." Richard made a sound that could have been assent. Then, because he'd been super intrusive and the least he could do was share something personal, Mateo said, "And it would have gotten awkward, so you were right. I was already in love with Sam then. If I'd started something with you, I would have blown it up when I went to find him."

"You've managed not to introduce us all this time." It sounded a little sharp, though Richard was smiling. "I promise I won't make a pass at him."

Mateo felt slightly guilty. It had been easy to get Sam to the studio at times he knew Richard wouldn't be there. "Next time we're all here. Anyway, this probably sounds completely offensive, but I'm starving and I've got my class in an hour. Do you want to go get something to eat with me?"

"It's not offensive. Thanks. Sure." A few minutes later they were out the door.

Mateo told Sam about it later. "Remember when you said you had that sort of dust-up with Cory, and you fixed it?" Sam gave him the look that meant Yes. Mateo nodded. "I fixed it with Richard. Told him why I didn't add him to the troupe. There was always this, eh, kind of uncomfortable thing because I asked him out a couple of time before I went to track you down."

"He didn't go out with you?" Sam couldn't believe it.

Mateo saw and appreciated the disbelief. "We were both already really active at Shall We Dance. It could have gotten awkward. So it's good he brushed me off. Also, the last time was the day I decided to stalk you. It was very motivational."

"He said no, so you came after me." Sam thought about that for a second, watched Mateo realize how it sounded, stifled a laugh as his lover's face changed. "Don't worry, baby. I know that's not why. So why didn't you add him to the troupe, really?"

"Too fragile," Mateo said bluntly. "Red said 'battles.' These numbers got brutal fast. If he hit the floor the way a couple of us have, something would break."

"Is he sick?"

"Not exactly. But also not exactly well. Anyway we had a good talk and now I think it won't be weird between us. He wants to meet you. Called me out for not introducing you."

"You know I don't want anyone but you." Sam reached for the back of Mateo's neck and pulled him into a kiss. "Lucky for me he turned you down."

"Sam, goddammit!" Mateo would have tried to argue but he was laughing, and Sam was kissing him, and pretty soon he forgot all about it.

***

August 2014

It was hot in Cleveland.

Mateo and Sam had traveled with Vicky and Sharon to the Games. Dmitri and his husband Patrick would arrive the next day to cheer them on. After the competitors got checked in, they went up to their adjacent rooms, leaving the connecting door open as they unpacked. "This was a good idea," Sharon said. "I'd be scared shitless if we were here alone."

"Me too," said Sam. "Feel okay about your dances?"

"You know, as much as I hate Dmitri every time he enters us in a competition, the experience has been good. But still. This feels hella big."

"Yeah."

"Let's get our stuff organized, then go and find the venue," Mateo suggested. "I think there's some practice time set aside."

"We can get a look at our competition," said Vicky.

Sharon flailed a little. "I don't *want* to get a look at our competition!"

Vicky laughed. Mateo said, "What I really want is some kind of program or schedule."

"Well, let's go find one," said Sam. "Everybody ready?"

"Give us five minutes. Girls, you know."

"We'll meet you down by the bar," said Vicky. "Bring your shoe bags."

When Vicky and Sharon joined Mateo and Sam at the bar, they had a venue map and schedule in hand. The venue for Dance Sport was within walking distance of their hotel and was open for practice that evening. "So here we go," Vicky said. "It's open until eight, we can come back and have dinner after."

Sharon read over her shoulder. "Our first round is seven o'clock tomorrow night. Standard Standard Latin Latin. You guys are up on day two."

"I thought maybe so," said Mateo. "Some of the couples will be doing all ten dances."

Sam said ,"My head would explode for sure."

Vicky patted his back. "You were born to dance Latin."

"So we have to wait all damn day. Great. Super. Awesome." Sharon sighed.

Mateo patted her back. "I don't know about you, but I'm gonna see if I can find a spa."

"*Good* idea!"

When they walked inside the venue, they stopped short. Dozens of couples were on the floor, a throng of Standard and Latin dancers doing a dizzying array of moves. Sam closed his eyes for a second. "Oh, shit."

"So much shit," Sharon said blankly.

"There's plenty of open seats," said Mateo, stifling a laugh. "Let's just put our shoes on and do a walk-through."

Vicky said, "Yeah. No point trying to go full-out."

Sharon gave her a resigned look. "You know I love you, right?"

"I love you too. Don't kill me."

After practice, they took a tour around the ballroom, noting the competitor roster posted behind the officials' table. "Look how many," Sam said.

Mateo was grinning. "It's fantastic. This is great. This is *us*."

They headed back to their hotel for dinner, discussing the floor, the number of competitors, and the variety of talent they hadn't been able to keep from noticing. "Are you nervous now?" Vicky asked Mateo. "I'm a little less so."

"No. Yes. Maybe a little."

"More," said Sam, and reached for his hand.

Sharon nodded. "It comes and goes. Should we go to one of these parties later on? If we're up in the room I'm going to start freaking out."

Vicky looked over her shoulder at the schedule, then kissed her cheek. "This is no time to watch HGTV. Let's party."

Being serious about their events, they didn't party too hard. A good night's sleep and a day spent relaxing, stretching, and walking through their routines had them feeling good (if still nervous) by the time they started getting dressed the following night. Walking back to the competition venue together, they joined a colorful parade that became a traffic jam at the entrance of the Grand Ballroom. Sam and Mateo were in costume, even though they wouldn't compete till the next night. Mateo wanted to be seen. Dark brown stretch pants with a vertical bronze stripe on the outside seam; bronze stretch velvet shirts with sheer sleeves, tiger stripes burned into the body fabric. Vicky was in a marine-blue sleeveless jumpsuit and Sharon in a matching backless gown with a divided skirt. She had glittery bracelets at the wrist and elbow, sparkling ornaments around her neck and in her upswept blonde hair. Vicky's hair was in a French braid to the nape of her neck, falling loose from there.

"You girls really look fabulous," said Mateo. "Did Kenji do those too?"

"He sure did." Vicky eyed the men. "I like your bling."

"There was no way I was coming to this without some bling!" He did a little twist, catching the light on the iridescent rhinestones encrusting the shirt collar, cuffs, and pants stripe. Sam had a matching rhinestone band around his ponytail.

"Those are much more tasteful than some of these outfits," Sharon said under her breath.

Sam answered, equally quiet. "I don't think I'd be comfortable in pink ruffles."

"You're just not a pink ruffles kind of guy," she said. They looked at each other and snickered.

Once inside and checked in, they looked around; the venue was so crowded there was little hope of spotting Dmitri and Patrick. A few rows of seats around the dance floor were supplemented by chairs on a mezzanine. Sam and Mateo escorted the women to the on-deck area, where there were over twenty couples waiting. "Yours may have to be split in a couple of heats," said Mateo. "I mean, this is a decent floor, but *damn*."

"Yours is gonna be worse," said Vicky.

"I know!"

A few minutes later, the announcer said, "Welcome to the Dance Sport competitions in the 2014 Gay Games! Let's hear it for all tonight's competitors!" A roar of applause crashed through the room.

Sharon and Sam said, "Oh my *God*!"

Vicky grinned. "It sounds like a rocket launch in here!"

"I *love* it!" Mateo bounced on his toes.

"Our first event tonight is the Ladies' Standard Competition." The announcer called each couple's number as they all went onto the floor. Vicky and Sharon were in the middle of the pack, waving at Mateo and Sam as they went. They secured a fairly favorable position near one corner of the floor.

Mateo yelled, "Go get 'em, girls!"

"We'll be separating the heats after this first introductory dance. Competitors, places please for your first dance, the waltz."

The first two minutes of waltz were a free-for-all. Many couples found themselves repeatedly stalled or blocked by the heavy traffic. Vicky was taller than most, making her way more successfully around the floor. She appeared to be swearing; Sharon was clearly giggling.

"Sharon's laughing again," Sam observed.

"I think Vicky just said 'fuck' again," said Mateo. "I don't blame her a bit."

"That's about the only word I'd be able to come up with." Then the announcer called the first dozen couples' numbers for the tango. The other dozen left the floor to wait their turn. With the divided heats, it took twice as long to get through the event. When Vicky and Sharon finally came off the floor after their quickstep, Mateo and Sam were waiting. "How do you feel?" Sam asked Sharon.

"Well, we didn't crash into anybody. Good driving, sweetie!"

"Good following!" said Vicky. They gave each other a high-five.

"Not crashing is more than a lot of people can say," said Mateo. "It was a *mess* out there."

"When will they post the callback?" Vicky squeezed past to grab a bottle of water from a service table.

"Probably pretty quick. They've got to run your next round after this." They watched the Men's Standard competition, which was also split into two heats.

"I can't believe how many people are here," said Sam. "It's great. It's like a Pride parade."

"Website said over sixty countries are represented in all the events."

"That's so cool," said Vicky. "I'm glad we decided to do this."

"Me too," said Sharon.

Vicky kissed her. Then she turned to the men and said, "You should go get seats on the mezzanine. Get four. If we don't make the final we can come up and sit with you and yell for those girls who won in Oakland."

"All right." Sam bent to kiss each of the women. "You're both fantastic."

"Truth." Mateo kissed them too. "Go do your thing." They made their way upstairs, waved to Dmitri and Patrick on the other side of the floor, and settled in to watch. "Oh, hell," Mateo said softly when he saw Sharon's reaction to the callback sheet for the final. "Well, maybe next time."

***

The girls swore they'd be making all the noise during the men's Latin competition. The ballroom was every bit as crowded, even noisier than the night before. When the Ladies' Latin began, Mateo and Sam went to the room nearby that was set aside for warmups. "You doing okay, honey?"

Sam pulled him close for a hug. "I'm fine now that it's started." A kiss, a squeeze, then back to their warmup.

They could hear the announcer through the walls. When he called the women's first heat for the paso doble, they got ready to go back into the main room. Sam stopped Mateo for a moment. "Hey baby. Whatever happens, thanks for this."

Mateo smiled. "My pleasure. Thanks for rocking that salsa. And taking my drunk ass home."

"I'm so glad I did. I love you a lot."

"I love you, too." One more hug, one long kiss, and they went in to compete. After the first round, they were mostly excited because there had been enough space on the floor for them to do their tricks. After the semifinal, they were so keyed up they could hardly speak. Then the callback was posted, and the girls must have seen them react because they heard a lot of screaming from up on the mezzanine. They both turned around, located their friends, and waved. Then they were hugging, kissing, and getting in other people's way. After a minute or two, Sam started making them a path through the throng. He held Mateo against his chest while they watched the women's Latin final. "You think Dmitri will put that on the website?"

Mateo laughed under his breath. "Made the final at the Gay Games? I think we can count on it. You're going to be famous."

"No way."

"Yes way." He rested his head on Sam's shoulder and looked up, turning a few degrees in. "Most awesome man in America. I'll tell Elena to put that in the caption." Sam laughed against his mouth. They stayed on their feet, moving around just enough to stay warm, waiting their turn. Waiting for their shot at a medal.

***

Much later, they kissed Vicky and Sharon goodnight and went into their room. The bronze medals went on the desk. Their clothes hit the floor. They should have been too tired to fool around, but they weren't. After a while, Sam rolled onto his back and sighed. "We're sexier than they are. If we switch leads, can we win?"

Mateo patted him randomly. "We might. Paris will be different. Probably bigger. There'll be a lot more Europeans. But even another bronze would be fantastic."

"Heh." Sam didn't feel at all bad about the bronze. Placing third tonight was so much better than he'd expected. More than he'd dreamed. "Yeah, maybe. Train for the gold and be happy with the bronze."

Mateo hitched up a little so he could see Sam's face. "You had fun, right?"

"Oh yeah. Of course, I still want to fucking *win*." Mateo laughed. Sam reached out and tugged a lock of that short, sleek black hair. "Switch leads, huh. That ain't nothing. We've been doing that all along."

Epilogue

Four years later

Paris. A second Gay Games. Vicky and Sharon along to compete again, Dmitri and Patrick along for moral support again. Kristine and her husband Hiro were along for their delayed honeymoon, new baby back home with Kris and Mateo's parents. "Tripping *balls*," Mateo said as they stood side by side at the top of the Eiffel Tower. "This is completely fucking *beyond*."

"It really is," Sam said softly. At times during the past two years, it felt like they were caught in a landslide. After 'Green Darkness' they kept going with the Underground Cabaret, becoming regulars and then headliners of the next three summer pro shows at Chrome. They had legit fans now, which never ceased to be a Thing at the gym (especially with Cory, who still made passes). Even before being featured in a low-budget tango movie this year.

The landslide, disorienting as it could be, was mostly good. They still had their same jobs, still lived in the same apartment. Some friends were gone, though. Elena moved to Italy with her husband, and they lost Ray forever due to a horrible accident outside Shall We Dance. Julia saw it happen and never came back to the studio. Since then, Sam hadn't looked for another pro-am partner.

Instead, he married Mateo. After Kris hooked up with Hiro and Mateo finally said, "I'd really like to be able to call you my husband."

All that time, they'd never really talked about it. Never even brought up the domestic partners option. With everything else they had going, it just hadn't seemed important. Until the accident.

Rory and Dana got married too, after living together for ten years. At least Sam didn't wait quite that long. He was glad they didn't wait another minute.

Mateo turned his head, catching Sam's eye. "Ready for tomorrow?"

"You decided what we're wearing yet?" They'd saved their two outfits from 2014, carefully cleaned and stored. No need to spend that money again.

"How about the brown to start with, and if we make the final, wear the purple?"

Sam bumped their shoulders together. "Great idea." After a second, because he knew his boy was already looking ahead at their calendar and wishing they had a next big thing, he said, "We could wear the purple when we do the same-sex event at the Salsa Challenge."

"When we what?!" Mateo grabbed him, squeezed him, lifted him off his feet. Sam was laughing. "When? Not this year. Next year?"

"Next year," Sam promised, getting control of the situation and leaning in for a kiss. "The one in L.A., in May."

"Oh my God oh my God oh my God." Mateo was so excited he wanted to run all the way down the tower and then all the way back up. But they were competing tomorrow, and he wanted another medal, so all he did was kiss Sam again.

THE END

Want more? Richard's story is **TAKE EVERYTHING**. If you can't get enough of dancing, try **FACE THE MUSIC**.

Discover this universe of romance at

www.thelastories.com

Author's Note:

The April Follies is a real thing, an annual same-sex ballroom competition. The event attended by my characters was held on Saturday, April 26, 2014 at the Just Dance Ballroom in Oakland, California. The couple winning women's Standard: Emily Coles & Kieren Jameson. The couple who won men's Latin here and at the Gay Games: Ernesto Palma & Nikolai Shpakov. You can see these couples dance and learn more about same-sex ballroom in the feature-length documentary *Hot to Trot*.

Prior to 2019, a few mainstream ballroom competitions, mostly collegiate, offered same-sex events alongside conventional events. As of summer 2019, the governing bodies for amateur and professional Dance Sport in the U.S. have changed the rules. A couple is no longer defined as a man (the leader) and a woman (the follower).

Competitive couples may now be any wonderful combination of genders, in any USA Dance or NDCA event. It's been a long time coming.

****

About the Author

Alexandra Caluen lives in a small purple house with her husband, a bottle of Laphroaig, a lot of books, and nine pairs of ballroom shoes. She is the author of over fifty contemporary romance novels and novellas featuring creative, diverse characters.

Connect with me:
Queeromance Ink: Alexandra Caluen
Instagram: @the.l.a.stories

www.ingramcontent.com/pod-product-compliance
Lightning Source LLC
Chambersburg PA
CBHW031703170626
46808CB00005B/1586

9 7 8 1 7 3 3 7 2 1 1 6 5